Do You Need Me?

Emmily Sorelle

Do You Need Me?

Copyright © 2024 Emmily Sorelle

ISBN: 9798320856735

Cover Design: Lucy at www.lucythings.com

Editor: Sorelle Romance

Copyediting: Ellie Race

Proofreading: Gennifer Ulmen

Beta Reader: Emma Harrison

emmilysorelle@gmail.com

emmilysorelle.com

Content Warning

This is a fun, heartwarming read. However, some readers may find the content upsetting.

If you have no triggers and want to avoid potential spoilers, please skip ahead... Now!

Please be advised that this book includes depictions of a family member suffering from cancer (minor character), death of a family member (minor character), scenes of threat to the female main character, mild violence, alcohol use, strong language, and explicit sexual content.

You've read the blurb... This spice is strictly 18+

To golden retrievers and the women who bring them to heel

Fifteen Years Ago

Emma

I wonder if I could get away with murder.

Could I lure Jamie to the top of the science building and throw him clear off the roof? Could I take him out with a well-aimed textbook right between his stupid eyes? Could I slip something into one of the nuclear sports drinks he guzzles between classes? Poison is a woman's weapon, after all.

Or maybe I could listen to my best friend, Cindy, and try to ignore him. Which I would totally do, except Jamie has made it his mission to make my life hell.

Everything about Jamie Payne gets under my skin. He's one of those people who never has to try. He was probably born under a lucky star or sold his soul in exchange for an easy life. I'm betting on the latter.

I've lost count of how many assignments Jamie has conveniently forgotten to hand in. Even when he does bother to do the work, it's rushed in the minutes before class. And lo and behold, he'll still get an A!

I actually *want* to learn. I want to do well. It's the only way I'll get out of here and make something of myself. I stay up late and pour hours into my homework because I'm playing the long game. One day, I'll be someone *important*, someone who's successful and has their life together.

And Jamie *Fuckface* Payne is getting in the way of that.

Take this afternoon, for example. Mr Hammond is trying his hardest to explain the different corporate structures in the UK. It's a losing battle, though. Not only is the content drier than burnt toast but he's lost control of the slides projected on his state-of-the-art whiteboard.

Every time he uses his little clicker to move on, the slides jump back three places. Or forward two. Even when Mr Hammond does nothing at all, the slides bounce around with no rhyme or reason, disrupting our lesson and driving him to madness.

He's blaming the spare clicker he found at the bottom of his bag, cursing the batteries under his breath while slamming his hand against the plastic casing.

Apparently, Mr Hammond's usual clicker went missing last week. Around the time of this exact class, in fact.

Coincidence? Hardly.

Not that I have proof, but I see this for what it is—a way for Jamie to get out of using his brain while dragging the rest of us down with him.

I sigh, bracing myself for yet another evening buried in my textbooks to make up for this lost time.

"Wait, I didn't get that," I hear Jamie's best friend—and fellow idiot—hiss behind me. "Make it go back a slide."

Slowly, Jamie reaches under the table and fiddles with something in his pocket. Sure enough, the slides jump back, and Anthony frantically scribbles down the difference between a nonprofit and a social enterprise.

I knew it.

For the next few minutes, I sit twisted in my seat and watch Jamie like a hawk. His head is bowed in apparent concentration, his dirty blond hair falling into his dark

2

brown eyes. He'd be the very embodiment of a studious pupil if he could keep his hand out of his trousers for more than two seconds. And wouldn't you know it? Every reach under the table coincides with the slides messing up.

It's confirmed. Jamie has the clicker.

I quickly weigh up my options. Do I wait until the end of class to turn Jamie in? Or do I say something now and save us all this painful experience?

My decision is made when the slides flick right back to the beginning, and poor Mr Hammond gives up, slumping against the wall in defeat.

Finally, someone who shares my frustration.

"Sir, Jamie has your clicker," I pipe up from my seat in the front row.

Mr Hammond looks down at his hand in bewilderment and my confidence that any of us will pass this business class plummets.

"The other clicker, sir," I clarify.

Understanding dawns on his face. "Good man, Jamie. Where did you find it?"

Oh, you've got to be fucking kidding me.

"On the floor, Mr Hammond," Jamie lies. He rises from his chair, his long legs carrying him to the front of the class so he can present the beloved clicker.

Seriously, how does nothing stick to this guy? No matter what Jamie does, he always gets away scot-free. Always.

"He's had it all along!" I screech in disbelief.

"Can we get back to the class at hand, Miss Drayton?" Mr Hammond responds dismissively. He then aims his new clicker at the screen and watches with satisfaction as the slides do exactly what they're supposed to.

"Yeah, Emma. Stop distracting us," Jamie mocks as he passes my desk, earning a titter from everyone in earshot.

I wish I'd kept my mouth shut. The class might be back

on track, but I've lost all hope of concentrating. There's an angry hum in my ears, and my jaw aches from clenching my teeth.

Then, when Mr Hammond's back is turned, it hits me. Literally. I'm hit in the head by a goddamn paper aeroplane.

With shaking fingers, I dislodge the offending article from my ponytail. I plan to crumple it up but stop myself when I spot the ink blotting through the flimsy paper.

Nice try, Princess.

Urgh! I don't know whether to scream or cry, but whatever I choose will be Jamie's fault.

That bloody nickname haunts me. Ever since our French teacher proclaimed my translation, *"Parfait!"* I've been *Princess Perfect* to Jamie. It's his own unique way of goading me, as if trying hard at school and getting good grades is somehow noteworthy.

And now, seeing the word *Princess* scratched in his shoddy penmanship is the last straw.

In a moment of pure madness, I scribble my own retaliation. It's not poetic. It's not smart. It's just a simple *"Fuck off, dickhead."*

I scrunch the paper into a ball and throw it straight at Jamie's forehead. My perfect shot catches him off guard, and he flinches beautifully.

Take that, Payne!

"Miss Drayton. See me after class," Mr Hammond snaps, his previously unseeing eyes now trained on me.

What?!

Oh, that is it. Mark my words, Jamie Payne is going down.

If it's the last thing I do.

Chapter One

Jamie

Vegas.

Motherfucking Las Vegas.

I mean, seriously, Anthony? Is a bar crawl in Newquay not good enough for you? Instead, you have to drag your entire stag party halfway across the world?

Usually, I wouldn't mind. In fact, I'd be jumping at the chance to explore what is arguably the most exciting place on earth for a single guy to visit.

But the problem is, we're not travelling five thousand miles to another country *just* for a stag party. Oh no. We're travelling five thousand miles to another country for a stag *and hen* party. That's right. The bride and groom have decided they absolutely cannot be separated and are having their last hurrah *together*.

I've kissed goodbye to my dream of watching Anthony slip dollar bills into a bored stripper's G-string and prepared myself to 'accidentally' run into the bride and her giggling gaggle of hens at every turn.

Still, I could have overlooked that. Just like I could have overlooked the time I need off work, the plane fare, the extortionate price of a hotel suite, the overexcited bridal party drowning their jealousy in tequila, and the slight chance I'm going to gamble away my flat. All of that is trivial—barely even a blip on the radar—compared to dealing with *her*.

Emma Drayton. The maid of honour.

I'd call her my arch nemesis, but I'm not twelve, and that title sounds way too cool for someone I once caught alphabetising books in our school library—for fun.

Emma will appreciate the delights of Sin City as much as I appreciate travelling on the London Underground with that one guy who doesn't believe in shoes. But Cindy wanted to go to Las Vegas, and Emma made sure that happened.

Because she's just so *perfect*.

Cindy is the long-suffering bride to my out-of-control groomzilla.

Did you know that's a thing? A groomzilla? I didn't until Anthony freaked out when I naively suggested that no one would notice if the napkins for the reception were a slightly different shade of yellow from our pocket squares.

Oh, how wrong I was.

Apparently, I didn't care if the wedding was ruined, and the photos were ruined, and our friendship was ruined, and his decrepit great-aunt died from shock after exposure to our clumsy fabric selection.

Did Anthony calm down after five minutes and apologise for being such a massive twat? Yes. Will I bring up the great napkin temper tantrum at every opportunity for the rest of his life? Also yes.

At this point, my best man's speech is practically writing itself. I have enough material from the last six months alone without digging into the vault of our twenty-year friendship.

While we were never the kids that got hauled into the

headteacher's office at every lunch period, the pair of us certainly clocked up an astonishing number of detentions.

But really, what thirteen-year-old boy *can* keep it together when the substitute teacher introduces himself as Mr Yanker?

Much to Emma's dismay, of course. She always took exception to our less-than-studious attitudes. While Anthony and I played ever more disruptive rounds of 'bogies' in assembly, Emma was busy becoming a flawless teacher's pet, handing in neatly stapled, double-spaced essays well ahead of schedule and volunteering to shepherd year sevens to the cafeteria.

Exactly when the hatred started between us, it's hard to say. For me, it was when I snuck Leonie Watton into the school gym after football practice, and Emma *helpfully* informed Mr Rowland that she was worried about the 'mysterious noises' coming from the boys' locker room.

Instead of a gloriously fumbled rite of passage, my first handjob ended with me unable to look my coach in the eye while spinning an elaborate tale about me, Leonie, a spider with a death wish, and my boxers.

Emma and I both breathed a sigh of relief on A-level results day, bidding each other farewell with a middle finger (me) and a glare cold enough to refreeze the ice caps (Emma).

I thought that would be the last I saw of her. Even when we both made the short move from Surrey to London for university, the city was plenty big enough for us to exist in blissful ignorance of each other.

That was until years later when Anthony bumped into Emma's best friend at a coffee shop. Apparently, he and Cindy collided when reaching for the last gingerbread muffin, and the rest is history. They're basically characters in a terrible rom-com.

Anthony was instantly besotted, and I can't blame him. Cindy is one of the nicest, most genuine people you'll ever meet. How she's put up with Princess Perfect all these years is beyond me.

Then again, Cindy also hasn't murdered Anthony during one of his wedding outbursts, so perhaps she just has more patience than I do.

Or maybe she meditates. Who knows?

When Anthony and Cindy got serious, it was time for my path to cross with Emma's again. Before our first reunion at Anthony's twenty-fifth birthday party, I was more than a little curious about how the teacher's pet had turned out.

A lot could have changed in the years since we'd left school, and it was entirely possible the girl I'd once hated had grown beyond our petty rivalry. *I* was certainly ready to turn over a new leaf.

I had mentally prepared myself to meet a stranger. Someone I only *used* to know. Nevertheless, it was still a shock to be faced with a stylish woman so different from the drab girl who haunted my memory.

All Emma's features were exactly as I'd remembered, but somehow completely different. From her arched brow, impeccably shaped to accentuate just how much she disproves of all fun, to her pursed lips, so perfectly glossed you can think of nothing but smearing your thumb across the plump surface.

The only real change was her once mousy hair, now falling in soft waves to her shoulders. It was a rich mahogany too inviting for someone whose expression implied the exact opposite.

But while her outer facade was polished and preened, the robot within was still running on the same program. Emma had completed the evolution from insufferable know-it-all to stuck-up bitch spectacularly.

You only had to look at her fingers tapping furiously over her phone to know that she was very busy, and very important, and had very pressing emails that needed to be answered *right now, goddammit!*

My scathing assessment was only proven correct when, after a few vodka shots for courage, I attempted to make peace for the sake of our mutual friends.

"So, do you still hate me?" I'd asked, sliding onto the barstool beside her.

She hadn't even bothered to look up, her slender fingers still flying across her screen. "Fuck off, fuck boy. I'm busy."

Now, I've always been an easy-going guy. I love my friends, I love my family, and I'm there for them, no questions asked. Need a wingman? I'm in. Need a shoulder to cry on? I'll buy the ice cream. Need an alibi? Well, *then* I'd probably ask what you did, but I'd consider it!

I'd almost forgotten how it felt to be truly hated, and I'm not ashamed to admit that it threw me off kilter. I mean, fuck boy? Sure, I'd been on my fair share of hook-up apps, but no more than the next twenty-five-year-old in London.

I was floored.

So, I shot back the only thing that would penetrate her cold armour. I accused her of being wrong.

"Don't you think it's rude to come to a party and then ignore every single person here?"

And there it was—that arched brow, so reminiscent of all those years ago. But now it was coupled with a slow up-and-down, her piercing blue eyes cataloguing my every flaw, from my worn Converse to my shoulder-length blond hair falling unhelpfully out of its band.

Emma's judgement was damning. Thoroughly unimpressed with the man before her, she didn't even dignify me

9

with a response. She just turned back to her phone and resumed her infuriating tapping, shaking her head as if *I* was the one being a dick.

I wish I could say things improved after that first party, but it would be the biggest of all lies if I did. That encounter was just the start of our rekindled animosity.

Anthony found our constant sniping funny... until Cindy's twenty-seventh birthday bash.

I'd gotten under Emma's skin all evening by shouting "Princess Party Pooper!" at the top of my lungs every time she went to touch her phone. *Hey, I never claimed to be mature.*

Eventually, she was so annoyed that she practically vibrated with rage, and I saw the exact moment she reached her limit. It happened in slow motion. Emma spun around, her arm outstretched to aim her full glass of red wine straight at my face.

What else was I to do? I ducked, not knowing that the birthday girl was standing right behind me. I dodged the attack. But Cindy? Well, she wasn't so lucky.

Emma was mortified, and to be honest, so was I. That apology bouquet still ranks as the biggest I've ever bought.

Of course, Emma and I still completely disagree about who is to blame for the incident. *She* was the one who threw the wine and ruined Cindy's birthday, not me. I don't see how I'm at fault.

That's when the four of us agreed it was better for all involved if Emma and I pretended the other didn't exist. Since then, the couple's every gathering has been carefully engineered to keep us as far apart as possible.

Birthdays, housewarmings, and new jobs, all celebrated with strict instructions that there must be at least ten feet between us at all times. It worked flawlessly... until the inevitable happened.

Through a veil of tears and snot, Anthony proposed on Christmas Eve, and Cindy leapt at the chance to become Mrs Carter-Reed.

Neither Anthony nor Cindy could imagine anyone but their best friend by their side on the biggest day of their life. Unfortunately, they also couldn't imagine how Emma and I would be in the same room long enough for them to say "I do".

Being the insufferable swot she is, Emma told Cindy she would ask me to put aside *my issues* for the sake of their happy day. As if I'm the only one adding fuel to the flaming pile of crap that is our relationship.

But I bit my tongue. I want to be Anthony's best man more than anything. He'll always be my ride-or-die, and I can't wait to stand up for him this summer.

I tried—I really tried—to work with Emma to make this Vegas trip a success. I even made a tranquil playlist to listen to while reading her many, many emails. But, in the end, we just grated on each other too much.

Where Emma wanted to forward plan every single second of our trip, I wanted to take a more experience-led approach. I've always found the best way to explore a new place is to walk around, get a feel for the area, and see what draws you in.

That attitude did not find favour with Emma.

"You just can't be bothered to spend twenty minutes looking up things to do in Vegas," she'd sneered down the phone.

Soon, my 'tranquil' playlist was full of heavy death metal, and even that didn't work. It was apparent that the only way we would make it to the stag-slash-hen in one piece was if Emma took the reins.

It was a beautiful moment. The first thing we ever agreed on.

And the last.

Emma taking the lead did not, as I soon discovered, involve me simply rocking up to the airport with my passport in hand and a suspicious number of one-dollar bills in my pocket.

No. It meant I had unwittingly demoted myself to 'Emma's bitch'. A role in which I'm not excelling.

Take today, for instance. It's the worst time of the week —hump day at lunchtime. The hour when your last weekend is a distant memory, and your next is just out of reach.

The bank I work for is getting absolutely crucified on every social media platform after announcing a series of branch closures in rural areas. It's a controversial move that will leave hundreds of elderly people unable to bank in person. As the social media relations manager, it's my job to neutralise our reputation and signpost people to the help they need.

After reading the fiftieth message likening me *personally* to Satan, I decide an overly large, overly expensive coffee is the only way to salvage my day. Honestly, if it weren't for the poor spelling and terrible punctuation, I'd assume most of the bank's DMs this morning were from Emma.

Stepping out of my office block and onto the swanky streets of Canary Wharf never fails to make me smile. Even on days when I'm up to my eyes in irate customers, being completely surrounded by intimidating glass skyscrapers reminds me that I'm just a tiny dot in a bigger picture.

All around me, chaos is being harnessed, tamed, and turned into something monumental. And I'm a part of that. Even on my worst day, I wouldn't want to be anywhere else.

It's a short stroll from my office to my favourite café. The warm spring sun shimmers across every shining surface, and there's a quiet hum in the air that's building across the entire city as we anticipate the surging summer months.

I let myself soak in the bustle around me, and by the time I've waited in the short queue and flirted with my favourite barista, I've almost forgotten user3937749 and their threat to find me and make me wish *I wos nevar born.*

I would even describe my mood as serene as I wait for my coffee, ready to tackle the rest of the day. Until...

Ring ring!

Without looking at my phone, I already know who's calling me. There's only one person who can telepathically sense my good mood and choose that exact moment to drag me back down.

Incoming call: Princess

I consider sending Emma to voicemail, but I know she'll only keep calling until I make the time to speak to her.

With a heavy groan, I answer the phone.

"Hi, Emma," I sigh, already tired of this conversation.

Emma doesn't bother with a greeting. "You didn't reply to my last email."

"Princess, you only sent it to me an hour ago."

"This is important, Jamie. I haven't got time for you to dither about."

"Aren't you at work right now? How are you even checking your messages?"

Emma dutifully ignores my valid question and jumps straight into the long list of everything I owe her. "Josh hasn't paid. Have you asked if he's still coming?"

"Er—"

"And only two of the stags have submitted their menu choices for the flights. I need the other options by tomorrow."

To be fair, I'm impressed the count is as high as two. I

haven't sent the menus around yet, so the number should stand at exactly zero.

"Right, but—"

"Also, excluding Josh, you're the only person who hasn't completed the ESTA for entry into the US. I'm shocked. You're usually so organised," she deadpans.

I don't know why Emma bothers to call. She never lets me say anything.

By the end of our conversation, I've been told to find out whether any of the guys have food allergies, to let her know if we're doing printed T-shirts (absolutely not), and to 'greenlight' the itinerary for day two attached to her last email.

"If you could pull your head out of your ass and actually do something for this trip, that would be great," Emma drawls. "Or not. I honestly have no problem with leaving you behind."

"Well, Princess," I say through clenched teeth, "as pleasant as this has been, I really need to go."

"Get this to me today, Jamie. I'm serious," she says before I hear the glorious chime of the phone disconnecting.

I take a deep, cleansing breath, count to ten, and still find myself wanting to hurl my phone across the café. There was no need for Emma to interrupt my workday with this. Everything on her list could wait until tomorrow. Well, except for my ESTA application. I probably should do that tonight, considering we fly on Friday. And I guess the outstanding payment needs sorting. And possibly the menu choices.

Alright, so I'm a little behind. The good news is I have an entire evening to fix this.

Pocketing my phone, I practically snatch my latte from the baffled barista and storm back to my office. I don't know what expression I have on my face, but given the wide berth the interns are giving my cubicle, it's probably not customer-friendly.

I know I'm in the wrong. I'm not pulling my weight for this trip. But having it pointed out by Emma really stings. Still, there's nothing I can do right now, so I shove the pent-up guilt to the back of my mind and focus on getting back to work.

I'll shoot off a text to Josh tonight on my way to the hospice, and hopefully, by the time I've left, one of Emma's problems will be solved.

To be honest, if it were up to me, I wouldn't be going to Vegas at all. My nan is losing her battle with cancer, and it physically hurts to think of leaving her when the number of days she has left is nowhere near enough.

I was even ready to cancel my place until my meddling sister, Bridget, let it slip to Nan. The feisty old lady said very sternly that she would haunt me from beyond the grave if I 'let that nice boy down on his special holiday'.

God, I love that woman.

So, while half my heart will stay in Nan's little hospice room, I suppose it's time I put the rest of it into this stag do. Tonight, I will tick off every point on Emma's ridiculous list. And I might even start packing!

Motivated by my new plan of attack, I turn my attention back to the shitshow waiting for me online. Sipping on what might as well be liquid gold, I lose myself in the hundreds of comments posted during my little excursion. I even manage a smile when constructing the perfect back-handed response to the delightful user3937749.

Then, just when I think my Wednesday is back on track, I hear it.

Ring ring.

Fuuuuuuuuuck!

Chapter Two

Emma

It only takes a moment for your life to change.

Just ask Issac Newton, who was just trying to enjoy his garden when a falling apple changed humanity's understanding of the universe forever. Or Alexander Fleming, who saved millions of lives after finding mould in his unwashed Petri dishes. Or Romeo Montague, who snuck into a party and triggered a series of events that led to a marriage and six deaths.

Okay, so perhaps Romeo and Juliet isn't the most aspirational example, but my point still stands. It only takes a few seconds to change your life.

It's something I fantasised about as a child. I'd lay awake in my tiny bedroom and dream about the day my life would change. The day I'd walk into a fancy London office and some pinstriped city man would say, "Emma, we need you!"

I studied hard at school, made sure I got good grades and walked into a top university. Then, in my second year, I managed to harass my way into an internship at one of London's biggest marketing consultancies. I put my blood, sweat, and tears into every minuscule task, working well into the night most evenings while my classmates were out partying. But it was so worth it.

At graduation, who sailed into the country's most coveted junior marketing role? Me.

Who is now working an average of fifteen hours of overtime a week for no extra pay and can barely keep her eyes open on the commute home every night? Also me. But I'm aiming for the executive suite, and nothing but complete devotion will get me there.

The point is I've never wasted a moment in my life, and I'm proud of where that's taken me. At thirty, I've accomplished more with my career than some people will ever manage.

It's this level of dedication that makes me the perfect maid of honour. Not only am I throwing aside my differences with the most infuriating man on the planet, but I have researched, designed, and managed the smoothest destination stag-slash-hen do ever.

Cindy should float from one activity to another with no idea of the extensive organisation behind the scenes. The seamless transitions from serene spa treatment to scandalous evening entertainment are works of administrative art.

Or they will be if this trip doesn't crash and burn before we've even left London. Because after all my micromanaging, there's still one thing I wasn't prepared for. Someone else fucking with my plan.

Case in point, Jamie. Or, more specifically, lack of Jamie.

His instructions were very simple. Meet us at Terminal Five of Heathrow Airport at six thirty a.m. That was it. The entire to-do list I gave him for today. All he needed to do was show up.

At Terminal Five.

At six thirty.

It's now three minutes past seven.

According to my itinerary, we should have already fast-tracked our way through security. Instead, we're stuck here by luggage drop-off.

I wish I'd pencilled in an earlier coffee stop. I don't think I can deal with this level of stress un-caffeinated.

"I can't believe Jamie's late," I huff, my gaze locked on the terminal entrance in case I can will him into existence. "I knew I should've told him an earlier time."

The bohemian beauty beside me rolls her eyes. "First of all, stop with the death glare, or Jamie will burst into flames the moment he gets here. Can you at least try to give him the benefit of the doubt this weekend? I'm sure he has a really good reason for being late."

"We'll see about that," I snort, pulling out my phone to send our missing globetrotter yet another text.

The best and worst thing about Cindy is that she sees the good in everyone. For years, I lived in fear people would take advantage of her pure heart. That's why I breathed a sigh of relief when she fell in love with Anthony. Sure, he's high maintenance, but he worships the ground she walks on.

"Hey, look at that," Cindy squeaks, pointing to the departure board with all the enthusiasm of a golden retriever. "Our flight's been delayed by half an hour. We're back on time!"

The other members of our group groan in unison.

"Yeah, that's not the good news you think it is, Cindy," Anthony laughs, draping his arm over her shoulder. "But I love you for trying."

I'm just contemplating whether this thirty-minute delay will be one of those that creeps up and up until your whole flight's cancelled when I hear it—the obnoxious slap of flip-flops on the polished floor.

"Last one here buys the first round!" Anthony yells across the airport, earning disproving looks from all the people who think it's too early for so much noise.

It's me. I'm people.

Jamie rushes over to us, looking every inch the beachboy in board shorts and a faded black hoodie, the drawstrings of which are jumping around in time with his long, hurried strides. His sandy, shoulder-length hair has long given up trying to look respectable and is, as always, already falling out of its knot and into his whisky-coloured eyes.

He skids to a halt in front of us, giving Cindy a quick kiss on the cheek before pulling Anthony in for a strong, one-armed hug.

"I'm so sorry I'm late," Jamie pants. "I overslept."

I raise my eyebrow at Cindy, wordlessly asking if this is the *good reason* she was hoping for.

"Don't worry," Anthony says, slapping Jamie on his muscular back. "You know I'm just happy you could make it."

"Me too," my traitor of a best friend adds, pushing her fiancé aside to embrace the man who is going to take years off my life. Her eyes are glistening as if she can't believe Jamie's really here.

Me neither, babe.

"I know, but I'm still sorry," Jamie murmurs into Cindy's hair. He stays there a beat too long before turning to the row of desks behind us. "Shall we check in and get this party started?"

Lord, give me strength and six vodka shots.

"Check in?"

"Yeah, check in," Jamie says slowly, as if I don't know how

an airport works. "I even put my passport in my front pocket so it'd be easy to get to." He swings his backpack around his body and proudly pulls out said passport to wave in my face.

"See!"

Oh, the poor deluded fool.

"Jamie, are you telling me you haven't checked in yet?"

He blinks at me gormlessly. "Come again?"

Anthony groans, squeezing Jamie's shoulder in commiseration while the rest of our group looks on with amusement and a touch of pity.

"You were *supposed* to check in last night. I sent you the link and everything."

"Did you?" Jamie asks cautiously.

"Yes!"

"Well, to be fair, you sent me about eighteen different emails yesterday," he scoffs derisively. "It was a bit much, Emma. In the end, they all kind of lost meaning."

My fists clench at my sides, my face hot with embarrassment. Sensing I'm either about to be arrested for assault or burst into tears, Cindy grabs Jamie by the hand and pulls him towards the check-in desks.

"Don't worry, Emma, we'll sort it now," Cindy says breezily, leading Jamie away so fast he leaves skid marks in his wake. "Why don't you get everyone through security, and we'll meet you later?"

I can only stare in disbelief as the pair join the short queue of unprepared travellers. Jamie's laughing a decibel too loudly, probably making fun of my regimented schedule and need to control absolutely everything.

God only knows how much he'll mock me when he finds out about the pink folder tucked neatly away in my backpack. It houses all the documents every single one of us will need today. It's pathologically organised with the papers stored in the order we'll need them, and then alphabetically among the group.

Jamie will probably call me a freak when he sees it. But too much can go wrong today, and clutching onto the things I can control is the only thing keeping me sane. Fuck him if he can't understand that.

I close my eyes and take a deep breath, reminding myself this is supposed to be fun—the trip of a lifetime. Never in my wildest dreams did I think Cindy and I would travel together, let alone to somewhere as exotic as Las Vegas. And if I have to put up with a man-bun sporting, self-absorbed dickhead to enjoy this experience, then so be it.

Pulling myself together, I plaster on a smile and head towards the group of near strangers I hope to soon call friends. Together, we navigate through security, our energy bouncing off each other as we eagerly embark on the adventure we've been planning for so long.

After a rocky start, we're back on track. If the best man turning up late is the only drama we'll face today, I'll take it.

"Come on, Emma. It's tradition!"

"*Tradition,*" I grumble.

Tradition is leaving a mince pie out for Santa, fireworks on Guy Fawkes Night, and your mum's roast dinner. Tradition is pancake day, wearing a bin bag cape on Halloween, and strawberries and cream at Wimbledon.

Tradition is *not* airport beer at eight in the morning.

We had a plan. One supposedly checked and approved by Jamie. Get through security, and then head to the largest coffee shop for breakfast while we wait for our flight to be called.

Sounds fine, Jamie had texted back after receiving the itinerary. *So why am I only just hearing about this mystical ritual now?*

Either Jamie didn't bother to read the original schedule, or he did and wanted to make this seemingly mundane alteration just to get under my skin. In any case, he's fucking with me.

Realistically, it doesn't matter if we're in a café or a bar right now. Both end with me getting my precious coffee. But it's hard to hold on to that fact when Jamie sits across from me with a superior grin on his face.

It seems the promise of beer turns him into an efficient machine. Within minutes of us settling down, he'd taken everyone's food and drink orders and logged them on the bar's app. Where was this dedication to alcohol when I was planning our bar hop along the strip?

The only thing stopping me from dumping my cappuccino over Jamie's lap is the memory of a terrifying security guard rummaging through his luggage to confiscate two oversized bottles of shampoo and conditioner. Two very expensive oversized bottles of shampoo and conditioner. Clearly, it costs a lot to look like you've been pulled through a hedge backwards.

But it was the optimistic supply of condoms unearthed in the search that really made the moment. Especially when the heavy-handed guard dislodged the box and accidentally sent it flying across security. It skidded over the floor in slow motion, only to be stopped by some poor old lady's foot.

Probably not the sort of action Jamie anticipated those condoms would see. Though judging by the twinkle in the old lady's eye, I don't think she minded one bit.

His not-so-secret stash came as a surprise to no one. Jamie's always seemed a bit of a player. At school, there was a line of eager girls before him and a trail of broken hearts behind. These days, he only has to walk into a room, and women are hooked on his every word, clambering over one another for just a sliver of his attention.

I blame his dimples. Thank God I'm immune.

Even now, the rest of the hens are staring at him with hearts in their eyes, completely oblivious to the bored waiter trying half-heartedly to serve our breakfasts.

"Pain aux raisins?" the teenager mumbles, holding up a small plate. I hope he hasn't actually touched the food. I'm not convinced he's showered this week.

When no one claims the pastry, he tries again, this time speaking loudly over the sound of wheeled suitcases and screaming children.

"Oh yeah, that's Emma's," Jamie says around a mouth full of masticated hashbrown.

I groan inwardly as the server plonks the disappointing breakfast down in front of me.

"I'm sorry. I think I ordered a pain au chocolat?" I have no idea why I'm apologising or why I seem to be asking a question.

"Yeah, that's not what's written on the tab," the boy says, glancing down at the printout on his enormous tray.

"You definitely said raisin, Emma," Jamie adds *helpfully*.

I definitely said nothing of the sort, but it doesn't take a genius to see Jamie's smirking face and put two and two together. I should have known volunteering to sort the breakfast orders was just another way to mess with me.

I want to kill him. I want to take my blunt airport knife and plunge it into his eye socket again and again until there's nothing left of his arrogant face.

Fortunately for Jamie, there's still a tiny part of my mind that's clinging on to sanity. I take a cleansing breath and ask myself, is this fight really worth it? Probably not, especially when we've got an entire weekend of this shit to live through. So, I assume the role of the bigger man and pick up my sad breakfast.

Defeat tastes even worse than baked raisins.

Well, almost.

Bloody fruit in my pastry.

But I'll be damned if I'm handing Jamie the win. I demolish every single crumb on my plate with a deceptive smile on my face. When our flight is finally called, I look so calm that no one would guess I'm contemplating the best way to dispose of a corpse.

At least I'd had the foresight to book our seats as far away from each other as possible. Jamie and I will be separated by two whole aisles. Surely enough room for me to forget about his existence.

Eventually, our group makes it onto the plane and straight into an every-man-for-himself battle for overhead lockers. This is why I wanted to pay extra for priority boarding. Of course, the Agent of Chaos had vetoed that idea weeks ago.

By the time Cindy and I are buckled into our seats, I'm ready for a holiday from this holiday. My body is exhausted, and my brain is itching at the thought of my bag stored three lockers ahead of me.

Though I did fare better than Anthony. His bag was taken from the cabin after a nimble old man literally climbed over him to secure the last overhead spot.

Luckily, our take-off is smooth, and in no time at all, we hear the welcome clink of the drinks trolley making its way towards us.

"What can I get you both?" a perky member of the cabin crew asks.

Cindy requests a white wine while another equally perky woman in the next aisle passes beers to the stags.

What the hell. If you can't beat them, join them.

"I'll have a red wine, please."

The flight attendant flashes me a painted smile before efficiently arranging my plastic cup, napkin, and a little bottle of red on the tray in front of me.

There's something alien about drinking before lunch, but considering we're headed for a city where time has no meaning, I write it off as training for the trip ahead.

As the plane flies higher, our wine supply drops to a dangerous low. The altitude must be kicking in because Cindy's tipsy after just one glass, her giggling alter ego making an earlier appearance than anticipated. Marta and Andi, two of Cindy's closest work friends, are engaged in a passionate debate about the best way to get sweat stank out of a yoga mat, while Patrick has roped Josh and Tom into a 'warm up' poker game. Josh looks as if he's already regretting his life choices.

As the wine works its magic, I feel myself drifting away from the excitement around me. I never sleep well before travelling, so the lure of a catnap is almost too good to resist.

My thoughts scramble, jumping from one nonsensical image to another as I slip into that beautiful dozing space. I don't think I've felt this calm in months, floating in and out of my surroundings, falling deeper and harder into tranquil peace, until...

"Oh my God! Your accent is adorable."

Did someone let a banshee on board?

My head snaps up, ready to stare passive-aggressively at the source of the supersonic squeal. She's not hard to find. In fact, you'd be hard-pressed to *miss* her.

The woman's hair is the same subtle shade of red as a fire engine, and her tan is as fake as the breasts bursting from her strappy top. She's accentuating her surgeon's work by perching her assets on top of her seat, leaning over her chair to talk to... well, who else?

She flicks her hair over her shoulder, giggling through her nose at whatever wonderfully witty thing is coming out of Jamie's mouth. I'm too far away to eavesdrop on their conversation, but Jamie's leaning in too, his tight, white T-shirt showcasing his flexed biceps.

I'm convinced I'm the only one paying attention to our best man-whore, until I hear Cindy scoff next to me.

"And here we have the horny male," she rasps in a terrible impression of David Attenborough. "See how he puffs out his chest in an attempt to woo the female of his species."

I can't help the loud snort that escapes me, unfortunately drawing the attention of said horndog. Jamie's eyes lock with mine, a cunning smile playing across his lips.

"Something wrong, Emma?" his raised eyebrow asks.

Alas, blessed with only b-cups, I have no hope of holding his interest for long. Jamie's new travel companion bounces in front of him, and our connection is severed.

I'd hoped Jamie and I would manage at least a day of civility before descending into pettiness. But four hours into our trip, and I realise that was just a stupid dream.

It's going to be me versus him. Right versus wrong. Good sense versus whatever the hell Jamie's doing right now.

Only one of us will leave Vegas victorious. And I'm going to make damn sure it's me.

You might have won this battle, Jamie. But the war? The war is *mine*.

Chapter Three

Jamie

Time flies when you're having fun. An idiom that's especially true when forty-thousand feet in the air. Because the only thing better than ten uninterrupted hours with cleavage shoved in your face is ten uninterrupted hours of Emma Drayton grinding her teeth because of it.

Kalista ("with a K") isn't even what I'd call my type. The women I date are usually less... obvious about their intentions. I'm more attracted to someone who'll make me work for what I want. I love the challenge of a welcome chase, and if I'm handed everything on a plate, I lose interest before the sheets are dry.

At first, I'd only intended to make polite small talk with the cute redhead before excusing myself to join Patrick's card game. That was until I felt the icy chill of Emma's stare boring into the back of my skull. For whatever reason, my talking to Kalista was grating on her nerves, and I wasn't about to look a gift horse in the mouth.

When Kalista flirted, I flirted back. When she flicked her hair over her shoulder, I made sure to respond by flexing my muscles. All for Emma's benefit, of course. I can't even remember what we talked about, but I sure as hell won't forget the way Emma's eyes promised payback every time Kalista trilled at something unremarkable I'd said.

I was starting to worry about giving Kalista the wrong impression. Fortunately, when I turned down her offer of 'drinks' at her apartment, she merely shrugged and gave me an unbothered finger wave before disembarking the plane.

I wouldn't usually drag someone else into our games, but Emma had hit a nerve this morning with her torrent of increasingly snide messages. So, I gladly climbed off my moral high horse, willing to do whatever it took to regain the upper hand.

Yes, I overslept. But I also broke about fifty traffic laws to get to the airport, all while my phone was blowing up with missed calls and texts from the devil herself.

I could tell Emma was getting more and more pissed off because the texts evolved from a simple: *Where are you, asshole?* to more deadly prose along the lines of: *You selfish fucking prick. I can't believe you would ruin Cindy's day. Wait, I can. I hope you miss the flight entirely and save us all the displeasure of your company, you massive twat. Go die in a hole.*

I'm paraphrasing, of course. Her language was *much* worse.

The absolute kicker is that I'm never late. Despite what Emma may think of me, I pride myself on being the guy you can rely on. I would never dream of ruining the happy couple's trip on purpose.

Not that I bothered to explain that to Emma. I'm sure no defence short of being dead would be enough for her.

I'll catch Anthony to apologise later, and that should be good enough for everyone involved.

If you can believe it, last night I had actually resolved to keep the peace between us. A Las Vegas truce, if you will.

But all my goodwill flew out the window after reading the poison she'd left on my phone.

It's game on, Emma. You've thrown down the gauntlet and have no idea what you've unleashed. We have until the end of our trip to find out if I can make you feel as small as you did me.

My first golden opportunity presented itself when I boarded the minivan to our hotel this afternoon.

Did Emma really think she could hide her secret folder from me? How could I have missed the pristine pink article that made an appearance at every checkpoint and barrier along our journey?

So, what else was I to do when I spotted it poking out of her bag on the minivan's front seat? I checked that Emma was still supervising the loading of our luggage, then quickly snatched the folder and stashed it in my own backpack.

I could barely keep the smug look off my face as we made the short trip to our hotel. Even now, as our group stares dumbfoundedly at the faux opulence of the lobby, I keep one eye on Emma, just waiting for her to realise that her precious documents are MIA.

"Jamie, I'm not going to make it," Anthony whines, crossing and uncrossing his legs in some bizarre jig beside me.

"I told you to lay off the coffee, mate. You know it goes straight through you."

"Urgh, what are you? My mother?" Anthony snipes, desperately holding his crotch. "Nope, it's no use. Look after my stuff. I'm going to find a bathroom." He scurries away past a bank of elaborate, marble-effect elevators that, I assume, lead to the hotel suites.

"Where's he off to?" Cindy shouts across the lobby. As luck would have it, she's standing right next to Emma, which gives me the opening I need to watch my juvenile prank play out up close.

"He's had too much coffee," I say, walking over to the pair just as Emma drops her brown leather backpack to the floor in front of her.

As she leans over to unzip its contents, I notice a shift in the stags' attention. Where they were huddled together, each with their phone out to plan which bars we should hit tomorrow night, they're now all hooked on the maid of honour. Or, more specifically, to the perfect view she's offering down her tight tank top.

Their wandering eyes leave a bad taste in my mouth. Usually, my sense of chivalry is pretty well buried when it comes to Emma, but still, I shift a few inches to my left and block her from view.

Not that I can blame them. Even I'll admit that Emma is objectively nice to look at. Okay, more than nice. Pretty stunning, actually. But that's hardly worth dwelling on when she ruins the effect every time she opens her mouth.

"It must be in here," Emma gasps, frantically searching through her bag and ruining its systematic organisation in the process.

"Maybe you left it on the minibus," Cindy suggests calmly.

"No, I checked the whole van before it left," she moans, depositing a handful of tampons onto the floor beside her. "It has all the papers we need. How could I have lost it?"

Suddenly, she stops her desperate search and throws her head back to the ceiling. "Oh my God, Cindy. Your passport's in there."

This is gold. I couldn't have planned it better if I'd tried. It's not until I see the first glistening tear in the corner of Emma's eye that I decide to put her out of her misery.

Unlike Princess Perfect herself, I'm not in the business of making people cry.

"What's wrong, Emma?" I ask innocently. "Have you lost something?"

"Not now, Jamie," Emma groans.

"It's just that, it seems you've misplaced all the paperwork we need to check in."

"Seriously, fuck off." Emma turns her empty bag upside down, shaking it ferociously as if a giant bloody folder has somehow concealed itself within the lining.

With as much showmanship as I can muster—we are in Vegas, after all—I drop my bag beside hers and flourish the missing documents. The folder has only been in my possession for half an hour, yet it bears all the marks of its jaunt to the disorganised side. All four of its corners are now dogeared, curling over like they've wilted in exhaustion, and there's a stain down the front that even *I* can't identify. A few of the inner sheets have come loose, but Emma still looks on as if I've brandished the winning lottery ticket.

She moves to snatch the folder from me, but I'm just too quick for her. I lift it way above my head so Emma has no hope of stealing it back, even on tiptoes.

"What the hell, Jamie?" Emma yells, yanking on my arm to try and reach her precious documents. "Hand it over."

"I don't know, Emma. I'm not sure if we can trust you with something this important. You've already lost it once." I wave the pink folder around, the contents threatening to spill out over the polished floor.

That's the taunting straw that broke the camel's back. A determined glint flickers to life in her eyes, and before I know it, she's launching herself at me, planting one hand firmly on my shoulder and hoisting herself high enough to grab the file.

Emma and I have been at each other's throats for years, but she's *never* lost control like this. Her knee digs into my hip as she reaches ever higher, and I have to wrap my arm around her waist to stop us from toppling back onto the stone-cold floor.

Whether it's our precarious position or my travel-addled brain, I can't help but feel everything. I try hard not to, Lord, do I try. But it's impossible to ignore the way she moves on top of me, the way her softness brushes against my hardened muscles as she attempts to scale my body like a tree. When that first telltale jolt of *something* shoots to my groin, I drop her, quickly stepping back and throwing the damned folder at her feet.

I blame the jetlag.

Before I can contemplate whatever the hell *that* was, Emma's snatching the folder up from the floor, her cold eyes promising murder.

"What's going on?" Anthony calls out, wiping his wet hands on his jeans as he walks towards us. Classy.

"Emma here lost all our documents," I say, studiously ignoring the queasy feeling in my stomach. "But don't worry. I saved the day."

"Aw, nice one. You always come through." Anthony slaps my shoulder, and even with my mind busy trying to erase the last twenty seconds from my memory, I still manage to laugh at Emma's indignant choke.

Figuring I've milked this ploy for all it's worth, I decide to join the other stags in planning tomorrow evening's entertainment. Except, when I step towards the bemused group, I'm stopped in my tracks by a tight grip on my wrist.

"You may have fooled everyone else, but I see you for the fuck-up you are," Emma whispers, her ghosted threat leaving painful goosebumps in its wake. "Stay the hell away from me."

I don't have the heart to tell Emma that her message has fallen on deaf ears, so I let her storm away, her long legs quickly devouring the distance to the hotel's trembling receptionist.

With more efficiency than I will ever hope to manage, Emma returns within minutes to dish out our keycards. Mine is thrown at me, of course.

And with that, our weary group disbands, most heading for a well-earned catnap, myself included until Anthony asks if I'll grab a drink with him before dinner.

I jump at the chance, still needing to explain why I was so late this morning. After a quick freshen-up in my room, I take the elevator back down to reception and meet my best friend.

Since we're in Las Vegas, all Anthony and I have to do is fall out of the lobby, and we're in a bar. Or, as it happens, an old-fashioned speakeasy.

The windowless room is decorated in rich velvets and dark wood, the sultry space lit by stained-glass lamps that stand on every table. We order a round of beer to see us through until dinner and grab a table at the back of the bar, where the music is quieter.

"So, how's your nan?" Anthony asks, carefully sipping the head of his draught beer.

"She's not so great." I shrug, trying hard not to dwell on missing an entire weekend with her. "The cancer's spread too far. There's nothing the doctors can do except make her comfortable. She's got a few weeks left at best."

"Shit, I'm so sorry," Anthony says, his eyes soft with sympathy. "I didn't realise she had so little time. You know I'd have understood if you'd bailed, right?"

"I know, but Nan insisted. She said she could feel it in her waters that I needed to be here this weekend." I laugh, my chest aching as my heart tries to break free and fly itself home. "She even threatened to haunt me if I cancelled on you."

"Well, I appreciate you being here. Even if it's only to avoid paranormal intimidation."

"I'm glad I'm here too," I smile. "Although, I'm sorry I messed up this morning. I can't believe I was so late. I spent most of last night at the hospice, and then I couldn't sleep because I was worrying about something happening to Nan while I was here. I swear I set an alarm, but I think I slept through it—"

"Woah, Jamie. It's fine," Anthony interrupts. "If anyone had a good excuse to derail my stag do, it's you. Besides, I knew you'd make the flight. How else would you be able to make Emma's life a living hell all weekend?"

"I don't know what you mean," I say innocently, slurping at my frothy beer.

"Right," Anthony drawls. "Are you telling me you haven't been trying to wind her up ever since breakfast this morning?"

"I merely took the opportunities that were presented to me." I pause, debating how low I'm going to stoop. "And she started it."

Quite low, apparently.

Anthony groans, his head falling back in frustration. "Okay, you know I love you, but can you pretty please try not to push Emma over the edge this weekend?"

"I'll ignore her if she ignores me," I concede diplomatically. "How's that?"

"Yeah, that's clearly not going to happen. No one else exists to either of you when you're in the same room."

I scoff uncomfortably. "That's an exaggeration."

"Is it? Can you even name any of the other girls here with Cindy?"

"Well... there's Emma." Is it hot in here? I feel like it's hot in here.

"Nice try. You're both obsessed with each other. If I didn't know how far back this little feud went, I'd swear this was all some kind of kinky foreplay."

"What?" I splutter incredulously. "This is not foreplay! Anyway, I just spent a whole flight flirting with Klarisa, remember? Why would I do that if I was obsessed with someone else?" There. A flawless rebuttal. I drink my beer in triumph.

"Kalista," Anthony corrects. "And we both know you were only talking to her because it was pissing Emma off."

"Nuh-uh!" I make the noise with all the dignity a man can muster when he's forgotten how to form words.

"All I'm saying is that underneath her mask and the armour—"

"And the condescension, the superiority, and the general hatred of humankind—"

"Under the armour," Anthony continues, "Emma's got a heart of gold. It's just she doesn't let many people see it. She'd do anything for Cindy, including putting up with your arse for an entire weekend. So, try not to drive her off the Grand Canyon, okay?"

"I make no promises," I sulk until Anthony raises his brow at me expectantly. "But fine, whatever, I'll play nice."

"That's all I ask."

"Unless she starts it. Then all bets are off."

"Fucking hell," he sighs. "We're doomed."

That we are, Anthony. That we are.

I really thought we'd be on time for dinner. After promising Anthony I'd be on my best behaviour, I even suggested leaving the bar with plenty of time to spare.

Of course, all my good intentions went out the window when we were heckled by a man and his exceptionally rude parrot. We'd thought he was a street performer who'd trained his bird to say all the best swear words until we tried to tip him and found he was just a crazy man with a foul-mouthed friend.

Either way, our twenty-second journey from the bar to the hotel turned into a twenty-minute adventure I can't wait to tell Nan about. If she were an animal, she'd definitely be a parrot that told you to 'fuck off, butt face' every time you spoke.

The only thing that saved me from Emma's wrath as we scrambled for the last seats at dinner was Anthony's astounding impression of said parrot.

Still, as the evening wears on, the glares she's been throwing in my direction have grown ever more deadly. She's furious. Late twice in one day? How dare I?

When our food arrives, we all pick at our plates, our stomachs confused at the prospect of food at this hour. It might be dinnertime here, but it's past one in the morning back home.

"So, Jamie, what's the worst thing you and Anthony did at school?" one of the hens asks as she chases peas around her steak. I think she's called Martha.

Oh, wait. Or is it Marta? Bollocks, maybe Anthony has a point.

I wrack my brain, trying to think of something exciting enough to share with the group but also tame enough to share with a group that happens to include Anthony's future wife.

"Oh my God," Anthony jumps in, obviously worried about whatever tale I'm going to pull out of my ass. "Do you remember when we raced skateboards down the hill next to the science block? You flew over the bonnet of Mrs Browning's new convertible and scraped all the paintwork."

"That was you?" Cindy squeals from the head of the table.

"Yep," I say, smirking at my best friend, who clearly doesn't want me to share how I once caught him wanking over a biology textbook in the teachers' toilet. "I sprained my right wrist when I landed and spent all summer trying to find inventive ways around my injury."

"Didn't Mrs Browning try to fail you at history after that?" Anthony asks.

"She tried, but Mum complained to the exam board, and our whole year had to have their coursework externally invigilated. They bumped me up to a B." If Nan's a swearing parrot, my mum's a bloodthirsty shark.

I don't need to look at Emma to know her eyes are on me. If I'm not mistaken, they're trying to burrow under my skin and burn me from the inside out. The truth is, since Anthony's *observations*, I've been watching Emma more closely, too. For years, we've avoided being in close quarters at all costs, meaning I've never really had the chance to see how she acts around other people.

The interesting thing is that whenever someone tries to draw her into conversation, she'll give a polite answer before returning to her food. She doesn't engage, and she certainly doesn't show any interest in what anyone else is saying. In fact, several times, she's looked like a startled deer in headlights, as if only just realising she has a role in this group beyond organising where people need to be.

The only time she's had any reaction at all is when I speak. She *notices* me, and that's more than anyone else can say.

It's a heady feeling, being able to affect someone this much. As soon as I open my mouth, I trigger a butterfly effect that changes her entire demeanour. Narrowed eyes, gritted teeth, clenched fists, even a huff if I'm being extra charming. At this dinner alone, I've earned five (yes, five!) eye-rolls from her. When Josh asked me about *the cute girl from the plane,* I honestly thought she would lob her steak knife at me.

I hate to admit it, but Anthony's right. Emma's a bit obsessed with me.

Ding!

The vibration in my pocket drags me down from my high, especially when I find a text from Bridget waiting for me.

My heart sinks. It's ridiculous o'clock in the morning in London, and my sister is hardly a night owl.

Please let Nan be okay. Please, please, please.

> Bridget: Nan was asking about you. Send me pictures so I can show her your ugly face tomorrow.

I breathe a sigh of relief. Thank God.

> Me: WTF, B? Why are you texting me at 2 a.m.? You nearly gave me a heart attack.

The little text bubble shows me that she's writing back.

Bridget: Shit, sorry! I fell asleep on the sofa and figured you'd still be awake over there in Tinseltown.

Me: Tinseltown is Hollywood, dickhead. Vegas is Sin City.

Bridget: Whatever. Send pictures. Night x

I smile, setting my phone down and feeling a hundred pounds lighter now that I know Nan's okay.

"Jamie," Tom slurs across the table. "Stop sexting with *Plane Pussy* and tell me more shit about Anthony at school!"

Okay, gross. Time to cut Tom off for the night.

I catch Emma's eye and find her trying her hardest to melt the skin from my bones. My best friend is deluded if he thinks I can behave now that I've discovered I'm the centre of her attention. It's addictive.

I clear my throat. "Did Anthony ever tell you he lost his virginity in the humanities cupboard?"

Our table descends into chaos, and I proudly earn my sixth eye-roll of the night.

Chapter Four

Emma

D ay one in Las Vegas has been a rude awakening. And I mean that in the most literal sense because I had a rude fucking awakening at four o'clock this morning.

At first, my sleep-muddled brain couldn't make sense of the intrusive trill ricocheting around my room. The noise mercifully stopped before I could come to my senses, tricking my strung-out body into a false sense of serenity, only to start again with a vengeance a few moments later.

Ring, ring. Ring, ring.

It was only then I could pinpoint the sound to the hotel phone sitting innocuously beside my bed. I scrambled for the handset, all manner of disastrous scenarios running through my head, only to be greeted by a far too chipper hotel receptionist ordering me to 'wake up and seize the day'.

I'd nearly snapped the phone in two when she'd explained our party organiser had requested an alarm call to my room. Apparently, *Mr Payne* didn't want me to miss our sunrise tour of Red Rock Canyon.

That prick!

I'm not sure what's more infuriating. The wake-up call, the laughable use of the word *organiser,* or that Jamie had rejected that same tour the second I'd suggested it.

Despondent at losing the first battle of the day, I crawled back under my covers to cram in a few more hours' sleep before breakfast.

Fortunately, when my *actual* alarm sounded at a reasonable hour, I felt more human and less like a rabid dog ready to maul anything in its path.

I'd almost describe myself as awake now that I've had a steaming shower and a whole mountain of caffeine. Dressed in a blue linen jumpsuit that will complement the bags under my eyes, I'm as ready as I'll ever be to meet the others for breakfast.

I totter into the elevator on platformed sandals that will absolutely be the death of me this morning and stab the button for the rooftop restaurant more viciously than is warranted.

The warm, dry air hits me the moment I step out onto the spectacular patio. The white tiles shine in the strong morning sun, and a glass wall allows an almost unobstructed view of the Vegas skyline.

The panorama is breathtaking, the city an impressive shrine to splendour and gaudiness. Pristine skyscrapers built of columns and windows surround extravagant fountains and manicured gardens. The sharp lines of the hotels are a stark contrast to the soft ruggedness of the mountains beyond. It's a recipe for pompousness, the ingredients at risk of taking themselves too seriously, if not for the miniature global landmarks dotted garishly throughout the strip. Instead, the city promises me glamour, debauchery, and a time I'll never forget.

I spot Cindy and most of our party at a circular table in the middle of the bar. It seems everyone's employing a different tactic to counter jetlag. Anthony's bouncing in his chair, hopped up on coffee, Cindy and Andi both have plates full of chocolate-covered pastries, and Tom has fallen asleep in his chair.

I breathe a sigh of relief when I realise Jamie's not among them, and there's a brief glimmer of hope that I can make it through an entire meal with my nerves intact. Of course, that dream dies when he emerges from behind the overstocked breakfast bar.

He's wearing a loose white tank top, and a pair of red beach shorts that I'm sure were painstakingly selected to showcase his toned calves and muscular thighs. In homage to douchebags everywhere, he's paired the ensemble with a black backwards cap, as if he isn't a grown adult with a job at a fucking bank.

Jamie's flooding a pancake stack with syrup, his tongue poking out as he tilts his plate this way and that for maximum coverage. How is it possible for him to be so effortlessly annoying all of the time?

Before I can decide how to best confront his childish ass, my legs are already marching towards him, my jaw clenched, and my hands fisted at my sides.

Welp. His morning's about to take a turn for the worse.

Jamie's eyes light up the second he spots my furious advance, his mouth twisting into a triumphant grin. "Good morning, Princess. Nice of you to join us."

I don't even dignify that with a response. Instead, I yank the syrup pot from his hand, hopefully pissing him off and saving America from a national syrup shortage in the process.

"Wow, someone's woken up on the wrong side of the bed. What's the matter, Emma? Bad night's sleep?"

I grind my teeth, reminding myself that throwing Jamie

off the top of a building will only cause more of a headache in the long run.

"You're an asshole," I spit for want of a much better insult.

"Well, that's a bit uncalled for. All I'm doing is making some breakfast."

"Cut the crap, Jamie. You know exactly what I'm talking about."

"I'm not sure I do," Jamie says, turning back to the buffet and ferreting out the biggest blueberries to scatter across his plate. "What's got your knickers in a twist this morning? A crease in your planner? A speck of dust on your suitcase?"

"Call my room again, and I'll slip laxatives into your beer when you're not looking."

Jamie gasps with fake realisation. "Oh, is that what this tantrum is about? I thought you'd love my wake-up call. I'm sure you said you wanted to visit that canyon thing?"

It takes all my resolve not to knock the plate from his hands and onto his stupid flip-flops. I take a deep breath, trying to rein in the anger that threatens to burst out of me.

"Just leave me alone, okay? Don't talk to me, don't look at me. If you so much as breathe in my direction, I swear I'll skewer you with the nearest sharp object."

"Don't tempt me with a good time, Princess." Jamie puts down his plate and casually leans against the breakfast bar.

"Do you have to be so insufferable?" I hiss, the tenuous grip I have on my control failing by the second. "Why not channel all this energy into your best friend? Anthony? Remember him? He's sort of the reason why we're all here."

There's a lively challenge sparkling in Jamie's dark eyes. He leans in, inching towards me so he can whisper in my ear. "But, Emma, why would I do that when you look so pretty all worked up for me."

His playful words cast a malevolent shadow, and I flinch away before I'm tainted by their devilish promise.

I don't have a response. No witty reply or scathing barb. For the first time, Jamie has rendered me speechless. And with that, the scoreboard shows I've lost our first morning in Vegas.

"Emma," a melodic voice chimes from across the rooftop. Thank God Cindy's seen fit to swoop in and save me from this nightmare.

"See you later, Princess," Jamie taunts, fleeing the scene of his crime with a spring in his step and a victorious wink over his shoulder.

It's unfair how easily he immerses himself back into our group. It's like he never left, laughing with the others while discreetly prying another cup of coffee from Anthony's unsteady hands.

"What happened?" Cindy asks as she steps up beside me, concern marring her sunny features.

I'm convinced Jamie's trying to make this trip all about him, so I bite my tongue and wave off his pathetic cry for attention. I'll be damned if I give him what he wants.

"Oh, nothing. Our dear best man was just being his usual, irritating self."

"So, I spotted one of those really American coffee houses across the street," Cindy says, grabbing my hand and tugging me towards the elevator. "Want to check it out? I could murder one of those blitzed-up coffees with all the whipped cream and sprinkles on top."

"Have you ever had a blitzed-up coffee with all the whipped cream and sprinkles on top?" I ask dubiously. She's typically more of a green tea sort of girl.

"Nope, that's the fun of it."

It's not until Cindy hits the button for the ground floor that I realise what's happened. Jamie and I have been separated. Again. Yet another event where people need to bend over backwards to accommodate our stupid animosity.

Guilt settles heavily in my stomach. I'm just as bad as Jamie. Why do I let him get to me? If I'd ignored him, I could be eating breakfast with the others right now instead of being marched away like a naughty child. And by the bride of all people.

Jamie and I are toxic, and nothing is going to fix that. I need to take the moral high ground and stay as far away from him as possible. My best friend's hen do is riding on it.

Hell, my sanity is riding on it!

The next time Jamie goads me, I'll be ready. He's not going to get the better of me again. I'll make damn sure of it.

Chapter Five

Jamie

Emma's ignoring me. Not a single scoff or scornful glare has been shot in my direction for over twenty-four hours.

It's infuriating, and certainly not through lack of trying on my part. I've thrown everything I have at Emma. I've bulldozed her carefully laid plans by sending the stags on completely spontaneous and unscheduled activities. I've single-handedly ensured Anthony's been late for every meal. And I've even lost an entire human being.

Seriously, none of us have seen Tom since yesterday.

I've shamelessly flirted with everything that moves, and even stole her towel and robe from the hotel spa. But still, she's giving me *nothing*. Not even an eye-roll. I'm worried she's had a personality transplant overnight. *My* Emma would never stand for such blatant disregard for meticulously organised fun.

The whole situation has me feeling itchy. We've always been tit for tat. Without Emma's tat, my tit is just pathetic. If I'm not careful, I could end up looking like that loser who doesn't know when to quit.

After a day of following her around the strip, I need this night out. I've had to watch from afar as she relaxes into the group of girls, laughing at their conspiratorial whispers and starting to make friends. It's a softer side of her I've never seen, and it's throwing me off-balance.

Yes, a night out at a Vegas club is exactly what the doctor ordered. If only the hens weren't joining us too...

"You're quiet tonight," Anthony observes as we trail behind our group.

We've decided to walk to the club since it's only ten minutes away from our hotel. Well, Emma decided, and everyone—including me—went along with her plan. I didn't have the energy to argue. Her aloofness has really knocked me off-centre.

"Sorry, mate. I was just thinking about Nan," I reply. It's not exactly a lie. Bridget is tearing her hair out with my almost hourly check-ins.

"Everything okay?"

"Yeah, Nan's good. By all accounts, she's keeping the finest nurses in London on their toes."

"Only another couple of days, and you'll be able to see for yourself," Anthony says, throwing his arm around me. He's already polished off a lethal-looking cocktail at the hotel bar, so our nighttime stroll is taking slightly longer than anticipated.

We're all following behind Emma's gold, strappy heels like obedient little ducklings. Tonight, she's wearing a pale pink dress that reaches her knees but is tight enough to be anything but modest. Her bouncy hair falls in soft waves around her shoulders, and the hens must have found a stray can of glitter because all of them, including Emma, are sparkling under the flashing Vegas lights.

The girls are putting us to shame. The stags have all

opted for the same boring shirt and jeans combo. Who knew there were so many shades of denim blue?

When Emma turns to cut through a flawlessly green park, Patrick breaks away from the herd, catching up with Emma's determined stride in just a few overreached steps.

I've not known Patrick long, but he's not the sort of guy I'd usually hang around with. He's alright in small doses, but he can be a bit of an ass. I know he's got a girlfriend at home, yet he's been trying it on with anyone who catches his eye this weekend. I don't think he's gone as far as to actually cheat, but it still doesn't sit right with me.

Emma is almost startled by Patrick's sudden appearance, though she quickly recovers and moves closer to him when he starts to speak.

Why does Patrick need to talk to Emma? Have they become friends? Is something wrong? Maybe he has some sort of problem with the trip? It's only prudent I check what's happening here. I am the second in command, after all.

I hear Anthony's groan the moment I quicken my pace, but I'm undeterred. I easily overtake the rest of our group to fall in behind the leading duo.

"So, how far away did you say the club was, Emma?" I hear Patrick ask, far too innocently.

"Only a few more minutes," comes Emma's soft reply.

Urgh, it's so weird when she's nice.

"And what time do we have the VIP booth from?"

"The email says eleven, but I think they'll let us in from ten thirty."

"And what about breakfast tomorrow? Exactly what time did you book the table for?"

And it goes on and on. Question after inane question that Patrick already has the answer to. I'd think he was flirting, except I've seen the guy in action. This is not his brand of sleaze.

When Patrick circles back to his original question, I have all the evidence I need that he's being a dick.

A quick look around tells me I'm the only one who thinks something's off. The other girls are immersed in their own secretive conversations, and the stags are laughing raucously, each offering lewd suggestions as to where Tom, our missing stag, has ended up.

Not even Emma has cottoned on to the fact that Patrick's making fun of her. Because that's what he's doing. He's asking these questions to *mock* Emma for her precise plans and careful timings.

It's hard not to see red. I needle at Emma because she needles at me. After almost twenty years of rivalry, our scorecard is pretty even. I'm an annoying dick to her because she's a pretentious bitch to me. She bites me, and I bite back. We give as good as we get, and it's fair. It's how we work.

Well, it was until yesterday.

Patrick, on the other hand, doesn't have that excuse. All Emma has ever done to him is organise an entire holiday for his enjoyment. *He's* never had to suffer her judgement or condescending sneer because Emma's never said a bad word to him. Hell, she's never said *any* words to him, as far as I can tell. So what game is this jackass playing?

"Could you email me tomorrow's schedule? I just want to make sure I know what's going on."

Unfortunately for Patrick, he asks his latest dickhead question just as he passes a very elaborate-looking fountain.

Poor, poor Patrick.

I speed up, reaching out so I can shove the prick in the back. Hard.

I catch him by surprise, easily knocking him off course and into the cool, blue depths of the water feature beside us.

He falls into the fountain with an almighty *splash*, the water sloshing over the side of the marble basin to rain over me and Emma.

"What the fuck?" he gurgles while Emma stands frozen to the spot, tiny drops of water running down her bare legs.

"Oh my God, I'm so sorry, Patrick," I lie, rushing over to haul him out of the fountain. "I tripped and went arse over tit. Are you okay?"

The guy looks stunned. Soggy and stunned. As if on autopilot, he stretches out his hand to accept my help. I pull him up, drawing him in for what will look to the others like a backslapping hug between friends.

Of course, that's not what this is.

I angle my head, speaking directly into Patrick's ear so no one else will hear my blatant threat. "The next time you mess with Emma, it'll be my fist you accidentally fall into. Got it?"

I force Patrick's breath from his chest with a final smack across his back and step away from his dripping form. My jeans and shirt are damp, but it's worth it.

"We good, man?" I ask, my charm returned for the benefit of the group.

Patrick nods dumbly.

"Jamie, what the hell is wrong with you?" Emma fumes, finally snapping out of her daze. "Can you seriously not go five minutes without ruining everything?"

"I tripped!" I protest indignantly, gesturing behind me to evidence the perfectly flat paving stones.

Luckily, everyone else seems to have missed my not-so-subtle sabotage, and they take my story at face value.

Anthony steps up beside me, looking almost as amused

as Emma is furious. "You always were a clumsy drunk," he snorts. "You alright, Pat?"

"Yeah, fine. No harm done." Patrick laughs nervously. "Er, I'm going to head back to the hotel and change. I'll meet you later?"

I'd rather he didn't come back at all, but I guess I'll compromise.

"Do you want me to come with you?" Emma asks with far more concern than is necessary in this situation. Patrick's wet, not dying.

I narrow my eyes, daring him to accept the offer.

"No, it's fine," he quickly replies. "It won't take long. I'll see you at the club in a bit."

As soon as the dripping husk of a man becomes an insignificant blight on our periphery, Emma turns on me. Colour has flooded her cheeks, and her cool eyes are full of vengeance.

Damn, I've missed that look.

"What is your problem?" she spits venomously. "Are you really that desperate for my attention? Or can't you stand the thought of someone else wanting to talk to me?"

The first option. Definitely the first option.

The rest of our group is peeling away, probably to seek shelter from our inevitable explosion. Only the long-suffering bride and groom remain, ready to step in if this gets ugly. Well, *when* this gets ugly, I suppose.

"You're paying for Patrick's dry cleaning," Emma demands, challenging me to argue. I'm only too happy to oblige.

"Oh, please. Patrick was wearing jeans and a shirt. He'll chuck them in the wash, and they'll come out just as drab as before."

"You really are the biggest prick I've ever met."

"Rant all you want, Princess. This time, I was doing you

51

a favour." It's feeling kind of lofty up here on this moral high ground. I'm not sure I like it.

"Go fuck yourself, Jamie," Emma snaps, her temper reaching fever pitch. Cindy tugs at her elbow, sensing we're about to cross into *possible public offence* territory.

"Take your own advice, sweetheart. It might make you more bearable," I yell at her retreating back.

Anthony knocks me around the head, but still, I can't keep the satisfied grin off my face. All I care about is that Emma's mad at me again.

I'm back in the game. And the play has never felt so good.

The club is loud, hot, and filled to the brim with twenty-somethings, all in various stages of undress. With its generic pulsing music, sticky floors, and the smell of stale alcohol permeating the air, I could be in any club in the world. Only the rogue feathers and sequins adorning almost every surface give its location away.

I'm still riding the high from my earlier altercation with Emma. So, I've not felt the need to touch the ridiculously overpriced bottles of alcohol standing in an ice bath at our equally overpriced booth.

I'm sitting with the guys at a low round table, the club's lights continuously flashing across its pitch-black surface. From our prime spot on the balcony, we have a bird's-eye view of our girls. They've been swallowed by the surging dancefloor, their formation morphing as the crowd undulates and sways to the DJ's beat.

Anthony and Josh are busy pouring our next round of drinks, but I'm content watching the dynamics of the club below. The humming energy of the place settles in my veins, and despite the unbridled chaos, I feel a sense of peace.

Perhaps that's why when Anthony hands me what must be a triple shot of neat whisky, I sip at the contents rather than knocking it back like my overexcited comrades.

Josh and Anthony slam down their tumblers, each spluttering clumsily before collapsing into a fit of giggles and reaching for another round.

I smile to myself. This is going to get messy, and I can't wait to watch it happen.

"Ah, there he is," Josh suddenly yells across the bar.

Oh, joy, it's Patrick. Significantly drier and infinitely more pissed off than when we left him.

I think it's time to stretch my legs. You know, get the lay of the land, soak up the atmosphere, put as much distance as possible between me and someone I physically assaulted earlier this evening...

"I'm going to do a lap," I shout at Anthony, waving in the general direction of *over there* so my point translates over the deafening music.

"Alright, catch you in a bit, man. If you see Cindy, can you tell her I've made her a drink?"

I spot said concoction on the table and decide it's best if I 'forget' that particular message.

"Of course, mate," I fib before taking my leave and weaving my way across the balcony.

I skirt along the glass railing, finding myself a quiet corner by the stairs. The dark spot gives me the perfect vantage point across the whole club.

Maybe I should find a pretty girl to talk to. Someone cute and sweet who'll find my accent charming and laugh at my subpar jokes. It's been a few months since I've felt the need to hook-up, and what better place to end my dry spell than in Sin City itself?

There's certainly no shortage of beautiful women here. I even spot a few trying me on for size, their pouted lips and hooded eyes beckoning me closer. I might be on foreign soil, but body language is universal.

All the same, no one is really holding my attention. I'm still pumped from my altercation with Emma, and it'll take more than cute to satisfy me tonight. I'm too keyed up to play nice.

It doesn't help that my eyes are constantly drawn to the devil herself.

Emma and Cindy are right at the centre of the enormous dancefloor, the rest of the hens nowhere to be found. Cindy's having the time of her life, her head thrown back and her hands in the air, screaming the words to some pop song I haven't heard since school.

But it's Emma who's captured my interest. She might not be wailing at the top of her lungs, but she seems to be having fun. It's... unnerving.

This is not the aggrieved woman who greeted me at Heathrow Airport. No, this Emma is *alive*. There's an indulgent smile on her glossy lips, and her eyes are sparkling brighter than the club lights cutting across her pale pink dress.

I never would have pegged Emma as someone with rhythm, but her hips sway with flawless grace, and she moves in perfect time with the pulsating beat. As her hands glide through her loose tresses, I find myself standing up straighter to get a better look.

The vision is incongruent with everything I know about my adversary. Who is *this* Emma, and how do I conquer her too?

It's only when Emma throws her arms around Cindy's neck that I notice I'm not the only one ensnared. The pair are encapsulated by a band of eager admirers, each of them calculating their odds of getting lucky while trying to look indifferent.

The first brave soul breaks away from the safety of the crowd, approaching Emma with hope in his eyes and lust in his pants.

Don't do it, bro.

I wait on tenterhooks, curious to see how Emma turns down this interloper. A subtle shake of the head or a full-blown slap in the face? I imagine the former since extreme reactions are reserved for me and me alone.

If my eyes pop out of my head when Emma turns and gives him the time of day, then I'm absolutely floored when she allows him to put his hands *on her fucking waist.*

Seriously, has Emma been body snatched?

The pair sway together, moving closer and closer as the song reaches its chaotic climax. It's honestly a little dirty, and a part of me feels like an unwelcome voyeur.

Of course, another part of me is really fricking curious, so I study this unearthed side of Emma, looking my fill from the safety of my darkened corner.

I've never really thought about Emma having sex before. I mean, I guess she must. I just assumed it was more of a scheduled event. A boring roll in the sheets with an equally boring guy, probably organised via a shared calendar invite.

But now, as I watch Emma taunt her prey, I'm confronted with a different reality. Maybe Emma's not the good girl she'd have us all believe. Maybe she plays with her food. Maybe the Vegas population will be down by one come tomorrow morning.

The guy manages to entertain Emma for an entire song before she's bored. To be honest, that's longer than I thought he'd last. As the track winds down, Emma whispers in his ear before turning back to Cindy, who's been happily jumping around on her own.

As the night plays on, the same thing happens over and over again. Some chancer will peel himself away from the crowd, and Emma will put up with him for as long as she wants. Most last a song, some last less. One particularly douchey guy lasts two entire tracks, and my mind starts to fry.

Why this guy? Sure, he's the most confident of the bunch, but honestly, he seems a bit of a knob. I mean, who wears board shorts and a vest to a *club*?

I don't know what criteria Emma's using to cast her judgements, but I need to find out. And if I can remind her of my existence in the process, that's just a bonus.

Slowly, I take the stairs to the dancefloor, keeping Emma in my sight the entire time. She's dancing with Cindy now, blissfully unaware of my presence as I circle closer, chasing her smiles and stalking her every step.

Winding my way through writhing bodies, I coil in tighter to my prize. When I slide up behind Emma, the sly movement catches Cindy's eye.

Mischief must be written all over my face because she narrows her eyes at me in warning. *Too late, Cindy.*

Reaching out, I subtly drag my fingers across the small of Emma's back, the silky material smooth beneath my skin. That's all it takes to steal Emma's attention. She spins around, almost losing her balance in those ridiculous shoes when she comes face to face with the last person she expects.

"What are you doing?" Emma asks, too taken aback to remember she's mad at me.

I smirk at the confusion on her face, leaning in so close that I can smell her floral perfume.

"Just making sure I'm the one you'll be thinking about in bed tonight, Princess."

Emma's lips part, her face darkening as my curse washes over her.

Slowly, I take a smug step back, and then another, until the crowd swallows me back into its incessant tide.

Tonight, I am the victor.

Your move, Emma.

Chapter Six

Jamie

E mma's there. Right there in front of me on the dance floor. Her body sways to the music, captivating and enchanting anyone who dares lay eyes on her. She's so close I can reach out and skim my fingers across the material stretched over her taut stomach.

I don't think I've ever seen her in pink before. The colour seems too fun, too frivolous for her. This dress should be grey. Or black, to match her cold heart.

I clutch at the jarring material, wanting to tear it from her stirring body. Then, my face twists into a taunting smile, ready to goad Emma into our next sating collision.

Except, when her eyes lock with mine, it's not loathing reflected back at me.

It's need.

Hunger.

A deep desire so desperate it steals the breath from my lungs. Because I feel it too. An all-consuming want humming through my veins, clouding every one of my senses.

The bass throbs around us, hundreds of faceless bodies pulsing in time to a song I've never heard but is familiar all the same. I'm jostled by the crowd, the sound of the club deafening yet so quiet I can hear every breath Emma takes.

My fingers play over the silky softness of her dress, running from the slope of her waist to the dip of her pelvis. I'm mesmerised by the way her muscles jump under my ministrations, and I trace my fingers back and forth until she grips onto my arms, halting my teasing trail.

I brace myself for rejection, but it never comes. Instead, Emma pulls me closer, her eyes fluttering and her head falling back to bare the glistening flesh of her neck.

Emma's exposing herself to me, yielding to me... tempting me.

And I've never been one to deny myself.

I step closer, dropping my head to run my nose up the length of her neck, her floral perfume flowing from her sweet skin all the way to my heavy cock. My teeth ache with the need to mark her, to prove to myself I was here.

I graze across her thumping pulse, then soothe the bite with a gentle kiss.

"Jamie," she whimpers, her fingers digging ruthlessly into my biceps.

Her chest rises and falls, and my own tumbles in line with her staccato rhythm. She looks mindless, lost, hooking her arms around my neck and clinging on for dear life. I'm the port in her storm, her anchor. But it's hopeless when I'm lost, too.

I drop my hands to Emma's ass and pull her into me.

She fits so perfectly, my broad frame completely encompassing her lithe figure. The moment my body melds with hers, Emma's eyes fly open, burning with desire, want, and something else I can't quite make out but has my cock twitching nonetheless.

Her dress is still wrong, the pink too sweet and innocent.

She should be draped in blood red to match the wicked gleam in her eyes, or better yet, wearing nothing at all.

My dick swells painfully in the prison of my jeans, a throbbing, hopeful member I've no chance of hiding from Emma. Not that I want to.

I roll my hips forward, my silent moan echoing around the pulsing club.

Emma meets my next thrust, the sinful grind of her body driving me to madness. I need more. I need to be so close to her that she'll never forget I was here. That for one shining moment, we made sense.

I grab onto the back of her thigh and wrap her leg around my waist. Her tight dress protests, the material bunching around the tops of her thighs and cupping her biteable ass exquisitely.

We rut harder and harder, each thrust faster and more crazed than the last. We push each other to our limits—and ever closer to the stupidest best decision we've ever made.

I'm so close, desperate for release, and Emma's breathy moans tell me she's close, too.

Her fingers tangle in my hair, her tempting mouth parted, just daring me to accept the invitation.

I lean in, feeling her breath across my lips and—

I wake with a start, gasping as my mind struggles to make sense of the desperation coursing through my body. Sucking in a lungful of air, I slam my eyes shut and wait for my world to stop spinning.

What in the ever-loving fuck was that?

One moment of obsessive insanity at a club, one minuscule hint of something more simmering inside that ice sculpture, and my mind betrays me like this?

I kick my legs against the crisp hotel sheets, willing my body to behave and forget everything it thinks it's discovered tonight.

Emma and I? Infeasible. A recipe for disaster, homicide, and potentially the end of time as we know it. How could a sane world continue to stand when Emma and I tear down the very foundations on which we've built our lives?

No, I'm better off forgetting this night ever happened. I'll blame it on the spell of Vegas and draw a line right underneath it.

If only my dick would get the message.

I take several meditative breaths, each more useless than the last. I'm a lost cause, and there's only one way to reset the board.

Hating myself all the while, I throw off the covers and fist my aching cock. It only takes a few frantic pumps before I'm coming all over my chest, Emma's name in my throat as I finish the job she started.

Chapter Seven

Emma

My time in Vegas can only be described as an assault on my senses. Whichever way I turn, I'm blinded by the lights that glint off almost every shining surface. I can't hear over the roar of a hundred different crowds as they merge into a screaming symphony. And no matter what I try, the overpowering taste of the sambuca shots Marta ordered at lunch still lingers on my tongue.

I'm in love. Las Vegas has stolen my heart, and I'm not even mad about it. Who'd have thought that the risk-averse introvert, who gets a migraine from just thinking about too much artificial lighting, doesn't want to go home tomorrow morning?

I've sung my heart out with drag queens, been a referee for a water volleyball match, and unwound after it all at the hotel spa. Cindy and I even spent a very surreal hour feeding coins into one of those old-fashioned slot machines. Originally, we'd tried to turn it into a drinking game, taking a gulp of our mojitos every time the wheels came to a mismatched halt. But we quickly abandoned that idea.

We both have too much to live for.

For the first time in almost a decade, work hasn't been at the forefront of my mind. Yes, my heart momentarily stops whenever I think about the sixty-eight unread emails haunting my inbox, but the marketing world didn't collapse without me. Consumers bought products they didn't want, and clients raked in profits they didn't need, all while lining my boss's deep pockets. The well-oiled machine continued.

I'm sure I should be having some kind of existential crisis over my complete lack of work-life balance, but my capacity for meaningful introspection took a hit when the words 'Marines' and 'water volleyball' were uttered in the same sentence.

Las Vegas would be perfect if it weren't for one thing.

Well, one person, to be exact. Because for every dimpled, All-American smile aimed in my direction, there's a snide comment waiting for me from my very own British super-villain.

It's as if Jamie misread the best man's job description and somehow confused it with a mission to make the maid of honour's life hell. He's done everything in his power to belittle, inconvenience, and embarrass me from behind his mask of a bumbling idiot.

Pushing Patrick into a fountain was a new low for him. And the way he taunted me in the club was borderline cruel, seeking me out just to make fun of me when my guard was down.

Even this morning, on our last full day of the trip, he had nothing better to do than annoy me.

We'd all decided to spend the early hours basking in the sun, driven to the poolside loungers by our lingering hangovers. Uninterested in sitting still for more than five minutes, Jamie took to walking up and down the infinity pool, trying to convince someone to play with him. He was on his third pass when he happened to slip right next to my sun lounger.

Thankfully, he caught his fall on the little plastic table beside me, but not before he swiped its entire contents into a lovely puddle of pool juice. My fresh cappuccino and the paperback thriller I'd nearly finished were both lost to its soggy depths.

His over-exaggerated apology was drowned out by the swarm of concerned women who flocked to his side to check he was okay. Marta even gave *me* the side-eye, as if it was *my* fault the table didn't save him completely.

My only respite from Jamie's campaign comes during the moments he's buried in his phone. It's in those precious seconds where I'm not the focus of his attention that I let myself really *look* at him. Gone is his carefree persona, replaced by a man who has the weight of the world on his shoulders.

Seeing the tense set of his jaw and the dark circles under his eyes, I can't help but think something's going on with Jamie. But given how sly he's been over the past few days, I can't bring myself to care.

After this trip, I've vowed to wash my hands of him. I'll see him on Cindy's wedding day, and then I have no interest in ever hearing his name again. My attention only adds fuel to his fire, and I intend to cut off his supply.

In practice, my new stance is taking some getting used to. Even now, as he saunters into the hotel bar to a round of catcalls and sarcastic applause, I have to remind myself to ignore the fact that he's late for dinner. Again.

What's harder to overlook is the way every light in the room bounces off his tanned skin, or more specifically, the second-hand glitter smeared in haphazard patches from his head to his waist.

How the hell did that get there?

Wait. I don't care. It's not my problem. And given Jamie's secretive smile whenever he's asked about it, an answer is not forthcoming.

The mood around the table is subdued tonight. Maybe I'm projecting, but it's as if we're all lamenting the end of our adventure.

Even Jamie, still sparkling ridiculously at the other end of the table, seems content to just sit back and eat his ginormous burger and fries.

I want to kick myself when I spot my oldest friend giving her husband-to-be the biggest heart eyes I've ever seen. I want to kick myself when Marta smiles at me, acknowledging the start of a fragile new friendship. But most of all, I want to kick myself when I realise I *have* to leave the table. Because, as much as I should be making the most of this, I need some time alone to savour the last few hours of holiday bliss.

Once our plates are cleared, I wait for an opportunity to excuse myself. Luckily, it doesn't take long for a lull to fall over the table. I think Vegas has finally beaten us.

"Right," I say, inwardly cringing at how awkward I sound. "I think I'm going to call it a night. See you all down here tomorrow morning at six?"

To my surprise, I'm met with a resounding chorus of *me too's*, with a few *thank God for that's* thrown in for good measure. Our time here has come to a natural close. Even Jamie doesn't seem bothered about the party ending, his eyes glued to his phone so intently that the carefree smudges of glitter on his jaw are jarring.

I share the elevator with Josh and Patrick, listening to them bicker about Tom and whether we should consider a search party.

Mere days ago, the knowledge we were missing a whole person would have sent me spiralling. Now, I'm placing that issue in a box marked *'not my problem'*. Tom is a grown man. He is capable of getting himself onto a plane without my help. And if he doesn't, that's his crisis to manage.

Besides, I have something more important to do than worry about a missing stag. After successfully orchestrating this whole trip, I think I deserve a little self-indulgence.

You see, I have a secret. Something no one else knows about. Something I will hide from my boring work colleagues and uptight clients at all costs.

Because I, Emma Drayton, am an addict.

A romance addict.

The serious paperback thriller that Jamie knocked into a pool puddle? That was nothing. A decoy. I've been trying to finish it for the past five weeks, but it's an uphill battle. An arduous slog. If I can't sleep, I don't need drugs. I simply pick up that book.

But put a romance novel in my hands, and I will sit there and ignore all my biological functions until it's finished. The trashier, the better. Porn with a plot? I'm in. Taboo relationships? Say no more. Stockholm syndrome? Just shut up and take my money.

Patrick and Josh barely register the wave I throw in their direction when we reach our floor, the pair still arguing about Tom's likely whereabouts. But I'm beyond caring. I'm about to get my fix, and anything else is irrelevant.

Letting myself into my room, I head straight for my minibar and pour myself a very overpriced vodka cranberry. I'm still on holiday, after all. Then I grab my phone, prop myself up on my bed, and open my reading app.

I've devoured enough romances to know this story is about to get juicy. The big scary CEO—that no one can stand—has just called an impromptu companywide meeting. The heroine is hiding at the back of the room, shaking in her stilettos while she waits to hear if the rumours are true. Has the tyrant she's been crushing on for three years proposed to his gorgeous but awful ex-girlfriend?

I sip my drink, the hotel room fading away as the utterly predictable story reels me in.

Page after page, the tension reaches new heights. The CEO and his secretary are about to rip each other's clothes off and give in to the lust that's been building for three whole chapters. Then, just as the domineering boss pushes our heroine up against his office wall—

I get a text.

Damn it!

I'm sorely tempted to swipe away the notification, but the American number tells me this is probably something important. With a sigh, I open the text, only to groan at the opening line.

> Unknown number: Hi, Miss Drayton. It's Frank from Bright Light Cabs. I'm so sorry, but we have to cancel your transfer tomorrow morning...

Fuck.

When researching the best hotel transfers in Las Vegas, I chose Bright Light Cabs because of its rave reviews. As a small family-run firm, they offer a more personal service, and their customers seem to love their friendly drivers and reliability.

Of course, the downside of such a small operation is when two drivers come down with the flu, there's not much that can be done. I just have to accept the full refund and thank Frank for the links he's sent to other companies that might be able to help.

I scroll through the information, trying to remember if any of the firms came up in my initial search. Usually, it's the kind of task I'd relish, but in the last moments of my holiday, the prospect of more research couldn't be less appealing.

Today, I'm in the mood to cut corners. Why spend hours online when I can get the information straight from the horse's mouth?

After all, back in the UK, I didn't have access to a receptionist in my lobby who deals with hundreds of transfers a month.

I thank my lucky stars that I'm still wearing my tank top and denim shorts from dinner, and throw my legs over the side of the bed. All I need to do is slip my feet into my wedged sandals, shove my keycard in my pocket, and I'm marching out the door.

There's a smug spring in my step as I wind my way to the elevators. Was a cancelled transfer really going to break me?

Bitch, please. After dealing with Jamie Payne for a whole long weekend, a cancelled taxi is child's play.

Now, I can handle *anything*.

Chapter Eight

Jamie

Just one more drink. That's all I want to mark the end of my holiday. Or that's what I'm telling myself, anyway. In reality, I'm avoiding my hotel room. The naked walls and foreign bed are a stark reminder of how far away I am from home. At least in this bustling bar, I can pretend I'm in London, pretend I'm not a million miles from a certain hospice—and the little old lady waiting for me there.

The only thing keeping me sane is messing with Emma. Ever since I realised I'm the only one who can steal her attention, I've wanted more. I'm obsessed. I want to find out exactly how many of her waking moments she'll dedicate to hating me before she snaps.

Every huff, every eye-roll, every grind of her teeth and murderous look, each of them a beautiful moment I've earned. Now I'm greedy for her, an addict, hoarding every marker of annoyance bestowed upon me.

Her barely concealed anger when I turned up for dinner tonight, covered in someone else's body glitter, was the icing on top of the Vegas cake. I thought she was going to erupt with the need to ask me how it came to be there.

It might be hard to believe, but there's a completely innocent explanation. I simply crashed into a man wearing nothing but a pair of silver Speedos and body paint at the casino this evening. No one else saw, so why not enjoy the air of mystery it afforded me? Especially when it was driving Emma crazy.

Oh shit, that reminds me. Is the glitter still there?

Luckily, our hotel is one of the gaudiest on the strip, so I have my pick of reflective surfaces in which to check.

Yep, I'm still sparkly.

I reach over the bar for a napkin and scrub at the oily smears on my face until I'm glitter-free. Then, deciding that's probably my sign to bid Vegas adieu, I down the rest of my beer and call it a night.

As luck would have it, there's an elevator waiting on the ground floor, and I manage to slip inside just as the doors start to edge their way closed. I nod to the only other guy in the car before pulling out my phone and rereading the text Bridget had sent me earlier.

Bridget: She's fine. Stop worrying and do something outrageous.

Inspired by my sister's pearls of wisdom, I set my mind to devising one last way to mess with my nemesis. A parting gift, if you will.

When I step out of the elevator, I'm so preoccupied with my thoughts of tyranny that I almost don't register the distant sound of drunken laughter down the hall.

And why would I? This is Vegas, after all. It's not until I

round the corridor that I finally realise something's not right...

Because I'm not hearing the sound of a couple of guys goofing around. I'm hearing a pack of predatory wolves going in for the kill.

Ask anyone—except Patrick—and they'll tell you I'm an easy-going sort of guy. I don't have a temper or a short fuse, and the only punches I've thrown are in the boxing ring. But that fact pales into insignificance when my brain makes sense of the scene before me.

Two tanked-up men have cornered a frightened woman, their seedy eyes leering while they tower over her small frame. That alone would stop anyone in their tracks, but it's the sight of mahogany hair and stylish sandals that really has me seeing red.

It's Emma. Those assholes are terrorising *my Emma*.

The look on her face is a kick to my stomach. There's no irritation there, none of the exasperation or infuriation I'm used to. Instead, Emma's skin is blanched, her fierce blue eyes wide with fear. She's hunched over as if she might be able to disappear, making herself as small as possible in the presence of these *men*.

I'm overcome by such a powerful wave of fury that my body coils into action, my blood reaching boiling point so fast that my head spins.

My approach goes unnoticed, which works in my favour, especially when the more foolish of the two men reaches out to trace his finger along Emma's trembling jaw.

This guy must have a death wish.

And I'm more than happy to satisfy it.

I move faster than I ever thought possible, catching the asshole's wrist in a painful grip just as his slimy fingers touch Emma's perfect skin.

I yank his arm back violently, spinning the unsuspecting man around so it's *me* he's facing. My evil grin is the only warning he gets before I ram my hand into his throat and pin him against the wall.

I check on his cowardly companion, ensuring he's not going to be a threat while I deal with the scum who laid his hands on Emma. But his snivelling accomplice is rooted to the spot, not so cocky now there's someone bigger and infinitely more murderous than him on the scene.

Emma whimpers, and I watch as she staggers away from us. Her eyes are shining with tears, and she's looking at me with something other than contempt for the first time in our lives.

And I hate it. I want to kill the person who put that frightened look on her face.

Adrenaline burns through me, charging my muscles with a wired energy that's begging for release. I'm frenzied, and judging by the way the cowards shake before me, I look just as unhinged as I feel.

I'm so amped up that my voice is nothing more than a low rumble when I lean in to spit in my captive's face. "How fucking dare you?" My hand flexes menacingly around his throat, my knuckles white from my tight grip.

"I'm s-sorry, man," he slurs, tugging at my wrist in a panic. "We were just messing around."

"I think you might be apologising to the wrong person," I sneer, moving in close enough to ensure he smells the stale alcohol on my breath.

The two men stare at me with fear in their eyes before turning to Emma and murmuring their pathetic apologies.

That's as good as it's going to get, so with a final squeeze of my hand for good measure, I drop the lowlife to the floor. I don't want them around Emma for one more second. They don't deserve to breathe the same air as her, let alone exist in her proximity.

"Now, fuck off before I knock out your teeth and shove them so far up your arse they'll end up back in your mouth."

Being the spineless twats they are, I don't need to repeat myself. I watch as the pair scurry away until the crackle of material hitching down the wall reminds me there's someone more important in need of my attention.

Emma has sunk to the floor, her arms around her shins and her head buried in her knees. My first instinct is to throw myself around her, to shield her from the world and tell her no one will hurt her again. But I hold back. She's already suffered one unwelcome touch tonight, and I'm not willing to add another. Instead, I crouch down beside her, letting her know she's not alone.

The stagnant hotel air is still, but the rasp of Emma's laboured breath is deafening. Her entire body shakes as she wheezes and gasps into her knees. Emma's having some kind of panic attack, and I haven't a clue how to help her.

"Breathe, Emma," I say stupidly. "Come on, in and out." I take slow, exaggerated breaths, unsure if this is the right thing to do or if Emma can even hear me.

I seriously second-guess my plan when I start to feel lightheaded, but I persevere regardless, inhaling and exhaling in case I can suddenly breathe for two.

My heart leaps into my throat when Emma uncoils herself from her protective ball and rests her head against the cold wall behind us. Her skin is still worryingly pale, but her wide, bloodshot eyes lock with mine as she follows the measured rise and fall of my chest.

We sit there for what feels like hours while Emma's breathing falls in time with mine, the tension leaching from her body with every passing minute.

"I froze," she finally whispers. "I can't believe I froze."

I don't think there's anything I can say that will make her feel better right now, not while her emotions are so raw.

All the words that spring to mind are worthless, empty platitudes.

I'm sorry.

It wasn't your fault.

Anyone would have done the same thing.

I wish I'd got here sooner...

The only thing I can do is give her a safe space to come down. So, I sit in vigil, listening to Emma grow stronger and steadier while I keep the outside world at bay.

Then, just as my ass cheeks fall asleep, she lets out an almighty groan and slams her face into her hands.

"Are you okay?" I ask like a complete idiot.

She sighs. "Just perfect."

I give her what I hope is a reassuring smile, and she tries to return the sentiment. Although it's more of a grimace if I'm honest.

"Where were you going? I thought you'd gone to bed?"

"Yeah, I had," Emma mutters groggily. "But our transfer was cancelled, so I was going to reception to order a new one."

The clear directive is a life raft in this unchartered ocean, so I jump to my feet and offer Emma my hand. After her shock, I consider suggesting that I deal with the task myself. But I know Emma better than that. She'd never trust me to organise something as important as an airport transfer. And rightly so.

Of course, instead of taking my outstretched palm like any normal person, she looks at me as if I've lost my mind.

Ah, it's good to be back on familiar ground.

"Come on," I say, giving my hand a shake. "Let's go and get this sorted."

Emma must be coming back to herself because she stubbornly pushes herself up the wall without my help. Still, she doesn't object when I fall in behind her, nor when I join her in the empty elevator. We remain in awkward silence until we reach the reception, both of us unwilling to acknowledge our apparent ceasefire.

It's not until Emma hands over her credit card to the receptionist that I notice how her fingers are trembling.

She's trying to come across as unaffected, but it's just another act. The calm and collected Emma who makes my life a misery is a far cry from this version of my foe. Her heel bounces restlessly as she waits for her payment to process, and her usually shrewd eyes dart nervously around the lobby, just waiting for some unknown spectre to strike.

I can't let her go back to her room alone like this. What if her blood pressure drops from the shock? What if she falls over and cracks her head on a sink? Anthony would never let me hear the end of it.

"Do you want to grab a Coke or something?" I ask when the receptionist hands back Emma's card. "The sugar might help with the adrenaline drop."

I've no idea if that's true because my medical knowledge is based on the murder mysteries my parents watch on Sunday. There's always a sympathetic neighbour passing sweet cups of tea to anyone who's stumbled across a corpse.

Nonetheless, the offer works because Emma stops fidgeting and looks at me suspiciously. Her clear eyes fix on mine, trying to unearth my non-existent ulterior motive.

Whatever she sees on my face must pass her test for bullshit because she turns abruptly, striding past me and straight into the empty hotel bar.

Even my six-foot-plus frame is no match for her determined pace. By the time I catch up with Emma, she's already folded her long legs over a barstool at the chrome counter.

Thanks for waiting. It's not like this was my idea or anything.

I signal to the barman, ready to order two of the biggest and sweetest sodas they have, when—

"A tequila, please," Emma says before I can get a word in.

The barman nods, pulling out a large shot glass from beneath the bar. Then he turns to me, his brow raised expectantly.

Fuck it.

"Better make that two."

The barman pours, and we waste no time in shotting the earthy liquid, both ignoring the salt and lemon wedges placed in front of us.

I slam my glass back down, wincing at the woodsy burn that slides down my throat. Emma adopts a more refined approach, delicately lowering her drink before signalling for another round.

The silence between us is killing me. I've never before been in the presence of someone who has managed to order so much alcohol with so few words.

"Should we drink to something?" I ask, just to break this roaring tension.

Emma ignores my question, picking up her shot and leaving me with no choice but to keep up. In my rush, I swallow the potent liquid the wrong way, and it takes every trick I learnt as a student not to spray the contents back out of my nose.

Bloody hell, how is it possible that Emma's beating me at *drinking*?

"Thank you," Emma finally says, her voice barely audible over my clumsy splutters.

"Yeah, no worries," I gasp hopelessly. There's a reason I rarely drink spirits.

"No, really. Thank you, Jamie. I don't know what would have happened if you hadn't..." I'm glad Emma trails off; I don't want to think of the alternative, either. "I know it probably killed you to come to my rescue."

"We both know you'd have done the same for me."

And I really believe that. No matter how childish we are, I'd like to think Emma would be there if I really needed it.

"I'd have stepped in and saved you from two drunk men who couldn't take no for an answer?" Emma snorts.

I play along, leaning in to flutter my eyelashes at her. "What? You don't think I'm pretty enough to attract all the drunk boys?"

"How are you still such an idiot?"

"Sorry to disappoint you, but I think it's a permanent affliction."

"I figured." Emma smiles shyly. She rocks her glass on the counter, grating it back and forth while choosing her next words. "I've never seen you like that before. You were terrifying. I thought you were going to kill that guy."

Yeah? Well, that guy touched you, my mind immediately responds. Thankfully, I swallow the possessive words before they can escape and hang over us for the rest of time.

"I'd say I wouldn't want to get on the wrong side of you, but I think that ship sailed years ago," Emma laughs wearily.

"Hey, let's call a truce tonight. We can go back to hating each other in the morning." I nudge Emma with my elbow, overshooting slightly and only just catching myself before I topple off my stool.

Bloody tequila.

"Besides," I continue, hoping we can move past my ungainly stumble. "You and I aren't bad people. We just don't get on. Those guys earlier? They were bad fucking people, and they deserve to rot in hell."

Emma studies me intently. I'm a mere specimen under her microscope, and it takes all my willpower not to squirm under the scrutiny. Her eyes narrow, and her lips purse, chewing over what she wants to say. I think she's debating whether or not our tentative ceasefire is strong enough for her to share whatever's on her mind.

"Can we not tell Cindy about tonight?" she finally asks. "I don't want this to ruin her hen do."

I let out a defeated groan. Cindy will blow a gasket if she finds out I was involved in this and didn't tell her. She's always been protective of Emma, and she'd hate to know her best friend went through this without her. Still, this isn't my story to share. Not even close.

"Don't you think she'll want to know?" I ask gently.

"Please? I'll tell her after the wedding. I promise."

"You don't need to promise me anything," I reassure her. "This is your choice. But I am going to let the hotel know what happened."

The least I can do is make sure those cretins don't take advantage of anyone else while they're here.

Emma takes a moment to contemplate my compromise before nodding reluctantly. This brings the total number of agreements we've had up to two.

Not wanting to wait until more of the tequila hits my system, I quickly hop off my stool to talk with reception. The front desk team records my version of events with little fuss and a firm assurance they'll act as necessary.

Emma's eyes seek me out the entire time, her body tight with tension until I'm back by her side.

"They'll take care of it," I tell her, climbing awkwardly back onto my stool. I've always thought it cruel to make chairs so unstable in establishments that serve alcohol. "And the hotel is going to cover our drinks tab tonight."

Considering what we went through to earn it, I won't say the perk is good news, but it's better than nothing. Something else Emma and I seem to agree on because she's already leaning over the counter to catch the barkeeper's attention.

"Hi, excuse me?" she shouts. "Can you get us the bottle, please?" Emma gestures to the empty shot glasses in front of us just in case there was any doubt as to which bottle she's referring to.

The tequila the barkeeper pulls from the fridge is far fancier than any I've seen before. I glance conspicuously at the bar menu and wince when I spot the outrageous price tag. You'd have to do really well in the casinos to consider buying a shot of that, let alone an entire bottle.

Oh well. They did say our tab would be covered. My head is going to hate me tomorrow.

Emma meticulously pours two generous shots, leaning down to ensure each glass contains the same amount of liquid. When she's satisfied, we both wordlessly pick up our pricey poison and knock it back in one.

We've barely lowered our glasses before Emma's pouring again. Except, this time, she looks up at me from beneath her lashes, a wicked glint shining in her eyes as she fills the shots to the brim. Princess Perfect's mask has finally slipped.

I can't help it. I smile back roguishly before necking the shot once more.

God, Emma's pretty. Why does she always look so pretty?

Should the spawn of Satan really have such shiny hair?

I love how the lights are making it all shimmery tonight.

I wonder what shade of blue you'd call her eyes. Midnight iceberg? Frozen galaxy?

She smells like flowers. I really like flowers.
Especially daisies.
I bet Emma likes daisies.
Shit, I think the tequila's starting to work...
And there lies my last coherent thought.

Chapter Nine

Jamie

Dear lord, I'm dying. That's the only explanation for the screaming pain ringing through my head.

Or is it coming from outside my head?

Wait, what the hell is that noise? Is someone strangling a seagull in my room?

WHY WON'T YOU SHUT THE FUCK UP!

Unfortunately, whatever is making the unholy screech cannot hear my internal monologue and carries on regardless.

Jeez, what the hell happened last night?

"Urgh." That's the only warning I get before I'm slapped in the face.

All of a sudden, I'm awake. Wide awake. Because an arm that is not mine has flung itself across my bed in the vague direction of the terrible, terrible sound.

I bolt upright with a manly shriek, grabbing the sheets and hoisting them up to my chin. In my heart, I already know who's just done the exact same thing on the other side of my bed.

I almost can't bear to turn and face the music, but I do.

Her hair is matted around her shoulders, and there's mascara smeared down her cheek, a matching streak embossed on my white pillowcase.

But despite all the imperfections, it's undeniable.

Emma Drayton is in my bed.

We both stare at each other in wide-eyed horror, unable to move while the shrill hotel phone continues its incessant monologue beside us.

I blindly reach over to the bedside table, fumbling around until I find the offending object, never once taking my eyes off *her*.

"Hello?" I croak into the phone.

"Good morning, Mr Payne. This is your wake-up call," a bright voice screams at me.

"What?"

"It's five forty, Mr Payne. Have a great day."

And the line goes dead.

"It was a wake-up call," I explain absurdly.

"I ordered you one," Emma whispers, the whites of her eyes stark against the dark room. "I didn't want you to be late."

That's it. The cherry on top of the fucking cake. My mind reaches breaking point, free-falling over the cliff of sanity and into the choppy waters of madness below.

It's impossible to hold back any longer. I take one big, fortifying breath and burst into uncontrollable laughter. I'm hysterical, tears rolling down my cheeks as Emma looks on in disbelief.

She's done it. She's finally driven me out of my mind.

"It's not funny, Jamie," she snaps haughtily. Which is hilarious, given the crust of drool at the corner of her mouth.

I snort.

"Christ almighty, it's like dealing with a child," she

laments to the ceiling. "Do you remember *anything* about last night?"

"I remember tequila?" I offer unhelpfully, wiping away my tears.

Damn my intolerance of hard liquor. I've no trouble reliving the first half of the evening. I remember the jack-asses harassing Emma and then ordering a fancy bottle of tequila at the hotel bar. I remember several very large shots, and then... it gets hazy.

I squeeze my eyes tight, trying to fish the memories from my alcohol-drenched brain. If I concentrate hard enough, there are some moments that float to the surface, debris from a catastrophic shipwreck.

A glimpse of Emma's long, tanned legs crossed elegantly over a barstool. A carefree giggle as we walk along the strip. Emma's face alight with a blinding smile, and her soul freer than I've ever seen before.

Fuck, she was beautiful.

But it's the disjointed snippets of conversation that paint a more disturbing picture. I remember commiserating our shared experience as the last singles amongst our friends, the questions about when you'll settle down, and the patronising assurances the right one is just around the corner.

I remember wondering aloud what's so good about tying yourself to someone else for the rest of your life and why people put so much weight on whether you possess that important piece of paper. I remember Emma sharing that she sometimes lies to people so they stop trying to set her up with their weird friends.

And, in the dregs of my mind, I remember a very official-looking building. And then a very tacky one.

A very *church-shaped* tacky one, filled with laughter and a lot of ruffles.

Oh shit.

Given Emma's strangled choke, I can only assume her memory has led her to the same little chapel.

We both look down at our hands, specifically the ring fingers.

"MOTHERFUCKER!"

That was Emma. Her mouth really is filthy. But I echo the sentiment. Because there on my finger is a shining gold band.

Fuuuuuuuck. Please tell me we didn't.

But alas, we did.

Slowly, Emma reaches over to the bedside table, a haunted look on her face. The crisp sound of rustling paper confirms my worst fears.

"Wow," I say, snatching the official document from her shaking hands. "We really are a giant cliché."

Emma springs from the bed, and I'm relieved to see she's fully clothed. Although, she is missing a shoe.

"Oh my God, oh my God, oh my God, oh my God," she chants, frantically pulling the ring off her finger and throwing it at my chest. Of course, it misses and hits me right between the eyes.

Son of a bitch.

"Hey!" I whine, rubbing my forehead. "What was that for?"

"What was that for? Jamie, we got married!"

Yes. That's absolutely a problem we need to solve. But I've just realised that while Emma is fully dressed, I'm stripped down to my boxers. My clothes are strewn haphazardly around the room, every article hanging off a different piece of furniture.

"Er, Emma. Did we..." I hope my awkward gesturing at the bed means I don't have to finish that sentence.

She gasps, looking repulsed. "Ew, no!"

Okay, rude. "How do you know?"

"Oh, for God's sake, Jamie. Just trust me. We didn't."

"Are you sure?"

"Yes, I'm bloody sure," she snaps. "Why? Are you so small women tend not to notice?"

Ouch.

"I've had no complaints, thank you," I mutter to appease my wounded pride. "But considering I've woken up half-naked and *married*, I think my question's justified."

Bloody hell, this is typical. I do a good deed by saving Emma, and *this* is how karma repays me. I groan, throwing myself back against the pillows. Maybe if I try to go back to sleep, this will have all been a terrible dream.

Obviously, Emma opts for the exact opposite strategy. I can hear her pacing around the hotel room, and my stomach revolts at the thought of so much circular motion when my blood is still forty per cent alcohol.

Okay, let's think about this logically. How much damage have we actually done? I'm sure we can annul this, *gulp*, marriage, especially if Emma says we've not slept together. Isn't that one of the qualifying conditions?

Yes, it'll be a pain to undo, but this is far from unfixable. To be honest, if I had to accidentally marry anyone, Emma is probably the perfect candidate. She despises me, so there's no chance she'll be blabbing about our little mistake. And she's hardly going to get clingy. In fact, I'm sure she's already plotting the best way to get rid of me.

"I can't *believe* you got me into this mess," Emma hisses, grabbing a pillow to bash me square in the face.

Or maybe not.

"Me?" I laugh, finally jumping out of bed. "How is this my fault?"

"Oh, come on," Emma scoffs. "In what world would this have been my idea?"

"I beg your pardon?" *Is she serious right now?*

"We both know I wouldn't go near you with a ten-foot barge pole, let alone stand next to you at a fucking altar."

"Oh, because I so famously pine over you?" I retort, grabbing my shorts off the floor lamp.

"Out of the two of us, who's more likely to be responsible for this disaster?"

"*You* were the one who ordered a whole bottle of tequila!"

I can't believe she's blaming me. Like I said. Karma sucks.

"Don't you *dare* pin this on me," she seethes, rounding the bed to jab at my chest with her sharp fingernail.

"Why not?" I knock away her accusing hand. "You're pinning it on me."

"You're insufferable."

"Don't change the subject!"

Knock, knock, knock.

For the second time this morning, we both freeze. Great, someone else to bear witness to this mess.

I creep over to the peephole, cursing silently when I see who's on the other side.

"Who is it?" Emma whispers.

"Shut up."

"Excuse you," she replies, throwing her hands on her hips.

"No, I mean, be quiet. It's Anthony. Quick, hide!"

"Where?"

Give me strength.

"I don't know. Figure it out!" I hiss.

Emma frantically searches for a cupboard to crawl into, or even a body bag to call her own. Of course, neither are forthcoming, being that this hotel spent its entire budget on faux marble and not actual furniture.

Suddenly, her eyes land on the door, and she moves with such determination that I'm momentarily worried she's given up and is going to walk straight out of here. But then, she plasters her back against the wall so she'll be hidden behind the door when it opens.

Well, it's better than nothing.

I take a deep breath, gearing up to lie to the person who knows me better than anyone in the world.

"Er, hey, man," I yell through the door, betrayed by my cracking voice. "What's up?"

"Well, you're going to be late for a start," Anthony shouts back. "And Emma's missing. Have you seen her?"

Shit. Busted.

"Are you sure she's not in her room?"

"No, Cindy went to check. She's definitely not there."

Emma looks at me in a panic. *Do something*, she mouths unhelpfully.

"She probably just went for a run. You know how she is."

Run? I don't run! Emma manages to argue soundlessly.

I'd laugh at the disgust on her face if we weren't two seconds away from being discovered in a very compromising position. I shrug in apology. I'm hungover and married. I'm not exactly functioning at full capacity.

"Really?" The surprise is evident in Anthony's voice, even through the hotel door. *Fuck!*

"Yeah. She probably needs to burn off all that pent-up aggression, am I right?" I laugh nervously until Emma kicks me in the shin. "Oof!"

"Jamie, is everything alright?" Anthony asks. "Look, can you open up? I feel weird talking to you like this."

My mind has gone blank. I can't think of a single excuse to keep Anthony out of my room. "Um, sure."

I crack open the door before slipping through to lean against the jamb. I keep one hand on the handle and raise the other above my head to grip the wooden frame.

Is this position natural? I feel like it's not natural. What do I usually do with my feet?!

I obviously fail at nonchalance because Anthony looks at me as if I've grown a set of horns. Before I can block his view, he peers under my arm and gasps dramatically when he takes in the dishevelled scene beyond.

"Did you finally get laid?"

Oh, fuck my life. Just fuck it all the way to hell.

"You totally did, didn't you?" Anthony squeals, far too invested in my love life.

I groan, swallowing my encroaching anxiety and the hangover that will have me vomiting on Anthony's shoes. "If I say yes, will you go away and let me get dressed?"

"Sure, sure," my irritating friend says in direct contradiction to the way he's edging himself further into my room. I plant my hand on his forehead and push him unceremoniously into the hallway.

"See you in the lobby," I shout before slamming the door in his face.

I watch Anthony leave through my little peephole, holding up my forefinger to Emma so she keeps quiet.

"Okay, he's gone," I say when Anthony finally rounds the corner to the elevators.

"So, having a bit of a dry spell, huh?" Emma drawls, folding her arms across her chest and looking far too pleased with herself.

"Oh, shut up and get out of here before Cindy sends a search party for you."

"How am I going to explain not being in my room?"

"Say you found a library and went to memorise every minute of today's schedule. That's believable."

"And what about"—Emma motions between us—"this?"

"Well, you'll have to take my last name, and you should probably know I want eleven children," I deadpan. Considering she's the one who micromanages everything, I'm doing more than my fair share of thinking this morning.

"You know what I mean," Emma whines. She's close to stamping her foot. I can feel it.

"We'll talk about it later." I check that the coast is clear one last time. "But at the risk of sounding like you, we're going to be late."

"Fine. We'll talk about it later."

That's literally what I just said.

"Goodbye, darling," I say stoically, opening the door for her. "I'll count the seconds until we're together again."

I don't hear what Emma mumbles as she brushes past me, and it's probably better for my self-esteem if it stays that way.

When she's gone, I release the breath I've been holding since I woke up next to Princess Perfect herself. Of all the people who would drunkenly agree to marry me, I'd have thought Emma would be at the bottom of the list.

What the hell happened last night? I always knew Drunk Jamie was an idiot, but who'd have thought Drunk Emma was just as chaotic?

Perhaps Emma's subconscious has a fun side? Perhaps we lost a bet? Whatever the reason, our past selves decided to tie us together. Now is not the time to question why. I have a plane to catch and a reality to return to.

Grabbing our wedding certificate and Emma's discarded ring from the bed, I scramble the rest of my belongings together and shove them into my carry-on. I can freshen up at the airport.

I take a quick glance around my room to check I've not forgotten anything, turn back to grab the phone charger I've left hanging from the wall, and make a hurried dash for the elevator.

It's time to face my loving wife.

Oh God. What have I done?

Chapter Ten

Emma

I've never been this late for anything in my life, let alone something as important as an airport transfer.

Thankfully, I'd had the good sense to pack yesterday morning. It meant when Jamie unceremoniously threw me out of his room, all I had to do was brush my teeth and splash my face before running to meet a very worried Cindy in the lobby.

By some miracle, I'm not the last to arrive. Jamie isn't here yet, not that I can judge him for that today, and we're still missing a stag.

"Has anyone seen Tom?" I ask Cindy. She's standing next to Anthony, but I seem to be having trouble looking him in the eye.

"Apparently, he's been casino-hopping this entire time," Cindy yawns. "He tried to find us after dinner yesterday but forgot which hotel we were in."

"Not that he made much effort to remember," Anthony chimes in, wrapping his arms around a sleepy Cindy. "Instead of texting one of us for the address, he decided to spend the evening at a blackjack table."

Wow. I have so many questions, but considering what I did last night, I decide to keep them to myself.

"Do we need to pick him up from somewhere?" I ask Anthony's forehead.

"Nah, he's going to meet us at the airport."

Well, that's a stroke of luck because I don't have the brainpower required to organise a pitstop. God knows where we'd end up.

A crash from across the lobby heralds Jamie's late arrival. I watch as he flies out of the elevator, his small suit-case clattering to the ground as if he'd propped it against the closed doors and forgot they would open again. He's still getting himself dressed, tugging on his hoodie and dislodging his sunglasses in the process. They skate across the marble floor before rattling to a halt right in front of Anthony.

"I'm sorry, I'm sorry," Jamie pants, struggling over to us. It's an eerie echo of the first day of our trip.

"You know what? I'm sort of used to it," Anthony laughs indulgently. He bends down to rescue the undoubtedly scratched sunglasses, and I cringe when I spot the designer label on the side.

A hush falls over our group, and I notice everyone is staring at me expectantly. Shit, I'm supposed to make a sarcastic comment about him being late. Even Jamie is waiting for me to reproach him.

Oh God, I can't do this. I'm far too hungover to act like everything's normal.

I knew he'd be late. He knew I knew he would be late. But the rest of our group doesn't know I knew he was going to be late, nor that he knew I knew either.

Damn, I have a headache.

"Does anyone have any paracetamol?" I ask weakly.

I must look worse than I thought because five different

packets arc thrust upon me within seconds. Grabbing the nearest, *thanks Josh,* I gesture half-heartedly to the reception desk. We all drop off our keycards and make our way to the minivan outside.

"Are you okay?" Cindy whispers as we watch the taxi driver load up our luggage. "You've only told us what to do once this morning."

I'm too exhausted to figure out if she's making a joke or not.

"I'm just tired," I lie, giving her a smile that'll fool no one. "I didn't sleep well."

"Is that why you went out so early this morning?"

"What?" It takes me a beat to remember she was looking for me earlier. "Oh yeah, I thought a walk might clear my head."

A guilty blush floods my cheeks. I have no experience in lying about something this big. It goes without saying I have never done anything so stupid before. My inebriated alter ego has some serious explaining to do.

In my defence, I've not been that drunk since Cindy bought us a porn-star martini tree on my twenty-sixth birthday. I don't remember much of that night either, just waking up in our bathtub with a wet foot, and Cindy passed out on top of me. But at least the only lasting consequence then was an aversion to passionfruit.

No such luck today. No, today I woke up with a freaking husband to remember my bad decisions by.

I'm the most boring person I know. I risk-assess every element of my life. Last year, I needed a new freezer, and it took me weeks of deliberation and a dedicated spreadsheet to choose the most cost-effective model.

Shit, I put more thought into buying white goods than I did into getting married. What's wrong with me?

Breathe, Emma. This is fixable. You can resolve this.

We speed past the towering hotels and glistening streets of Vegas. In a desperate bid to reassure myself that I'm not in this alone, I steal a glance at my dear husband. It does little to settle my nerves. Because while I agonise about how we can fix this as quickly as possible, Jamie's asleep, his mouth gaped open, and his neck bent at an unnatural angle against the window. This is going to be like every group project I've ever been a part of.

For a split-second last night, Jamie was bearable. Gallant even. He rushed to my side and rescued me from a situation that would have been much worse if it weren't for him. Grateful doesn't even begin to cover how I feel.

I don't remember much after those first tequila shots, but there's a lingering sense of fun, laughter, and mischief. For a few beautiful moments, Jamie and I existed in a happy truce. And then, true to form, we went and destroyed it all.

"Are you sure you're okay, Emma? You really don't seem like yourself this morning," Cindy says from the seat next to me. Her eyes follow mine to land on sleeping beauty himself. "Did something happen with Jamie?"

"What?" I nearly choke on my own tongue. "I mean, no. Definitely not. No! Nothing happened."

Smooth, Emma. Guilty rambling isn't at all suspicious.

Is it possible Cindy can tell we spent the night together? Maybe Jamie's chaotic energy has infected my aura. That sounds like something Cindy would pick up on. It probably doesn't help she caught me staring at him while he slept, either.

"Did you guys have another argument?"

"No, I'm just annoyed. How is he always late?" I sigh.

There. That's what I'd normally say. *Good job, Emma.*

"Hmm," Cindy replies, narrowing her eyes at me. Okay, so maybe my delivery was off.

Fuck. How am I going to keep a secret as big as this

from her? If she gives me just one more sceptical look, I'll crack. I'll spill my guts quicker than a snitch in a mafia romance novel.

I feel so guilty. I came here to support Cindy as she prepares for the biggest day of her life, and instead, I've made a mockery of everything it represents. I've used her wedding to tie myself to a man who baulks at the very idea of commitment.

Are people going to think I've tricked Jamie into this? That I'm some kind of desperate spinster who gets men drunk to trap them into a relationship?

Urgh, I think I'm going to be sick.

The ground lurches violently beneath me, and I squeeze my eyes tight as if that will keep my stomach contents from spewing out of my mouth. It's not until the engine cuts out that I realise the minivan has come to a blessed stop. If only my insides would get the memo.

I don't know if it's my guilty conscience making me paranoid, but I swear Cindy's watching me as our group trudges through security. We're a pack of zombies in dire need of caffeine, growing wearier and heavier with every step, all desperate to get back home.

I make sure to stay as far away from Jamie as possible, not only for the sake of our secret but also because of the strange stab of remorse in my gut when I think about blaming him this morning.

Yes, an idea as insane as getting married must have come from his brain. But I obviously went along with the scheme. It takes two to tango, after all.

The churning, twisting, vomity guilt is *not* helped by our turbulent takeoff. Weren't the abusive men, accidental husband, and killer hangover punishment enough without adding a rough flight into the mix?

To avoid Cindy and her supernatural intuition, I've

taken an aisle seat next to Patrick. I didn't think he'd mind now that we know each other better, but I was painfully wrong. Patrick's spent the last two hours in uneasy silence, looking at me sideways whenever he thinks my eyes are closed. Maybe my hangover's showing, and he's worried I'm going to throw up all over him?

On any other day, I'd analyse and stress about why Patrick doesn't want to sit next to me. But right now, I just don't care. I have bigger fish to fry.

I can't believe I'm going to say this, but I need to find Jamie. We should probably settle on a plan to reverse our stupidity as quickly as possible. And I guess I need to apologise to him, too. How annoying.

I get my chance an hour later when Jamie wakes up from yet another nap. I don't know how he can sleep when there's so much at stake. Apparently, he's not plagued by the same feelings of guilt and betrayal that I am. *Figures.*

I watch Jamie frown at Josh, who is fast asleep and blocking Jamie's only exit into the aisle. I can practically see his thought process. To wake, or not to wake? That is the question.

Don't do it, I plead.

Of course, even telepathically, Jamie never listens to me. He clambers over Josh like a deranged spider, his long legs bringing his crotch dangerously close to places I'm sure Josh would not appreciate.

Idiot.

I take a more standard approach with my own neighbour, giving Patrick an awkward smile and pointing towards the back of the plane by way of an explanation.

The man looks relieved, which, again, I don't have time to read into today.

I take the long way round to the bathrooms on Jamie's side of the plane, through the little cabin crew area filled with hundreds of tiny lockers. Passing a bored flight attendant, I grab a much-needed cup of tea and four sugar sachets.

Do I feel like a stalker while waiting outside the toilet for my husband? Yes. But I won't be able to relax until we have an action plan in place.

"Jamie," I hiss as soon as he opens the toilet door.

Worryingly, he doesn't look surprised to see me. Instead, he looks over his shoulder, presumably to check that our friends are out of earshot, before joining me in the tiny corridor between the toilets and the back of the plane.

"Ah, darling," Jamie says, leaning against the wall as if he hasn't just made the biggest mistake of his life. "I've missed you."

I decide to ignore his sarcasm and thrust my scolding tea into his hands. If he's going to be annoying, he can at least be useful. "Here, hold this."

"Is this for me?" he asks, peering into the cup.

"No. Don't touch it."

"But you asked me to hold it. I *have* to touch it."

"Urgh, you're such a child," I scoff, opening the first sugar packet and upending the contents into the steaming drink.

Jamie scrunches his nose as the other three sachets follow the first. "Wow. Do you want some tea with your sugar?"

"Shut up. It's my hangover cure." I stir the contents with the little wooden stick the cabin crew gave me and snatch back the precious cup.

"I can't believe you've had enough hangovers to have a cure," Jamie says.

"Well, I can't believe I'm married to you. But here we are."

"Oh, but sweetheart. I love you so much," he says dryly.

"Here's what we're going to do," I continue, ignoring him once again.

"Oh yeah, baby," Jamie moans. "I love it when you take charge."

Just then, a very bewildered man with a baseball cap and a beer belly steps out of the bathroom. From the look on his face, he's heard every word of our strange conversation.

Jamie up nods our eavesdropper, folding his arms over his chest. "Wives, am I right?"

The large man grunts in agreement before turning away to navigate his protruding stomach down the narrow aisles.

Fucking men.

"Sorry, Emma," Jamie says, finally remembering that we were in the middle of an important conversation. "What were you saying?" This guy has the attention span of a flea.

"I was just about to say I'll start looking for solicitors tomorrow."

"My love, I am hurt," Jamie gasps dramatically, clutching his chest. "Do you really want to get rid of me so quickly?"

"Would you rather I moved in with you and played housewife?"

"No thanks. You wouldn't last a day before you tried to poison my coffee."

"And don't you forget it, darling." I smile sweetly. "I'll be in touch at the end of the week with some legal options and an idea of the fees."

"Fine, whatever. I'm sure you'll do a thorough job. Now, is that everything, or can I get back to my nap?" Jamie's hit his daily limit for serious conversation.

"No."

When I don't elaborate any further, Jamie cocks his eyebrow impatiently. "Am I supposed to guess, or..."

It's now or never. Time for me to be the bigger person.

"I'm sorry," I say quietly, picking at the seam of my cardboard cup. It's not until the awkward silence stretches on that I dare to look up at Jamie.

"For what?" he asks. For once, he's not goading me. He's genuinely confused.

"For blaming you this morning. It was really shitty, considering how you helped me last night. I think I was just in shock and hating you is my default setting. So, yeah. I'm sorry."

"Oh," he says, clearly taken aback by my genuine apology. "Well, I don't know which of us is to blame for last night, but I figure I'm at least fifty per cent responsible. So, for what it's worth, I'm sorry too."

We stare at each other for an uncomfortable minute, neither of us knowing how to handle our first-ever shared apology. Eventually, I crack, unable to bear the discomfort any longer.

"I'm going to go and drink this." I motion robotically to my cooling tea.

If Jamie has a response beyond stunned silence, I don't stick around long enough to hear it. I turn and flee the way I came as fast as my shaking legs will carry me.

Dropping into my seat, I let myself breathe my first sigh of relief. With every sip of lukewarm tea, I feel myself stir back to life, my body recharging as the sugar hits my system.

Jamie and I have a plan. It's basic—and I'm the one doing all the work—but at least we have a direction. A way out of this accidental marriage. I can finally relax.

I close my eyes, soothed by the penetrating white noise of the plane's engine. My thoughts grow heavy and sluggish. If I'm lucky, maybe I can sleep until London.

Then, just as I'm about to doze off, I hear those famous fucking words.

"Oh my God! Your accent is adorable!"

Kill me. Kill. Me. Now.

Chapter Eleven

Jamie

I'm officially too old to drink. What gave it away? Waking up accidentally married to my mortal enemy? Or reaching the age of the two-day hangover? Because I'm still feeling like crap.

I've said it before, and I'll say it again. Motherfucking Las Vegas.

It's lucky I don't have to go into the office today. My bank offers flexible working, and armed with my laptop, I can deal with internet trolls from any desk in the country—or, in this case, my cluttered kitchen table.

I'm not exactly feeling my best this morning. After landing at the ungodly hour of four a.m., I hightailed it out of the airport and headed for my bed as quickly as possible. I was asleep before my head even hit the pillow. When my alarm sounded a few hours later, I fell out of bed and staggered to my kitchen to log on with barely a second to spare.

Unfortunately, that was the extent of my efficiency. I've made huge typos in global social media posts, accidentally sent an email meant for my intern to the entire executive suite, and called my boss 'sir'.

Her name is Julie.

To be fair, I have a lot on my mind. I've read that getting married is one of the most stressful life events you can go through. I don't even *remember* my wedding, which should only serve to make my situation more stressful, *right?*

By the time lunch rolls around, I'm a nervous mess and one mistake away from catching my boss's attention. I can't afford to be making error after error while my mind is stuck on what happened in Vegas. So, I pick up my phone and call the one person I can talk to about anything. Yes, she'll tease me mercilessly, but she won't judge.

Much.

"Ah, the wanderer returns," my sister exclaims when she answers. "How are you?"

"I'm dying. Send help."

"Oh really? What are your symptoms?"

"Sore head. Aching muscles. Loss of will to live."

"That'd be a hangover, love," she says with zero sympathy. "Drink some coffee, you'll be fine."

"Gee. Why didn't I think of that?"

"Because you're an idiot."

"Well..." Okay, so I was going to ease into the whole, *surprise, I'm married,* conversation. But it's hard to pass up such a perfect segue.

"Oh my God. What did you do?"

"I'll tell you. But you have to promise not to laugh."

"No deal."

"Urgh, please?"

"Nope," Bridget pops. "Now tell me what you did, or I'll make sure Mum knows who really spilt coffee on her white rug last Christmas. And hurry up. I don't want to waste my lunch hour on you."

"Okay, fine..." I start. And then stop. Wow, this is hard. Where do I even begin? "So, you know I went to Vegas?" I ask pointlessly.

"Oh, for Pete's sake," she huffs. "Yes, I'm aware."

"So, on the last night, I got really drunk. Like, blackout drunk."

"How bad are we talking? Me on the night I broke up with Hannah drunk?"

"Not quite..."

"You're right. No one has ever been that drunk."

"No, I mean, I was worse."

"Worse than throwing up all over a bouncer, falling down an underground escalator, losing a shoe on the tube, and then waking up in a stranger's garden thirty miles away?"

"On par with that," I concede. "Except instead of waking up in a stranger's garden, I woke up... married."

"WHAT?" Bridget chokes, the sound of her spluttered coughs filling the line.

"We had a bit of a bad experience at the hotel, and they gave us an entire bottle of tequila to make up for it."

In hindsight, I should have pushed for better compensation.

"I don't remember much after that. I have a vague memory of visiting one of those little chapels, and the next thing I know, we're waking up with rings on our fingers."

"Oh my God. Is that even legal?"

"Apparently so," I sigh. "I looked it up. You can apply for a wedding licence until midnight in Vegas."

"Shit, that's just asking for trouble," Bridget quips. "Wait. Who's 'we'? Who did you marry?"

Bridget's shock at finding out I'm married will pale in comparison to her reaction when she learns *who* I married. Bridget's been listening to me bitch and moan about my dear wife for the best part of twenty years.

"It was Emma," I admit reluctantly.

"Emma? As in Emma Drayton?"

"Yes."

"The Emma Drayton you've hated since puberty?"

"Do you know any other Emma Drayton?" I drawl.

"*The* Emma Drayton, who threw an entire drink over you the last time you came within two metres of one another?"

"Well, she actually hit Cindy—" I say before I'm drowned out by Bridget's hysterical laughter.

"Oh my God!"

"Bridget," I whine, switching to loudspeaker to save my precious eardrums. "It's not funny. Help me."

"I can't breathe. I honestly can't breathe," she gulps between relentless cackles.

"You're the worst."

"Shit, I'm going to pee myself," Bridget hiccups. "How the hell did this even happen?"

I give her a rundown of that fateful night in Vegas. It's an embarrassingly short tale, considering I don't want to share what happened to Emma without her permission and my tequila-induced amnesia. Nevertheless, with every word I *can* share, I feel lighter. It's been killing me to keep this secret, and being able to unburden is a weight off my shoulders.

"Jamie," Bridget sniffs, having laughed herself to tears. "You're a fucking idiot."

"Yes," I agree. I thought we'd already established that.

"Good, as long as you know. Right, gotta go. Love you."

"Wait!" I shout, bolting upright in my kitchen chair. "Aren't you going to help me?"

"What do you want me to do? I'm a physiotherapist, not a solicitor. Anyway, my lunch break is over. Love to the misses. Bye."

And with that, Bridget's gone. I'd be offended if I wasn't so used to my sister's trademark bluntness. The fact that she even took my call is practically a declaration of love.

Rushed farewell aside, confessing to Bridget has worked wonders on my frazzled mind. I can finally concentrate.

My fingers soar over my keyboard, catching up with overdue emails and deftly unravelling the mess I made this morning. For a few blissful hours, my tragic Vegas wedding and nagging wife are a distant memory.

I should have known it wouldn't last.

Bolstered by my good mood, I decide to finish my day with an impromptu run. I'm just changing into my workout gear when my phone vibrates angrily across my worn wooden dresser.

Bridget: We have a serious problem...

Shit. Jinxed it. Looks as if my good mood's about to take a nosedive after all.

Emma

There's nothing better than a London morning. The city is alive with potential, the streets teeming with promises of new beginnings and continued adventure.

It's my favourite time of the day. When I walk down the impressive streets of Chelsea, I imagine I'm weaving my own tiny thread into the rich history of the city.

My office is a gorgeous Edwardian redbrick townhouse nestled in the heart of the borough. It's surrounded by a wealth of other businesses, from cosmetic surgeons to high-brow solicitors. From exclusive real estate agents to lifestyle coaches pandering to the rich and famous. If you can charge a few hundred pounds an hour for your time, there's a place for you here.

This is exactly where I'd dreamed my career would take me.

Unfortunately, after catching less than an hour of sleep since landing, I don't feel I'm living up to my notable surroundings.

From the moment I collapsed at my desk, my day hasn't stopped. After four client meetings, two written proposals, and an unknown number of emails, the call of my bed is deafening.

Alas, there is no rest for the recently wicked. This evening marks step one in my plan to get rid of Jamie. My first priority? To find a solicitor who's professionally competent and experienced in dealing with things that didn't stay in Vegas. So, I settle down on my sofa with a large glass of wine and get to work.

Surprisingly, there are plenty of options for me to choose from. Undoing drunken mistakes must be a bigger business than I'd realised. After half an hour, I have two strong contenders on my list, one of which is just a stone's throw away from my office.

That likely means an eyewatering bill, but can you really put a price on your sanity?

This fiasco might be easier to undo than I'd thought. At this rate, I could be legally single by Christmas. Feeling pretty pleased with myself, I set down my tablet and decide on a well-deserved bubble bath. A steamy soak in some lavender-infused water seems the perfect way to unwind after a hectic day.

While my tub fills, I carefully choose the right combination of bath salts, oils, and bubbles to end my night. Then, just as I'm about to crumble a fragrant bath bomb into the water, I hear my phone ringing in the lounge.

Damn.

I quickly turn off the taps and run into the other room to catch whoever's disturbing my peace.

To my surprise, Jamie's name lights up my screen, and for one brief, insane moment, my stomach flutters, a sensation that I'm going to blame on my excitement about sharing the news of our legal leads.

"Hey, Emma," he says when I answer the phone.

"Jamie, I'm glad you called." Well, there's a sentence I never thought I'd say. "I've just started a shortlist of solicitors for us."

"Yeah, er, that's great," he says nervously. "Listen, can I talk to you about something?"

My stomach drops at Jamie's sheepish tone. He didn't even sound this uncomfortable when we woke up married!

"What's wrong?" I ask. "Has someone found out about us?"

Please say no. Please say no. Please say no.

"Yes."

Dammit!

"But I promise I'm going to fix it."

"Jamie! What the fuck?"

"I know," he groans. "But honestly, it wasn't my fault."

"Oh, I highly doubt that," I say. I can practically feel my blood pressure rising. "Who knows? Is it Anthony? Cindy?"

"No, no," Jamie reassures me quickly. "It's my nan."

For a moment, I don't think I've heard him correctly. Is he really this nervous because his *nan* knows about us?

I'm so relieved that I burst out laughing. "No offence, Jamie. But I don't think that's a big deal."

Would I rather she didn't know? Yes. But who's she going to tell? Her knitting club?

There's silence on the other end of the line. A pause that stretches on for so long I check we're still connected.

"Jamie?"

"My nan's been really sick," he finally admits quietly.

"Oh, I didn't know. Is she..." I trail off awkwardly. How do I finish that sentence? Is she better? Is she going to be okay? Is she... not?

"Yeah, it's cancer," Jamie says, taking a deep breath. "It spread too fast to treat. She's got a few weeks left if we're lucky."

Flashes of Jamie in Vegas play through my mind. The memory of the imperfect juxtaposition of him. One moment, the master of revelry, rallying the stags and dancing until dawn. And then, the other Jamie—the one with a dark cloud hanging over him, weighed down and glued to his phone or staring into a future that's coming too fast.

I can pinpoint every time his mask slipped because I saw it happening. And, to my shame, I never bothered to wonder why.

"Jamie, I'm so sorry," I say earnestly. We might not be the best of friends, but I can hear how much this is hurting him. I wish I could make it stop.

"Can you keep that in mind when I tell you the next bit?"

Oh, the sly git.

"I swear to God, Jamie, if you're about to use your nan as a get-out-of-jail-free card, I will kick your ass into next week."

"No, it's not like that, I swear," he says.

"What is it like?"

"Erm..."

Sick nan or not, Jamie's wearing on my patience. I've had more forthcoming conversations with my kettle.

"Jamie, why are you phoning me?"

"Did you know I almost pulled out of the Vegas trip?"

Oh my God, I swear I'm going to hit my head against a brick wall.

"I didn't want to leave Nan for so long," he continues. "It seemed wrong to miss so much time with her, you know? Anyway, Nan was furious when she found out I was going to cancel on Anthony. Have you ever had a woman in her eighties give you a death stare? It's terrifying.

"Nan wouldn't hear me out. She said she had a feeling in her waters that I needed to be in Vegas, and she'd never forgive me if I backed out. To cut a long story short, I agreed to go."

"Jamie, this conversation is the exact opposite of cutting a long story short."

"That bit was important, I promise," he assures me. "Anyway, this morning, I was on the phone with my sister, and I happened to mention we got married."

"You happened to mention it?" I ask incredulously. "Like, it just accidentally slipped out into the conversation?"

"Okay, so I may have phoned Bridget to tell her about the wedding." *That's more like it.* "But listen, I needed to talk to someone. It was eating me alive. I could barely function!"

"Urgh," I scoff. "We agreed this was a secret. You didn't even last two days!"

"I'm sorry I'm not as stone-faced as you," Jamie snaps. "I happen to have emotions. Anyway, Bridget thought the whole thing was hilarious, so she told Nan about it this afternoon."

"Let me guess. You didn't tell Bridget this was a secret either?"

"Not in so many words," Jamie mumbles. "The trouble

is, while Nan knows you can get drunkenly married in Vegas, she doesn't understand why you would do that with someone you don't actually like."

"That makes two of us," I say under my breath.

"Nan's built our wedding into a whole epic story. She thinks we got married because we're desperately in love. In her mind, that's why she had a feeling that I needed to be in Vegas. It was so you and I could fall in love while she was still around to see it."

"But Bridget set her straight, right?" I don't know why I'm bothering to ask when I already know the answer.

"She couldn't! Nan was just so excited. Bridget said she lit up when she heard about the wedding. Apparently, she can now pass happy. It would break her heart if she found out it wasn't true.

"Luckily, I've convinced Nan to keep this quiet for a while, so we shouldn't have to worry about my parents finding out."

Well, look at that. Jamie does understand the concept of secrecy.

"I explained that we want to keep the news under our hats for a few weeks until we've visited your mum. But, the catch," Jamie pauses, taking a fortifying breath, "is that she wants to meet you."

"Wow." That's the only word I have right now. All others have fled my lexicon.

"Yeah, so now I need you to come to the hospice tomorrow night and pretend to be my wife."

"I am your wife," I remind him weakly.

"You know what I mean. Pretend we're in love or what-ever. Nan really wants to meet you, and the sooner, the better. You know, for time."

I must have been a dictator in a past life. Or a mass

murderer. That's the only explanation for my recent run of bad luck.

"Please, Emma," Jamie begs. "I know this is a lot. Probably more than I deserve. But I wouldn't ask if it wasn't really important. Please. I don't want her to spend her last days worrying about me."

His voice breaks on those last words, completely shattering any chance I have of saying no. What am I going to do? Tell him to bugger off and break a dying woman's heart? I can't live with that on my conscience.

I quickly wonder if Jamie's backed me into a corner on purpose, but he does seem genuine. I've never heard him so unsure. So broken.

And I guess I owe him. He was there for me when I needed it.

Damn. I can't believe I'm going to do this.

"Fine. Text me the details," I grumble.

"Oh my God, thank you," Jamie gushes. "You're the best wife ever!"

Jamie thanks me again and again until I can't stomach his gratitude any longer. I hang up when he's mid-sentence, uncaring that I've yet to tell him about the solicitors I've found.

I'll email him tomorrow.

I can only deal with one insane problem at a time.

Chapter Twelve

Emma

Is it wrong to antagonise someone while arranging to meet their sick nan at a *hospice*? I hope not, or else I'm going straight to hell.

In my defence, I had to do *something* to restore the delicate balance of my relationship with Jamie. We've strayed too far from our usual path. Over the past few days, we've helped each other through some incredibly tough moments, and if I'm not careful, I'll give Jamie the impression that we're... *friends.*

I shudder at the thought. Or maybe from the late spring chill swirling around me as I follow the directions on my phone to the hospice.

I'm still wearing my work clothes, an emerald silk shirt tied in a loose bow around my neck and a tailored but tight black pencil skirt. The outfit seemed a good idea this morning when I had a meeting with the CEO of a high-end fashion chain in my calendar. But now, my decision to forego a jacket is coming back to haunt me. At this rate, my goosebumps are threatening to become permanent.

Not to mention, my feet are killing me after ten hours squeezed into four-inch heels. Still, there's nothing better than the click of stilettos on a polished floor to boost your confidence before a contract negotiation.

I did briefly wonder if Jamie's nan would rather see her grandson with a soft and homely sort of woman. But, considering I've had less than twenty-four hours to prepare for this ruse, I'm hoping the elaborate bouquet of pale pink peonies I'm clutching will be enough to sway her first impression in my favour.

It's impossible to miss the hospice when I turn into the handsome street in Croydon. The impressive building stands out even amidst the manicured houses and rows of trees trying their hardest to grow in line. It's easily the width of three mansions, with a stark white exterior broken up by warm brown beams that zigzag across its facade. Cars are haphazardly squeezed into any available space on the grounds, a remarkable feat considering the number of trickling water features and beautiful flower beds dotted all over the place.

The building would almost feel inviting, if not for the ambulance parked around the side, its doors flung wide open to welcome a new patient.

Against all odds, Jamie is already here waiting for me. I even check my watch to see if I've somehow lost time on my route from the tube station. But no, it really is a miracle.

He's casually leaning against the low drystone wall surrounding the hospice, wearing the same battered black hoodie, athletic shorts, and flimsy flip-flops he favoured in Vegas. Jamie's sandy hair is, as always, escaping from its half-hearted knot, brushing over the light stubble on his chin. I'm so glad he's made an effort.

The contrast between us is ludicrous. Perhaps I should have changed because our outfits alone showcase everything wrong with this match.

At first, I think my approach has gone unnoticed,

Jamie's mind miles away as he stares blindly into the distance. That is until he intentionally scrapes his foot across the ground, sweeping gravel in my direction with the edge of what can barely be described as a shoe.

"I know what you were doing," Jamie says in lieu of an actual greeting.

I sidestep the scattered stones and school my features into a mask of innocence. "What do you mean?"

That's a lie. I know *exactly* what he means. Late last night, I sent Jamie a couple of texts asking about his nan. I wanted to know basic things like her name (Maggie), where she grew up (Camden), and the best train to get here from Chelsea.

I settled in to wait the obligatory twelve hours it usually takes for Jamie to get back to me. Except, to my surprise, he replied straight away.

Not one to pass up a golden opportunity, I sent off a few more messages to test the parameters of Jamie's newfound responsiveness. And wouldn't you know, the replies kept coming, even if each was more terse than the last.

I quickly realised I was annoying Jamie, but there was nothing he could do about it. He *had* to play nice because, let's face it, I'm doing him the biggest of all favours. The least he could do was answer my overzealous questions that only ended when I lost signal on the underground less than an hour ago.

I'll give him his due; he lasted until lunchtime today before he stopped replying altogether. Judging by my unde-livered texts, he either turned off his phone or slammed it against a wall. Who knows?

"All the questions, Emma. Did you really think I wouldn't figure out you were trying to piss me off?"

"I don't know what you're talking about," I sniff with

just the right amount of indignation. "I only want to make a good impression."

Jamie pulls his phone from his pocket (it survived!) and reads my last text aloud.

"What is your nan's favourite operatic concept album from the last decade?" Jamie recites stoically. "You know, in case it comes up."

I have to bite my lip to stop myself from laughing. "Well, I thought it might be nice if your nan and I had the same answer. Don't you want her to like me?"

Jamie mutters something that sounds suspiciously like *give me strength,* while diving into his back pocket to pull out a small gold ring. To my surprise, it's the wedding band I threw at him in Vegas. I hadn't given a single thought to what had happened to it.

The simple ring is dainty and elegant, exactly what I would choose if I were getting married for real. And isn't that a kicker?

Drunk Emma: Good taste in jewellery, bad taste in men.

"You kept the rings?" I ask stupidly. Now that I look more closely, I see that its larger counterpart is already sitting comfortably on Jamie's left ring finger.

"I'm not made of money," Jamie scoffs. "You need to hook me up with your boss if you can afford to throw away precious metal."

"Not a chance," I say, balancing my bouquet under one arm and holding out my hand for the forgotten band.

I expect Jamie to drop the ring into my palm, so, of course, he does the opposite. I scarcely hide my gasp when he takes my hand, turns it over, and gently slides the ring onto my outstretched finger.

Beautiful, a faint voice echoes in the recess of my mind. A deep, commanding cadence that has the hair on the back of my neck standing on end. A teasing shiver snakes down my spine as a forgotten memory taunts me from the depths of my subconscious. It's floating just out of reach, and given its likely origin, I think that's where it should stay.

"Your hands are freezing," Jamie says, breaking the spell that's rendered me speechless. He must be immune to whatever freaky déjà vu is in the air.

"Come on, let's go," he says, turning towards the vast building behind us.

I give myself a stern talking-to as I scurry through the sliding doors of the hospice. The dangerously smooth voice was probably a figment of my tired imagination, right? I bet the symbolism of Jamie putting a ring on my finger triggered a recollection of a hundred identical scenes in a hundred different romance novels.

Yes, let's go with that. I knew my romance addiction was unhealthy.

I don't pay attention to the kind receptionist when he directs us to Maggie's room. I assume Jamie's been here enough times to know the way.

The corridors of the hospice are warm and cosy. Someone's clearly worked hard to make the atmosphere inviting, though the copious flower arrangements and little bowls of potpourri still struggle to overcome the sterile smell that hangs in the air. It's this overwhelming dichotomy between the feeling of home and hospital that puts into perspective the significance of what we're about to do.

Jamie's nan is sick, and I'm here to make her final days as happy as they can be. For both of them. I have never felt more underqualified for a task in my life. There's a persistent swarm of butterflies upsetting my stomach, and I ask myself, not for the first time, how the hell Jamie and I are going to pull this off.

What if Jamie's nan doesn't like me? What if she doesn't approve? If Jamie and I fail to play the part of loved-up newlyweds, will she spend her last days worrying needlessly about her grandson?

"Jamie?" I ask hesitantly when he leads us to a narrow flight of stairs. "What if your nan hates me?"

"How is that possible when you've memorised her favourite brand of dishwasher tablet?" he replies wryly.

"I'm serious. Am I walking into an interrogation? Am I here so she can see for herself if I'm a gold digger or something?"

"If that's the case, you're a pretty shitty gold digger," Jamie chuckles. "All I can offer you is an astronomical mortgage on a one-bedroom flat, a collection of vintage games consoles that don't work, and a savings account that will get you all the way to Cornwall if you use it wisely. I don't even have a car, but you bet I'll let you share my oyster card."

"Please don't tell me you use an oyster card," I gasp, horrified. "You know the barriers take contactless, right?"

"Of course I know that," Jamie says, rolling his eyes. "Hence why I've got a card to spare. But honestly, you don't have to worry about my nan thinking you're a gold digger."

Well, that's something, at least.

"She just wants to see if you're good enough for her favourite grandchild."

What?!

"YOU'RE the favourite grandchild? How is that possible? Are all your cousins serial killers?"

"You'll see," Jamie says smugly.

We've stopped in front of a smart, white door that reads *Maggie Payne,* and Jamie knocks loudly before bursting in, entirely uninvited. In two long strides, he's made it across the room and engulfed his frail nan in a bone-crushing hug.

Jamie and Maggie are chalk and cheese. Maggie is tiny. Everything about her is petite, something only accentuated by her thin skin and ashy complexion. Even her wispy grey hair is secured by a bejewelled clasp that seems far too heavy for her head.

However, more striking than the differences between them are the similarities. Because what Maggie lacks in size, she certainly makes up for in presence. She has a wicked glint in her watery eyes that reminds me so much of Jamie that it's startling. I even recognise her shaking smile, one that's playful and blindingly bright, just like her grandson's.

There is so much of Jamie in Maggie that I'm surprised to find myself immediately falling in love with her. And when she turns that brilliant beam on me, I can't help but smile back.

Maybe this will be easier than I thought?

"It's very nice to meet you. I'm Emma," I say, approaching the bed.

"Well, aren't you pretty," she rasps, her eyes roaming the length of me. "I'm so glad I can finally put a face to the name. Our whole family's been hearing about you for years."

I wince. Whatever Jamie's told them, I bet none of it's good.

"Don't worry, darling. It was always going to take someone with spirit to hold Jamie's attention," Maggie smiles mischievously.

I decide it's safer to sidestep that comment and divert Maggie's attention with the peonies in my arms. "These are for you."

"Oh, Jamie, look. Flowers!" she cries, clasping her hands together. "Let's put them in the window and see if they'll outlive me." She sounds unduly excited, given the morbid sentiment. I don't know whether to laugh or cry, so I settle for staring in disbelief.

"Nan," Jamie scolds. "For the last time, you have to stop saying that. You had Aunt Brenda in tears last time."

"I can say what I damn well please, Jamie," she snorts. "I'm the one who's dying. Emma, would you be a dear and find the vase in the cabinet over there? It might need a bit of a rinse. It's been a while since anyone's brought me flowers."

"I wonder why," Jamie mutters to himself.

I jump up to source the admittedly very dusty vase and quickly arrange the bouquet on the windowsill. Thankfully, the florist tied the flowers together well enough that all I have to do is plonk them in the water and add the feed.

Of course, all this means I've turned my back on Jamie, which is his cue to do something inappropriate. Sure enough, by the time I sink into one of the overstuffed armchairs by Maggie's bed, Jamie has pulled out two bottles of light beer from his backpack.

I'm no doctor, but I'm almost certain beer doesn't interact well with whatever pain medication Maggie must be taking. And based on her sly grin when she snatches the bottle from her grandson, she's well aware of this.

My thoughts must show plainly on my face because Maggie rolls her eyes, the move so reminiscent of Jamie I nearly burst out laughing.

"Well, it's hardly going to make me worse, is it?" Maggie says snarkily, taking a healthy gulp of the beer.

I take a moment to think it over and realise she's right.

"Do you want one?" Jamie asks, his hand hovering over his backpack.

"No thanks," I say, hoping my refusal doesn't come across as judgy. "I'm still recovering from the weekend."

"Ah, finally," Maggie says, wriggling excitedly in her

bed. "We're getting to the juicy stuff. How was Vegas? Tell me *everything*."

"Well, I didn't lose the groom, and there are no loan sharks after me. All in all, I'd say it was a successful trip." Jamie shrugs. "I did come back with a wife, though. So, it's swings and roundabouts."

"Oh, Jamie. You are wicked," Maggie says, swiping at him as if he's making a good-natured joke. I, of course, know better. It's best to hide a lie behind the truth, after all. "Poor Emma! And from what Bridget tells me, you let your new wife plan that whole trip by herself."

Instead of looking ashamed that he lumped me with all the organisation, he gives his nan a cocky grin, one that's probably got him out of all sorts of trouble over the years.

"Yes, I did. And it meant I had more time to sneak in here and bring you contraband. Besides, Emma *lives* for planning."

I offer Jamie a simpering smile that I hope belies how much I resent that statement. "Let's just say I've known Jamie for long enough to know we'd end up in Nova Scotia instead of Nevada if I let him anywhere near the arrangements."

"See, that's smart," Maggie agrees. "Emma is just the person you need, Jamie. Someone to keep you in line."

"Hey, I'm not that bad," Jamie protests.

"Sweetheart, the last time I went to your flat, you were cleaning your dishes with shampoo because you'd forgotten to buy washing-up liquid."

Oh, dear lord.

"That was one time," Jamie moans.

"And that was one time too many. I bet Emma's never done anything like that."

Wow, I think I love this woman.

Jamie sullenly flops back into his chair. I want to stick

my tongue out at him, but that might contradict the point Maggie's trying to make. I am the pinnacle of maturity, the bar by which all other grandchildren should be judged.

Suck it, Jamie.

"At last, you've found someone who can rein you in. That's what your dear grandpa did for me." Maggie's face softens, her eyes staring dreamily into the past. "We always teased him for being a stick in the mud, but I couldn't have functioned without Ronnie. He was my whole world and loved me like I hung every star in the sky. I'm just glad that when we reunite in my next adventure, I can tell him you've found the same happiness.

"I could feel it in my bones that you needed to be in Vegas, and now I know why. It was so you could find your way to Emma." Maggie knowingly taps the side of her head. "I have a fifth sense about these things."

"Don't you mean a sixth sense?" Jamie asks.

"No, my psychic ability is very finely tuned, so I bumped it up a place. It only seemed fair after all my food started to taste like cardboard."

Jamie nods as if that's perfectly reasonable. I, however, struggle to school my features into something resembling comprehension. You'd think after twenty years with Cindy, I'd be used to getting in touch with my spiritual side, but that's not the case. I have enough trouble dealing with what's right in front of my nose, let alone worrying about things I can't see.

"My only regret is that I didn't see this happening sooner. Maybe then I would have been around to meet my first great-grandchild. Who else is going to teach them all the rude words?" Suddenly, Maggie's eyes widen. "Wait, that's not why—"

"Definitely not!" I say at the same time as Jamie cries, "Hell no!"

Maggie laughs at our twin masks of horror. "Well, there's plenty of time for babies. You should travel first. Go see all the places your grandpa and I could only dream of."

"We will, Nan," Jamie promises, reaching out to jostle her knee through the thick duvet. "You can count on it."

It seems the day (and possibly the beer) is catching up with Maggie, and she stifles a yawn behind her shaking hand. I have to remind myself that she's incredibly sick. Her mind and her spirit are so full of life that it's easy to overlook her greying pallor and the number of tubes winding their way in and out of her body. When the time comes, the world will lose one of its brightest lights.

"So, if it wasn't a shotgun wedding," Nan says, her tired eyes twinkling with mischief, "how did this happen?"

I hope she can't see her grandson's face because his expression is one of pure panic. Jamie was so focused on getting me through the hospice doors that he didn't consider what might happen once we got here. Like someone asking how we came to be married, for example.

I, on the other hand, am always prepared. I take a deep breath and channel an overeager newlywed, desperate to share her epic tale with anyone who will feign an interest.

"It was so romantic," I gush, shifting my chair closer to Maggie. "We were by the pool in our hotel, just lounging around in the sun. I'd tried to read, but I was so jetlagged the words kept jumping around on the page. So, I set my book down on the table next to me and settled in for a catnap."

So far, so truthful.

"Of course," I laugh, reaching over to slap my tongue-tied husband in the chest. "This oaf put a stop to that. As usual, he was ignoring the rules and running by the pool. What's worse is he was wearing those stupid flip-flops. He stubbed his toe right beside me, almost falling head over heels. Luckily, he caught himself on the corner of my little table at the last moment.

"He came out of it unscathed, but the same can't be said for my favourite book. It shot off the table and straight into the deep end of the pool. It was ruined. Half of the pages had disintegrated by the time it dried, and the other half smelt like chlorine."

I deserve an Oscar. Maggie is hanging on my every word. Even the klutz in question looks invested in how the story will end.

Be cool, Jamie. Remember, you were meant to be there.

"Jamie felt *really* guilty about it. He'd convinced himself that I would assume he'd done it on purpose. No matter how many times I told him it didn't matter, he wouldn't believe me. Eventually, he took himself all over Las Vegas to hunt down a replacement copy."

Note to self: Remind Jamie he still owes me a book.

"That night, Jamie came to my room with a beautiful hardback edition embedded in a bouquet of two dozen pink roses. He told me he was sorry, not just about the book, but about everything. For all the times he upset me at school or made fun of me in class. He admitted it was his immature way of trying to get my attention, and he'd like to take me out for a drink to start making amends."

Maggie nods knowingly. "It does take men a while to catch up with us, dear."

I don't have to look at Jamie to know he's furious. His glare is a laser beam, scolding me with every twist of my bogus tale. But if he didn't want the blame to land at his feet, *he* should have come up with our cover story.

"Well, a few glasses of wine later, and the rest is history. We finally realised we have so much in common. We both like..."

Fuck. What the hell does Jamie like? Apart from tank tops and making my life a misery, I mean.

"Arsenal!" Jamie shouts, hit by a moment of inspiration. "Emma is a huge Arsenal fan."

Err...

"And we both watch the same obscure horror movies," he rambles. "Plus, she's a secret adrenaline junkie. It turns out we've both done the one-hundred-and-sixty-foot bungee jump at Battersea."

The fuck I did.

"Emma's even going to join me on my fundraising skydive next year."

The fuck I am!

Do I look like the kind of person who voluntarily jumps out of planes? And given the bemused look on Maggie's face, I don't think she's buying it either.

"That night, I realised Emma was meant to be my person. She's my missing part. The piece that completes me."

I telepathically plead with Casanova to reel it in. The objective of this ruse is to make it *believable*. I'm just about to open my mouth and interrupt his cheesy retelling when he does the unthinkable.

I see it happen in slow motion, but I'm powerless to stop it. In one confident move, Jamie reaches out and rests his hand on my knee.

He holds still for a torturous moment before gently sliding his hand over my thigh. The light touch shoots erratic tingles of electricity wherever his fingers wander, yet the act is so casual that I don't think he's noticed crossing a line we drew decades ago.

I, however, can do nothing but notice.

Jamie's hand is large enough to command all of my attention. Even through the taut material of my pencil skirt,

I can feel the warmth of his simple touch. Under his fingers, my skin burns unbearably, a sensation only made worse when he circles his thumb back and forth, dangerously close to my inner thigh.

And when he draws his hand away, he makes sure to trail the faintest path across my lap, his fingers leaving goosebumps stinging in their wake. I don't even register I've stopped breathing, not until I suck in a shuddered gasp at the loss of *him*.

One look at Jamie's smug face, and I know my reaction hasn't gone unnoticed. "After that, Emma realised that no one else could make her feel like I do. Isn't that right, Princess?"

Damn him. Damn him to hell.

"My darling Jamie," Maggie chuckles, indulgently patting his hand. "What a load of tripe." *Oops.* Clearly, we weren't as convincing as we'd hoped. "But thank you for sparing me the grisly details of how you two really got together in Vegas."

Jamie cracks up as if this isn't the most awkward conversation that's ever happened. Meanwhile, I pray for the ground to open up and swallow me whole.

"Now, away with the pair of you. I need my beauty sleep," she says, her heavy eyes sparkling. "I hope I get to see you again, Emma. It was a joy to meet you."

"The pleasure was mine," I say, my voice wobbling. I want to see Maggie again, and it's hard to comprehend that I probably won't have the chance. This simple farewell seems unbearably overwhelming. I can't imagine how Jamie and his family do this every day.

Jamie kisses his nan goodbye, and we leave her to rest. I don't trust myself to speak as we navigate our way out of the hospice. Jamie nods at a few members of staff in passing but seems happy to walk in sombre silence. He doesn't stop, not until we cross paths with a nurse darting across the impressive front gardens.

"Ah, Jamie," she says warmly. "How many am I contending with tonight?"

"Just the one," Jamie says with a coy smile. "She finished up about five minutes ago."

"Congratulations. You've been upgraded to my favourite relative. Bridget brought her two bottles yesterday," the nurse shouts over her shoulder as she hurries away.

Jamie and I are left alone once more, our crunching footsteps on the gravelled path the only sound keeping us company.

"So, Princess," Jamie finally says, his words a heavy anvil falling between us. "Did your six hundred questions help tonight?"

"Not really," I laugh. "Your nan is incredible."

Jamie was right. No amount of questioning could have prepared me for the wonder that is Maggie Payne.

"Thank you for coming. I know it meant the world to her to meet you."

"Oh, no problem."

Jamie and I trade weak smiles, neither of us knowing how to react now our go-to taunts and snide comments are off the table.

"Um, I'll email you in a few days with a list of solicitors," I tell him clumsily. "I don't think getting an annulment will be as painful as we thought."

"Oh, yeah? That's great." *Christ, why does this feel so awkward?* "Listen, I'm sorry if it feels like I'm leaving everything up to you. I'm just not in the best headspace to deal with this right now."

I follow Jamie's gaze as it's drawn back to the hospice. Let's just say tonight's got me feeling a touch guilty about hounding him during our Vegas planning.

I brush off his apology as if I haven't just spent months nagging him to within an inch of his life. "Don't worry, I've got it under control. I'll let you know when I need something from you."

"Okay. Great. I'll see you soon," he says, seemingly ready for this stilted conversation to be over. "Have a good night."

"You too."

Jamie lifts his hand in a weird, half-hearted wave. I think he meant to try for a handshake but then changed his mind at the last second. I return the odd gesture.

It's not until we take a step in the same direction that we both realise we're heading for the tube station.

Oh, the horror.

Fuck. My. Life.

In the two weeks following our night at the hospice, I throw myself into finding the best way to annul this marriage.

The hardest part has been waiting for Jamie to approve my preferred solicitor. Usually, I'd pester him and prod him until he gave in and replied to my email. But now I know better. Jamie's going through a lot, and I'm probably the last thing on his mind.

Still, even with the process at a standstill, I can breathe a little easier. We're out of the woods. Our friends still have no idea what happened in Vegas, and Jamie's nan is convinced we're the real deal.

She can literally die happy. Job done.

Or so I thought.

The universe must have a vendetta against me because precisely fourteen days after our successful deception, my worse-for-wear husband appears on my doorstep.

"Jamie, what the hell are you doing here?" I gasp, ushering him into my flat before my neighbours see him and assume I'm taking in homeless people. Call me a snob, but it looks like he hasn't brushed his hair all week.

"Um," he says, rubbing the back of his neck uneasily. "Yeah, I'm going to need another favour..."

Chapter Thirteen

Jamie

The day has finally come. The end that's been hanging over my family for months. Today is the day of my nan's funeral.

She passed away peacefully in her sleep. I'm trying to find some comfort in the knowledge that she spent her last night surrounded by her family. She'd have heard Bridget and me argue over football lineups and felt Mum styling her thin hair just the way she liked, that ridiculous clip front and centre.

I should feel lucky. We had so much time to say good-bye. Whenever I left her side, I made sure nothing was left unsaid. Though, that doesn't soften the blow now that she's gone.

Everything reminds me of her. I can't even open my fridge without coming face-to-face with her packs of shitty beer.

Usually, I'd have bequeathed the impressive haul to my eighteen-year-old cousin, but after the panicked call I'd received from Bridget a few nights ago, I decided my need was greater.

You see, I have a problem. Emma is an overachiever. I've known this for years, so why, *why* did I not see she would have Nan falling head over heels in love with her?

Maybe it was the bouquet of flowers, which did happen to outlast Nan after all. Or perhaps it was because Emma reminded her of Grandpa. Whatever the reason, it was good enough for Nan to make Emma a named beneficiary in her will.

Yes, she was so enamoured with my lovely bride that she called her solicitor and had Bridget witness a last-minute change to her wishes. She cut every family member's share of her estate in order to give Emma and me an extra twenty thousand pounds to 'start our life together'. It's more money than I've ever had and almost double what each of my cousins will receive.

See, I said I was the favourite.

The icing on the cake is that Nan swore Bridget to secrecy, knowing all too well I would try to talk her out of it. Bridget folded like a pack of cards. She couldn't say no to Nan any more than I could. That woman should have been a hostage negotiator.

Thank God Bridget finally broke her silence before the will reading. It would have been pretty awkward for my family to find out about *my wife* in a solicitor's office.

Unsurprisingly, Emma blew a fuse when I showed up on her doorstep to share our joyful news.

"Why didn't Bridget stop her?" she asked, practically tearing out her hair.

Good question, wife of mine.

And how would Bridget have done that? Especially since we'd convinced Nan this was a real, legitimate marriage? It would have looked like the worst kind of sibling rivalry. Luckily, Bridget wasn't fussed by her reduced inheritance. Though considering this whole mess is her fault in the first place, she doesn't have much of a leg to stand on.

The guilt ate away at me. I felt awful that I would be pocketing more than my fair share. It was only once I decided to put half of my inheritance into a new bank account that I could finally sleep at night. I'm not touching a single penny of my ill-gotten gains. I'm going to save it for someone in my family who needs it and then swoop in like the Paynes' white knight.

That solution didn't placate Emma.

"Oh my God, oh my God, oh my God," she hyperventilated. *"I'm one of those awful people who scams pensioners out of money. You can't keep it, Jamie. You have to give it back!"*

"And how would that work?" I argued. *"Hey guys, funny story. I tricked Nan into thinking I got married, introduced her to my fake-slash-real wife, and then she changed her will in my favour. But don't worry, I'm not going to keep the money. No harm done, right?"*

"What's the alternative, Jamie?" Emma hissed through gritted teeth.

Ah yes, the alternative...

Bridget and I had not been idle in our grief. To distract ourselves from Nan's passing, we'd stayed up all night nursing a bottle of vodka and hatching an airtight plan. Well, if Emma and I pretending to be married for real, dragging her to family events, and then 'getting divorced' a year later, can pass as a plan.

I must have looked a desperate mess when I showed up at Emma's door, but that didn't mean I was off the hook. Far from it. We'd argued for over an hour before she'd finally agreed to my absurd scheme.

To add insult to injury, Emma wouldn't let me leave until I'd used her hairbrush.

Anthony's right. She's obsessed with me.

And that brings us to today. Nan's funeral. Or, more accurately, her wake. I've moved through the day in a haze, passing from place to place with no recollection of how I got anywhere.

Everything feels wrong. The sky is too dark, the people are too quiet, and time is bouncing around as if it's forgotten what linear means. Emma's presence in my parents' lounge seems normal in comparison, even if every member of my family is watching her with the same shell-shocked expression.

Perhaps announcing my marriage on the family group chat the night before the funeral wasn't my best idea. My mum was on the phone within minutes, the source of her anger switching from her exclusion from the ceremony and that there even was a ceremony to begin with. I took my bollocking like a man, promising she could meet Emma officially before the funeral.

The result? A very uncomfortable breakfast at my parents' house this morning, especially when I tried to heap a mountain of sugar into Emma's tea. Instead of swooning at the gesture, something I'm assured is the height of romance, Emma stared at me in utter disgust.

Apparently, sweet tea is only acceptable for hangovers. Like the sugar has some kind of magical properties that suck the literal poison out of your veins. How was I supposed to know that?

Tea-gate aside, I'm grateful to have Emma beside me today. She's been the perfect buffer between me and everyone else. Payne family events, by nature, are boisterous and messy. We talk too much, share too much, and very occasionally drink too much.

Usually, I love the chaos. Hell, half the time, I'm the

cause of it. But when I woke up this morning, I couldn't imagine anything worse.

I didn't want to see anyone, let alone talk to them. All I wanted to do was hide in my old bedroom and pretend the whole thing wasn't happening.

Emma took one look at me this morning and just knew what I needed. She straightened my tie, tightened the band in my hair, and led me to breakfast without so much as a word.

She's been my shield. An immovable and impenetrable barrier that's given me the space to breathe and survive this shitty situation. Anyone wanting to speak to me had to get through her first. If marketing fails, I swear Emma has a future as a bodyguard.

Even in the crematorium, when the kind words and sympathetic looks became too much, it was Emma's hand that sought out mine. I clung to her for dear life, wishing I could rest my head on her shoulder, just for a bit, to surround myself with her steadfast strength.

Now, with the cremation over, our small group of friends and family have descended on my parents' home. I'm starting to feel more like myself. I won't be bouncing on the trampoline with my younger cousins anytime soon, but at least I feel strong enough to hold a normal conversation. And just in time.

With the solemn business concluded, the Payne family gossip mill has resumed its unceasing grind.

The hot topic? Our Vegas wedding, of course.

"I just can't believe you didn't invite us, Jamie," Aunt Brenda croons, having cornered us just outside the kitchen. It's devastating. The appetisers are so close I can smell the cream cheese.

"I've a spectacular hat I've been saving for such an occasion. The brim has feathers and everything."

"It was more of a spur-of-the-moment thing, Aunt B," I say while trying to telepathically convince Bridget to bring me a sandwich.

"Well, at any rate, it's wonderful to finally meet you, Emma. We've heard a lot about you over the years. I must say, I'm surprised at how things turned out."

"Love will find a way," I mutter, watching sorrowfully as my uncle swipes the last salmon puff.

"So, where are you both living? Emma, have you moved in with Jamie?"

Emma falls seamlessly into our agreed lie. "Actually, Jamie's moved in with me in Chelsea. I turned my spare room into an office during lockdown, so it made sense when we both sometimes work from home."

"Very sensible, dear. And I'm sure it will make a lovely nursery in a year or two." Aunt Brenda winks, utterly oblivious to Emma's abject horror.

"I'm just so glad you were able to meet Maggie. She loved all her grandchildren, but we always knew she had a special place in her heart for Jamie. She was so incredibly proud of him. I'm sure seeing him settle down before she passed made all the difference."

Aunt Brenda's words slam into me with all the force of a speeding truck, the grief I'd barely managed to swallow making itself known in my throat. I can't breathe, suffocating under the weight of my own mourning. My vision swims, Aunt Brenda's soft form wavering before my eyes as they flood with unshed tears.

The only thing that pierces through my heavy shroud is a soft, melodic voice. "Brenda, would you excuse us for a moment?"

Emma takes my hand and gently guides me towards my parents' staircase. "Which room is yours?" she asks when we reach the landing.

Instead of using precious words to explain that mine is on the far left, I slip past Emma, keeping hold of her hand to pull her into my room.

When I collapse on top of my Star Wars duvet, I shut my eyes and let my familiar surroundings ground me. I can smell my mum's favourite fabric softener and hear the tick of the old grandfather clock outside my bedroom door. I can even feel the warmth of the afternoon sun shining through my blinds, hitting me just as it did when I was a child.

Here, I can believe nothing has changed, even if just for a moment.

I vaguely wonder what teenaged Jamie would think if he could see me now. With Emma in my bedroom. And the door closed!

As if summoned by my errant thoughts, I feel the edge of my bed dip, the old mattress springs creaking as Emma settles down beside me.

"Tell me a story about your nan," she whispers, covering my hand with hers. Her touch is light but anchors me to the present, even when her words send me hurtling back into the past.

There are too many precious memories to choose from. Like Nan teaching me how to haggle. She was a badass at any market stall and claimed that just because I was growing up in Surrey, it didn't mean I could turn my back on our London roots.

Or when Nan squared up to the coach of my junior football team, a young man well over a foot taller than her. He'd foolishly benched me because I'd missed the previous week's practice with the flu. I swear the man was quaking in his studded boots by the time she was finished with him. A lioness protecting her cubs has nothing on a little old lady whose favourite grandchild is upset. Nan was ready to throw down.

But there will always be one memory I'll treasure above all others. It was the day I learnt that just because you grow up, it doesn't mean you have to *grow up*.

"I was fourteen years old, turning fifteen," I say softly, my eyes tracing the familiar pattern on my childhood ceiling. "It was just before my birthday, and Nan and I were going to spend Friday night making a cake for my party.

"She was the shittiest baker," I laugh, a lonely tear streaking down my cheek. "But it was tradition. We never missed a birthday, not until she went into the hospice. Last year, we tried to make a lemon drizzle cake, and I nearly broke a tooth on the icing.

"Anyway, I was the kid with the absolute worst cake every year, and I loved it. Even as a moody teenager, I still made time for the tradition.

"For my fifteenth birthday, she asked me what kind of cake we should bake, and I said, 'Why not a lobster?' I can't even remember why. Maybe I'd seen a documentary on them or something.

"Nan didn't have the internet or anything like that, so we found a Victoria sponge recipe in a dusty old cookbook that was falling apart and relied far too heavily on lard. We made the body using two loaf tins but were stumped by the claws. Eventually, we figured we could use two round cakes, assemble the four bits together on a board, and just draw the lobster on top with icing.

"Of course, when we laid all the cakes out, a line of loaves with two balls at the end, we realised our mistake," I remember with a smile. "There was no way around it. We'd baked a giant dick.

"I was laughing so hard snot was coming out of my nose. Any normal grandmother would have chucked the project at that point. But Nan just said my cake had character.

"So, we loaded our piping bags with red icing and got to work drawing out this bloody lobster. The trouble was, neither of us could draw, let alone pipe. By the time we were done, it looked like a really angry, bright red penis. Especially when Nan tried to add a flared tail.

"When Dad came to pick me up, the pair of us were still in her cute little kitchen, covered in icing sugar and high off raw cake batter. He took one look at our creation and said he 'didn't want to know'." I laugh through my tears, squeezing my eyes tight to hold on to the memory. "And that is the story of how Nan and I baked an enormous penis for my fifteenth birthday party."

"Wow," Emma marvels. "You know, a few months ago, I wouldn't have believed you. But after meeting your nan, I don't think anything could surprise me."

I offer Emma a watery smile. It may not have been the heartwarming or profound remembrance she expected, but it's quintessentially Nan. My favourite memory of my adolescence.

As with anything Emma puts her mind to, she has succeeded. She wanted me to feel better, and I do. Honestly, my heart is lighter than it's been in days.

"Thank you," I say, squeezing her hand with mine. "For making today easier."

"You're welcome," she says, chewing absently on her soft bottom lip. "Now we're even, right? You saved me from those drunk idiots, and I saved you from your nosey aunt."

"I'd say we're square. Although, your mission was slightly more perilous."

"Oh, for sure," Emma nods seriously. "Especially when you add the looks your parents have been throwing me all afternoon."

"To be fair, I think they were aimed at me."

"Yeah, you're probably right," Emma agrees. "I'm a delight. You're clearly the problem."

"Hey!" I gasp, sitting upright. "I thought we had a truce?"

"Dream on, Payne," Emma huffs, pushing me back down to the mattress. "Where's the fun in that?"

Chapter Fourteen

Emma

Why do I tempt fate? Have I learnt nothing over the past few weeks? If you so much as tempt that bitch, she'll leap at the chance to fuck you over without even breaking a sweat.

Take today, for instance. It's the Monday after the funeral, and I should be enjoying a well-earned break from Jamie Payne's chaos.

Everything is going according to plan. His family believes we're a real—if unlikely—married couple, and our next event as husband and wife isn't until Christmas.

This morning was perfection. I booked my and Cindy's final fitting for the wedding, and my boss assigned me three new, high-profile clients my colleagues would kill their own mother for.

Plus, when I arrived home, a book from my favourite author was waiting in my letterbox. I've been looking forward to this release for months. It has all my favourite tropes—a forbidden romance between a grumpy hockey player and his sunshine stepsister.

The evening is as it should be. I have a glass of wine in

my hand, and I'm just cracking the spine on my new book when...

Knock, knock, knock.

I consider ignoring whoever has dared disrupt my night when my doorbell joins the fray.

With a huff, I set my book down so that I can send away my annoying visitor. But when I stretch to my toes and look through the peephole, I wish I'd stuck to my original plan. I should have ignored the interruption after all.

It's Jamie. Again.

Two days. That's all it took for fate to lure me into a false sense of security before stabbing me in the back.

This hangover is the gift that just keeps on giving.

"What the hell do you want?" I demand, flinging open my door. I don't mean to sound rude, but whatever Jamie's here to say, I know it can't be good.

"May I come in?" he asks nervously. "We need to talk."

That's my first clue that something's wrong. Usually, Jamie would be the first to point out my incredibly bad manners. Instead, he ignores my offensive attitude and focuses his attention on my ankles like some Victorian pervert.

"Jamie, the last time I let you in, I ended up pretending to be in love with you at a funeral," I laugh. But the sound dies in my throat when Jamie flinches. "Oh God. What have you done now?"

"Can we...?" Jamie motions awkwardly into my flat instead of finishing his sentence.

I step back with a sigh and wave him inside with more flare than necessary. Does he even need an invitation? Perhaps he's a vampire. I'm powerless to keep him out because I've made the mistake of letting the bastard in once already.

Jamie brushes past me before I can change my mind.

He scurries into my lounge and flops onto my teal sofa, dwarfing it completely. His eyes dart unseeingly around my living space until they land on my precious wine.

"Do you want a glass?" I ask in response to his longing gaze.

"Have you got anything stronger?"

"I have a bottle of whisky that my boss gave me for Christmas." Howard is not the best at gifts. His strategy is to think about what he wants and then ask his secretary to buy exactly that.

"Whisky will work."

That's my second clue that something's amiss. Jamie is not a seasoned spirit drinker—as evidenced by his catastrophic reaction to tequila.

I narrow my eyes, trying to scare whatever has Jamie so harried out of him. But he remains tight-lipped. Well, for now, at least. I'm sure the long-forgotten bottle of alcohol I'm about to produce will go some way to rectifying that.

In my kitchen, I find the whisky hidden at the back of a cupboard. The cork is a little tricky to remove, but it eventually bursts free with a satisfying *pop,* and I pour what I guesstimate to be a double shot over some ice cubes.

When I return to the lounge, Jamie is gnawing at the corner of his thumb. Spotting the all-important elixir in my hand, the tension instantly melts from his body, his face lighting up as if I'm holding a cup of liquid gold.

Something is definitely wrong with Jamie. He has *never* looked at me like that before. My suspicion piqued, I hand him the drink and settle next to him on the sofa.

For the first time in three years, I regret buying a two-seater. We're sitting close enough that I can count the individual lashes lining his warm, brown eyes. A girl could get hopelessly lost in their swirling depths if she weren't careful.

Even with the small space between us, I can feel the searing heat radiating from beneath his black jeans, and try as I might, all I can smell is his sandalwood aftershave. It makes me think of autumn storms and cosy winter nights, a confusing contradiction to his beachy clothes and salt-sprayed hair.

We must have spent too much time together recently. That's the only plausible explanation for my wayward thoughts. I've become desensitised to Jamie's cocky attitude, giving me room to notice his other—less annoying—qualities.

Jamie, however, does not appear to be struggling with our proximity. No. He's far too lost in his own thoughts for that.

He downs his whisky in one smooth shot, the ice cubes clinking together as he upends the crystal glass.

Okay, there's my third clue.

"Come on, Jamie. What's wrong?" I ask, tempted to start biting my *own* nails.

"Do you think I could get a top-up first?" He coughs, raising his glass hopefully.

"Not a chance. Stop stalling."

Jamie worries his lip, unsure how to break whatever news has him turning to whisky on a Monday night.

"Do you remember at the funeral when Aunt Brenda asked us where we'd be living?"

"Vaguely," I reply. Aunt Brenda talked *a lot*.

"And you said I'd moved in with you."

"I suppose I must have done. That was the story we agreed on."

"Right, right," Jamie says absently. "Well, Aunt B kind of got it into her head that my flat was just, kind of, free."

"What do you mean?"

"Well, my cousin, Robby, is starting a tattoo apprentice-ship in Greenwich next week."

I groan, finally able to see where this is heading.

"Yeah..." Jamie sighs defeatedly. "Because she thinks I'm living here, Aunt Brenda's asked if Robby could move into my flat while he saves up for his own deposit."

Damn. I thought we'd been so smart. Jamie and I had thought of every conceivable question someone might ask us at the funeral. We had an entire email chain dedicated to getting our story straight.

Jamie moving into my flat would have been the most logical step for us if this marriage were real. Well, more real than just legally real. I have more space, and I haven't lived like a slob for the past however many years. So, we made that our official line.

Sod's law that all our careful planning has come back to bite one of us on the ass.

"Wow, that's awkward," I sympathise. "How did you tell her?"

"Tell her what?"

"That Robby wouldn't be able to move in."

"Um... I didn't."

I stare at him blankly. "Come again?"

"You met Aunt Brenda," Jamie whines, throwing his head back against the sofa. "She's a bulldozer in a frilly apron. I panicked. I couldn't think of a single reason why Robby couldn't move into my flat."

"Are you joking?" I ask in disbelief. "How about '*I'm sorry, Aunt B. I already have a tenant?*'"

I sometimes wonder how Jamie is able to pass as a moderately successful adult.

"I know, I know!" he cries, running his hands through his dishevelled hair. "But you weren't there, Emma. Aunt Brenda wouldn't let me get a word in edgeways. She just kept going on about how proud Nan would be and how much family needs to stick together at a time like this. She even brought up our share of the inheritance. She asked how our house hunt is going!"

"Oof, that sucks," I commiserate, taking a sympathetic sip of my wine. "So, what are you going to do? Check into a bed and breakfast or something?"

"I thought about that," Jamie says gloomily. "But it could be months before Robby finds another place. The rent he can pay me on his apprenticeship wage barely covers half of my mortgage. So, short of blowing through the money Nan left me, I can't afford it."

Wow, Robby's really getting a good deal out of this.

"What about Bridget? Can you stay with her for a bit?"

"She hasn't got enough space and lives more than two hours from my office. I can't even stay with Anthony because how do I explain intentionally making myself homeless so my cousin can live in my flat for peanuts?"

Jamie finally plucks up the courage to look me in the eye. He's holding his breath, waiting for me to do the maths and catch up with what he's trying to tell me.

Shit. Jamie thinks he's going to live here.

With me.

No wonder he looks so nervous.

"No," I say, shaking my head profusely. "No, no, no. Absolutely not!"

"Please, Emma," Jamie begs. "I've literally nowhere else to go. I'll give you everything Robby is paying me in rent."

Ha! I already know that amounts to the square root of fuck all. And that's not the only problem with this master plan.

"Jamie, there is no way you and I could live together. We'd end up killing each other. You must have someone else you can stay with?"

"Not in London. Everyone is either too friendly with Anthony or too close to my family to keep this a secret."

Why do his eyes look so big all of a sudden? Is he trying to puppy-dog me into letting him stay?

The most infuriating thing is that I know Jamie's right. There's no other option. If Anthony finds out Jamie's couch surfing, he'd start asking questions that would lead him right back to that Vegas hotel room.

And if Jamie's family found out? That would be even worse. Nothing says *sham marriage* and *gold-digging whore* like living estranged from your supposed husband.

"Oh my God, I don't believe this," I moan, draining my glass in three large gulps. Suddenly, the whisky makes sense. Maybe I should go and get the bottle? Jamie must need a top-up by now.

"Emma, please," he whispers shakily. "I don't want to tell my family what I've done."

This cannot happen. Jamie and I might be on more friendly terms now, but how long will that last if we live in each other's pockets?

Neither of us has had a personality transplant in the past few weeks. Put us in a confined space for long enough, and everything we've ever hated about each other will be magnified.

There's no way I can deal with his havoc infiltrating my organised life. I only have limited memories of his hotel room in Vegas, but I know that if he made that much mess in my flat, I'd smother him with a decorative cushion.

But I have to admit, there's a tiny, infinitesimal part of me that's curious. A lonely neurone firing at the back of my mind, wondering what it would be like to break out of my comfort zone.

Because, for as long as I can remember, my life has revolved around regimented routines and obsessive control.

And it's served me well. I have a good job, independence, and the security I've always dreamed of.

I also have a husband who's not really mine and *one* good friend who is about to start her own new chapter.

Is that *it* for me? Have I already achieved everything I set out to do?

I'm in a rut, and I'm starting to worry about what will happen if I can't claw my way out. Am I going to wake up in ten years and realise I've got money in the bank but nothing in my life?

Yes, my boss had enough faith in my work today to give me three huge accounts, but I'm stretched thin enough as it is. I've no idea how I'll manage the additional workload, and for the first time ever, I'm questioning whether I even want to.

Since returning from Vegas, I've lived the same day over and over. I've lain awake at night and tried to pinpoint the exact moment when all my days started to roll into one.

How long has my life been this way? Was it a slow descent into monotony, or did the insanity of Vegas cast my well-ordered life into dullness by comparison?

If I hadn't taken that trip, would I have lived in peaceful ignorance for the next year? Two years? Decade? Hell, would I have repeated the same day over and over until I keeled over from a stress-induced heart attack at forty-five?

The only break in the cloud of my existential crisis has been living out this ridiculous farce with Jamie. Maybe his brand of bedlam is precisely what I need to get myself out of this rut. Something in my life has to change, and Jamie has certainly proven himself to be life-changing.

Besides, if Jamie will give me Robby's rent money, I can start rebuilding my savings. They took a hit to pay for Vegas, and losing part of my safety net has been another thing playing on my mind.

Shit. Am I really going to do this?

"Jamie, I don't know..." I hesitate.

But it's too late. Jamie hears the resignation in my voice. He spots my moment of weakness and grabs onto it with both hands.

"Trust me," he promises eagerly. "You won't even know I'm here."

Famous. Last. Words.

Chapter Fifteen

Emma

Oh, how Jamie lied. *"You won't even know I'm here,"* he'd said. *"It'll be like living with a really clean ghost."*

Bullshit. I definitely know he's in my flat. There's no getting away from him!

Our new living arrangement has obliterated whatever tentative friendship we've built since waking up accidentally married.

Not that either of us is acknowledging that fact. Oh no. We've slipped into some weird, sickly sweet, passive-aggressive way of speaking to each other. Something that straddles the line between diplomacy and such thinly veiled loathing, I'm surprised neither one of us has been arrested for homicide.

"Perhaps you'd feel more at home if you unpacked the boxes stacked by the sofa?"

Move your boxes before I burn them.

"I'd love to take a shower after the gym. Could you see your way to leaving me some hot water?"

I hate cold showers, you selfish bitch.

"I find that not caring whether the dried pasta has ended up on the rice shelf helps me relax after a long day."

You're so bloody pedantic. I can't believe I have to live with you. You're insufferable.

Yeah, we're not doing such a great job of hiding how much we're getting on each other's nerves.

I've no idea how to describe our relationship anymore. We're not enemies, per se. We've been through too much to go back to genuinely hating each other. But we're not friends either.

Some would call us *frenemies*, but that doesn't quite capture how close I am to hitting my new roommate around the head with a blunt object. Also, it's way too cute to apply to *Jamie*.

It's been a week and a half since he showed up on my doorstep, and I'm tired.

I'm tired of constantly tripping over his shit.

I'm tired of being banished from my own sofa at night.

I'm tired of finding his sweaty gym clothes in with my washing.

I'm tired of smelling his spiced, woody aftershave wherever I go. How does he manage that? Does he spray it around when I'm not looking? Is he deliberately gyrating his stink all over my upholstery? Why can I smell it on my bath towel, for fuck's sake?

In short, I'm tired of Jamie.

It doesn't help that I've had a *bad* day at work—well, a bad week, if I'm honest. Fitting in those three new clients is proving even harder than I'd imagined. Short of inventing a time machine, I can no longer fit my weekly tasks into seven days.

I'm aware this stress *might* be contributing to how much Jamie-ness I can tolerate. And, to be fair, I think he's trying to be a good roommate. Yes, he's messy, disorganised, and sometimes forgets I'm there, but he's not actively trying to piss me off.

He even agreed to sleep on my sofa. Sure, it pulls out into a bed, but I'd have thought he'd at least fight me on it, especially when I have a spare room. It's technically set up as an office, but I could squeeze a double mattress next to my standing desk if I really tried.

Still, why should I lose my office space because Jamie couldn't think on his feet? He made his bed, and he can literally lie in it.

Although, that decision has come back to haunt me because Jamie seems to have an aversion to pyjamas. On our first morning together, I walked into my lounge to find him dead to the world and sprawled across my sofa in nothing but his tight, white boxers.

For the rest of the day, I was plagued with unwanted memories of his washboard stomach and chiselled pecs at the most inconvenient of moments.

Going over a proposal with my boss? *Boom. Jamie's abs.*

Important lunch meeting with a client? *Hey, remember that happy trail? Imagine if you licked it.*

I even caught myself wondering how it might feel to be pinned beneath him, his hard muscles moving over mine as he worked his thick length into my...

Luckily, I've become immune after a few mornings of repeat exposure. Whenever my mind drifts to the way his biceps flex as he hugs his pillow or to the impressive bulge in his underwear, I just think of the sound he makes when he blows his nose before bed, and I'm cured.

It's a snotty miracle!

And if I'm still preoccupied with Jamie on my commute home tonight, it's because he's only just remembered to text me about the post he put in the microwave three days ago. I am *not* thinking about how biteable his peachy ass looked on my sofa this morning.

At least thoughts of Jamie have kept my mind off my hellish day at work. I don't think I've ever been happier to be going home, even if my safe space has been infiltrated by a ridiculously fit snot goblin.

From the second my ass hit my desk, I didn't stop. Clients were complaining about campaigns we'd spent weeks perfecting, the decrepit CFO wasn't happy with our quarterly forecasts, and the stress of it all made our junior marketer so anxious he quit this afternoon.

You can pick up his tasks. Right, Emma?

I've been putting out one fire after another. All I want to do for the rest of the night is to slip into the world's biggest bubble bath, drink tea, and work out my angst with the darkest romance book I can find.

Trigger warnings? With the mood I'm in, I want all of them.

Wearily, I climb the stairs to my flat, mentally running through the most depraved books to ever darken my Kindle. I'm sure I heard about a new release that features kidnapping, Stockholm syndrome, and plenty of torture.

Ah, true love. Now, what the heck was it called?

I'm so preoccupied with trying to remember the title of said smut-fest—and questioning my life choices—that I don't notice when my front door sticks. I also don't notice the large cardboard box that happens to be blocking my entryway. Not until it's too late, anyway.

I tumble into my flat, catching myself on the wall opposite and banging my elbow hard on the doorframe.

What the hell?

Looking down, I find that a mass of wires has wound itself around my ankles like vines in a jungle.

"Have a nice trip?" Jamie snorts from my sofa. His eyes are glued to my television, his stupid little avatar running away from a hoard of obnoxiously loud zombies. Jamie's fingers mash furiously against his game controller as his mini-me ducks and weaves through a post-apocalyptic world.

Boom!

Jamie punches the air as a spray of detached, undead limbs flies across my screen. Based on his excited whoop, I guess he just won whatever game he's playing.

I close my eyes and count to ten, praying it'll be enough to quell the anger threatening to fracture out of me.

One, two, three, four—

"Oh, by the way. You're out of milk."

My eyes fly open, instantly landing on the massive bowl of chocolate cereal sitting uneaten on top of my iPad.

Great. I'm on the verge of a nervous breakdown, and I can't even unwind in my own home. Why? Because some teenager is killing zombies on my sofa and stealing my milk so he can have breakfast for dinner.

Hold on tight, folks. This is about to get messy.

"Jamie, are you serious right now?"

My infuriating roommate finally looks up at me, his lips downturned as my words run through his tiny brain. It's as if he genuinely can't see a problem with barricading me from my own flat, using the last of my milk, and turning my expensive tablet into a placemat.

"Huh?" he grunts.

This guy really is clueless.

I yank the wires off my ankles and use them to point out everything wrong with my lounge. "I know I said make yourself at home, but this is taking the piss."

Jamie looks around, still trying to put the pieces together.

"Is this because you fell over that box?" Jamie eventually realises, turning away from me to load up a new game.

"The box was right behind the door," I remind him, my self-control stretched to its limit. "Were you trying to break my neck? Or are you just an idiot?"

"You think I left it there on purpose?" He scoffs, twisting on the sofa to unveil his scornful sneer. "Sorry to burst your bubble, but I don't spend my time devising lame ways to sabotage you."

"Why was the box behind my door, then?"

"For God's sake, Emma! I got distracted by the updates on my PlayStation and forgot to move it. It's not a big deal." With every passing second, he's sounding increasingly like a petulant child.

"You can't just set up a games system in my lounge without asking me, Jamie." I stalk towards him, feeling more dangerous with every step.

"Bloody hell, it's one console. There are, like, two extra cables in your lounge."

"Then what the fuck are all these?!" I shout, throwing my collection of wires at his feet. "Do you ever think of anyone other than yourself?"

"You should be thanking me for making this place look lived in," Jamie snaps back. "It's not my fault your definition of a home doesn't go beyond somewhere to eat and sleep."

"Jamie, I swear I'm about five seconds away from tossing that box at your head."

I'm not a good shot. He's in no real danger.

"Alright, calm down," Jamie says in that condescending tone which has calmed down absolutely no one ever. "I'm not your live-in punching bag, so don't take your shitty day out on me. Whatever's put you in a mood tonight, it's not the box."

"You're right, Jamie. It's not the bloody box," I yell. "It's

153

you being a selfish fucking asshole. I have done nothing but go out of my way to help you since we've come back from Vegas. For Christ's sake, you're living in my home. And how do you repay me? You leave booby traps at my door and drink all of my bloody milk!"

"Okay, you need to find a better way to work out your stress, Princess. Because this," he waves his hand up and down in my direction, "this isn't healthy."

"How can I work out my stress when *you* are my fucking stress? And you're always here!"

"It's more than that, and you know it," Jamie spits. "You work, and you come home. That's your life. You're a robot, and you're going to put yourself in an early grave if you don't find a way to let off some steam every once in a while."

"I'm sorry if my methods of self-care don't meet your high standards," I coo. "Unlike you, I have to think about more than just what bar I'm going to visit on Friday night. Maybe you'd understand if you'd ever cared about someone other than yourself. But you don't. One day, you're going to die alone because everyone will have woken up and realised what a selfish, unbearable prick you are."

Jamie recoils as if I've struck him. I can pinpoint the exact moment my spewed hatred hits its mark. A fire ignites in his dark eyes, his anger fuelling the flames, and I have no choice but to step back before I'm burned.

"You know what, Emma," he growls, deliberately pushing himself off the sofa. "I'm going to leave before one of us says something we can't take back. And while I'm gone, why don't you think about everything you just said to me."

The loathing that glows in his narrowed eyes makes my stomach churn. But I don't look away. I can't. I'm caught in his stare, helpless to move until he sees fit to release me.

It's only when Jamie storms out of the lounge that I can breathe again. He marches past me, snatching up his gym bag and flying out of my flat without a backward glance.

My only consolation is that he fails to slam the door on his way out. Despite throwing all his weight behind it, the door simply ricochets back on its hinges in silence, one of Jamie's mutinous wires preventing it from catching.

I wait until I hear the elevator ding before moving to close the door myself. Then, I quickly round up the rest of Jamie's cables and twist them into the knottiest knot possible. My hands are shaking, and my jaw aches from clenching it so tightly, but I can't help it. I'm seething.

The anger inside me has burned so hot it's finding any release it can. I either grit my teeth and focus on cleaning up or give in to the tears of frustration threatening to spill down my cheeks.

When my lounge resembles its pre-Jamie state, I want to scream. It took me minutes to tidy up. Minutes. If Jamie had made the slightest amount of effort or spared me a single thought, then tonight would never have happened.

If only Jamie wasn't such a selfish prick.

And then, what I said hits me. The words I spat at Jamie crash into my chest so hard I stagger back under their weight.

Maybe you'd understand if you'd ever cared about someone other than yourself...

One day, you're going to die alone...

Shit.

Did I just say that? To a *grieving man?*

My poisonous speech sits like lead in my stomach, a bulking mass that will forever anchor me to a moment I can't take back.

Finally, the dam bursts. My shame, anger, and frustration spill out of me until all I can do is crawl into my bed and sob into my pillow.

Maybe tomorrow will be better. Or maybe it'll be so much worse.

And it's all my fault.

Chapter Sixteen

Jamie

I'm fuming. I can't remember the last time I was this angry. Dealing with those asshats in Vegas was a pleasant summer stroll compared to the trembling madness simmering inside me right now.

And over what? Some wires and a misplaced box? The only reason that fight turned nuclear is because Emma had a bad day and needed someone to take it out on.

And boy, did she get *mean*.

My collision with Emma has left me with a restless energy nestled beneath my skin, one that's propelling me towards my new workout spot at breakneck speed. Fighting with Emma might prove to be the most effective pre-workout I've ever taken.

I knew I had to get out of that flat before I said something I'd regret. Emma was brutal. She wasn't taking prisoners. Her words were meant to maim, and they hit their mark with precision. It's hard to believe the tender woman who talked me through Nan's funeral could be capable of such callous malice.

Emma's lucky she has Cindy because, at this point, I'm not sure anyone else would survive her.

I'm still stewing when I use my fob to enter the quiet gym. Thankfully, there's no one at the front desk. I'd usually stop to chat with the trainer on reception duty, but today, I'm in no mood for small talk.

I quickly stash my bag in one of the battered lockers and push through a turnstile into the cavernous space. The pungent smell of stale sweat and glass cleaner welcomes me, promising respite from the circus screaming in my head. After a few deep breaths of the musty scent, my mind shuts down, ready to relax into the mindless grind of a workout.

The gym is quiet tonight, so I easily snag myself a treadmill. I drape my towel over the empty cup holder and realise I've left my water bottle in Emma's kitchen. Oh well, tiny cardboard cups it is. Seems I can't catch a break tonight.

I'm just adjusting the belt's incline to a respectable tilt when one of the gym's personal trainers leans against my machine. I met Miles last week, and he seems a decent enough guy. He's a typical gym bunny, arms the size of tree trunks, with a buzzed head and a tank top about two sizes too small.

Miles also likes to talk. Or, more specifically, to gossip. Any other day I'd love to while away my tedious warmup listening to stories about people I've never met. But right now, I wish he'd kept on walking.

"Alright, Jamie?" he asks happily, his eyes skating around the room for any gym-related emergencies. Especially those affecting the fairer sex, I'd hazard to guess.

"Hi, Miles," I reply half-heartedly.

"How've you been?"

"Fine." I grit my teeth, upping the speed on my treadmill in the hope that my aggressive button stabbing will indicate I'm not in the mood for company.

"Cool, cool," he says, trying to fold his enormous arms

across his even more enormous chest. "I'm just with a client."

Unless said client is invisible, he's lost them somewhere in the gym.

"Don't let me hold you up," I puff. "I'm sure they're paying you a fortune to be here."

"Are you okay, dude? You don't sound like your usual self."

I'm tempted to remind Miles we've known each other for less than a week, but I hold my tongue. It's not his fault I'm in such a foul mood.

"Sorry, man," I apologise, stopping the machine to talk to him properly. "I'm having a bad night."

"Anything you want to chat about?"

"Nah, just roommate trouble. We got into a massive fight this evening."

"You guys don't get on?" Miles asks, his client long forgotten. This must be how he gathers all his intel.

"She's a she, and no. Most days, we can't even stand to be in the same room as each other."

"What? No way. Why'd you live together then? Is she hot?"

I am not touching that tonight. How do you say, *'because we accidentally got married in Vegas even though we hate each other. Oh, yeah, and she's hot as hell,'* without sounding a tad ridiculous?

"Shouldn't you be getting back to your client?" I deflect, hopefully.

"Yeah, I suppose," Miles sighs, reluctantly pushing away from my machine. "Later, man. Good luck with your roomie."

Thank fuck for that.

I restart the treadmill, ramping up the speed in a bid to outrun my awful evening. I break into a sprint, running faster and faster until my muscles burn, and all I can think about is my next gasped breath.

At least the anger boiling beneath my skin is a welcome change from the lingering sadness that's hung over me since Nan passed. It's like I've been wearing rubber gloves. I can feel what I'm doing, but everything's muted. Every emotion, every laugh, every day is quiet now that she's not here. Tonight is the first time I've felt alive in weeks. And that's not healthy.

How are the two of us going to survive this living arrangement? It's not even been two weeks, and Emma and I have already topped any argument we've ever had. We need to find a way to exist without blowing up at each other because this *has* to work. I've nowhere else to go.

Maybe Emma and I have messed with the status quo too much. We've been tiptoeing around each other, pretending to be civil, and look where it's got us. Perhaps we should cut our losses and restore our relationship to its factory settings before one of us really gets hurt.

Is it possible we need the familiar ground of snide comments and immature pranks to level us while we navigate this unchartered territory? To serve as a pressure valve that gradually releases the tension so it doesn't build and build until we can do nothing but explode cataclysmically?

Anything's worth a try, especially if I don't want to be homeless by the time Anthony's wedding rolls around.

The longer I'm on the treadmill, the more convinced I become that a regime of provocation is the way to go. Really, it's for the good of humanity. It's the only way to stop the pair of us from blasting the planet into smithereens.

I think it'll be good for Emma too. She's wound up so tight I'm scared of the day she finally snaps. No one will be safe. I wasn't lying when I said all I've seen her do is work since I moved in. Perhaps if she let off some steam every now and again, she wouldn't pick a fight over the slightest thing.

That's my story, and I'm sticking to it.

By the time I've stumbled off my treadmill and chugged six tiny cups of water, I'm a new man. I've worked out my pent-up anger *and* devised a foolproof plan to avoid a repeat occurrence.

There's even a skip in my step when I wave goodbye to Miles from across the gym. It's time to put my plan into action. I'm calling it *Operation Husband from Hell*.

I can't fucking wait.

To say I've spent the last few days being the worst roommate humanly possible is the understatement of the decade. I've become the adult embodiment of *I know you are, but what am I?*

I've never pretended to be mature, or inventive for that matter. But luckily for me, Emma is an only child and incredibly dull. She's easier to rile up than an old man who thinks believing in basic human rights makes you a snowflake. She just never sees it coming.

We're talking sticky tape over the bathroom taps and salt in the sugar pot levels of pettiness. I've rearranged her meticulously alphabetised bookcase, left my dirty washing in odd places all over the flat (my personal favourite was the random sock in the dishwasher), and linked a very desperate online dating profile to her email address.

One afternoon, when I was particularly bored, I wrapped her whole office in tin foil. The chair, the desk, the computer monitor—nothing escaped the metallic treatment. I even foiled every individual pen in her little stationary organiser. It took me over an hour and two trips to the corner shop, but it was worth it to see her turn into a living, breathing paint swatch. I saw every shade of red imaginable.

But the prank that really sent Emma supernova was when I managed to change her Wi-Fi password. On Friday night, she came home to an empty flat and couldn't connect to the internet.

I've been so relentless in my mischief that I didn't think that particular prank would even register on her radar. Except, apparently, she'd wanted to finish off some work emails after dinner and couldn't get the hotspot on her phone to play ball.

The way I see it, I was doing her a favour. What kind of psychopath pulls overtime on a Friday night anyway?

It appears my litany of annoyance has restored the natural order. Everything is the way it should be. We're back to communicating in taunts and insults, and Emma has eye strain from rolling them so often.

About sixty per cent of my waking hours are dedicated to finding new and innovative ways to be a pain in her ass. So much so that even as I email my team about the social media schedule for the next month, half of my mind is still fixated on my prickly roommate.

Today marks our first time working from home together since our big fight. So far, we've been lucky, and our schedules have meant that one or both of us have been going into London every day.

This Monday morning, our luck ran out.

I have to say, I'm not loving it. For starters, I've lost the use of Emma's fancy desk. So here I am, hunched over the kitchen table, every chiropractor's nightmare. Or payday, depending on how you look at it.

Secondly, I can't even sneeze without Emma poking her head out of her office and hissing at me like a feral cat. The flat is so deathly quiet that my ears hum in the oppressive silence. Even the traffic outside seems scared to make a sound for fear of Emma unleashing her fury on every motorised vehicle in Chelsea.

At least when I'm on my own, I can turn on shitty morning television and pretend I'm surrounded by gossiping colleagues. All my working life, I've thrived in the chaos of giant corporations. My brain has been conditioned to work amidst the clamouring background noise of a hundred different people doing whatever it takes to meet their targets.

No chance of that in House Drayton. Instead, I've resorted to wearing headphones to protect my ears from the angry slam of keys emanating from Emma's office. There's nothing that says *you're not working hard enough* more than someone else's uninterrupted typing.

It takes a few hours and a very heavy playlist, but I eventually manage to tune Emma out and lose myself in my mountainous inbox. I'm halfway through my backlog and in between songs when something catches my attention.

The typing. It's stopped.

I pull a headphone out of my ear and listen for signs that Emma is about to break for lunch. I wonder if she's going to cook something and, more importantly, if I can bug her enough that she makes me some too.

Except it's not Emma's determined footfall that greets me. It's a murmur so faint that I'm struggling to place it.

There it is again.

A choked sound, as if something's sucked the air out of a room, stealing the breath of everyone inside.

Tentatively, I rise from the kitchen table and inch towards Emma's office.

"No, no, no!" The desperate plea reaches my ears, and I abandon my soft approach, quickly rounding the corner into Emma's spare room.

Something is definitely wrong. Emma is standing completely frozen at her desk. Her wide eyes are glued to the computer monitor in front of her, and her tight grip on her desk is turning her knuckles white.

"Emma, what's wrong?" I step closer, worried that her desk is the only thing keeping her upright.

"It didn't send," Emma wheezes, completely oblivious to my arrival. "It didn't send, it didn't send. I'm going to get fired. Howard's going to fire me." Emma coughs, dropping her head to the wood, like the effort of holding it upright is suddenly too much. Her breathing is coming faster and faster, the sound rasping as she gasps for air.

Oh, shit. Is she hyperventilating?

"Princess, can you hear me?" I ask, gently shaking her shoulder.

Emma doesn't give any outward sign that she's heard me. She can't even catch her breath. That's when it finally dawns on me. Emma's having a panic attack. And this one's so much worse than Vegas.

Knowing she won't hear me in this state, I take her hands and slowly steer her away from her desk. The movement sends Emma into another coughing fit, so I wrap my arm around her waist and guide her to the floor against the wall.

Even as I kneel in front of her, she doesn't register we've moved. I almost start to worry that Emma will pass out when something surfaces from the dark recesses of my memory. A vague recollection of helping someone through a panic attack by focusing them on their surroundings.

For all I know, it's utter bollocks. But right now, I'll give anything a shot.

Cupping her cheeks, I lift her face so she has no choice but to look at me. "Emma, tell me something you can see."

She frowns like I've asked her to explain quantum

164

mechanics. Christ, even in her drained state, I can still piss her off.

"Something you can see," I persist. "Come on, Princess. Tell me anything."

"Your hoodie is blue," she finally croaks out.

"Good," I murmur quietly, pleased to hear her breaths evening out. "And what about sounds? Can you hear anything?"

Emma closes her eyes in concentration. "My laptop," she says. "I can hear it buzzing." She stiffens immediately, her chest heaving at an alarming rate.

Shit!

"What about touch?" I blurt out, trying to reroute her attention. "Can you feel anything?"

For a moment, Emma does nothing but gasp for air. I'm about to repeat myself when I see her slowly slide her hands along the floor beside her.

"I can feel the carpet," Emma whispers, and I breathe my own sigh of relief. "And the wall behind me is cold." She lifts her gaze to mine, her shining eyes finally *seeing* me. "And you. I can feel you."

"What can you smell?" I ask, gently stroking my thumbs across her jaw.

"Your aftershave," Emma moans, gently pulling her head out of my hold and leaning back against the wall.

Well, that's the last thing I expected her to say, especially when there's a ginormous mug of black coffee on her desk.

"Why can I always smell you everywhere? Do you bathe in cologne or something?"

I burst out laughing. I'm not sure if that's an intentional dig or whether Emma's mind is still running away from her. Either way, I'm so fucking happy she's coming back to reality.

Emma drags her hands down her face, groaning into her palms. "Oh my God, I'm so stupid."

"Yeah, that's not true," I scoff.

If Emma's stupid, my IQ would be around that of a slug. She's been running rings around me ever since we were teenagers.

"No, I am," she mumbles, still hiding behind her hands. "I can't believe how much trouble I'm in. Seriously, if I'm not fired, it'll be because Howard's already killed me."

"It can't be that bad," I reason. Maybe some distance will help put whatever problem she has into perspective.

"Oh, it can," Emma laughs bitterly. "I'm leading the bid for a portfolio of work my boss is desperate to win. If I'm successful, it'll bring in over two million pounds. It's taken me months to get the application together.

"I was so prepared. Everything was flawless. But my scheduled email failed on Friday night, and I didn't even notice. I've missed the fucking application deadline!"

I flinch. Yeah, I take it back. Losing a two-million-pound bid because you forgot to send an email is *bad*.

"There it is, mocking me," Emma says, nodding to the open email on her computer. "Unsent and perfect in my draft folder."

"I'm sure it seems worse than it is," I lie through my teeth. In all honesty, this sounds pretty damning.

Of course, Emma's not fooled by my fake optimism and fixes me with a glare capable of withering my internal organs.

"Okay, it's bad," I concede. "But here's what you're going to do. You're going to send the bid now with the cringiest apology ever written. Use me as an excuse if you have to. Lay it on thick.

"Tell them you've been supporting your grieving husband and had to take more time off than usual. You scheduled your application email well in advance, so whatever happened at home, you knew it would reach the right person in time.

"Slime all over it. Say how embarrassed you are that your tech failed and how you're mortified that you missed the deadline, especially when you're one hundred and ten per cent committed to this bid. End it by telling them how great they are and how much you admire everything they do."

Emma's hanging on my every word, and so she should be. I've been bullshitting my way out of missed deadlines since I was eleven years old. I'm a pro. This is *my* domain.

"You know what," I say, pushing to my feet and unplugging her laptop from the monitor. "It'll be quicker if I write it."

It takes me less than five minutes to draft out the most sickeningly sweet, ass-kissing email in the history of emails. I know it'll work. I'd bet my job on it.

"There," I say, folding myself onto the floor and thrusting the laptop at her chest. "Send that. Chances are they'll accept the bid, and your boss will be none the wiser."

"Wow," Emma says in awe as she reads my email over and over again. "This might actually work."

"I've had a lot of practice," I boast with a shrug.

"I know," she says, nudging me with her shoulder. "Even so, I think I'll need another coffee before I can deal with this properly."

"I'll make it. Just come to the kitchen when you're ready."

I leave Emma to have a moment to herself. If I'm being totally honest, I need a breather, too. That was fucking scary. I'm so full of adrenaline that I don't know whether I want to run a marathon or collapse on my bed and sleep for a week.

Obviously, I can't do either right now, so I shove a pod into Emma's elaborate coffee machine and watch as the thick liquid trickles into the tiny cup below.

Has Emma been spiralling this whole time? Have I been making it worse? The way I've been picking and plucking at Emma would drive anyone to madness, let alone someone already on the edge.

Shit. Am I the villain here?

Emma clears her throat behind me, interrupting my awful epiphany. She's still pale, but at least she looks steady on her feet.

"I'm sorry," I say, holding out my caffeinated olive branch.

"What for?" Emma asks, accepting the peace offering.

"For taking over your life. For distracting you. For all the childish shit I've pulled over the past few days." I try to run my fingers through my hair, only to remember I tied it back this morning.

"That was really frightening, Emma. I didn't know what to do. I'm just so sorry I've been making life harder for you. I thought riling you up would help relieve some of the tension between us. Let off steam in small doses, you know?"

"Huh." Emma tilts her head as if genuinely considering the merit of my idiotic plan.

"It was stupid," I hurry to add. "I'd no idea you were dealing with so much at work. I never would have pushed you so far if I did."

I really am the world's biggest twat. Emma's done nothing but help me since we got back from Vegas, and I've returned the favour by delivering her to a fucking nervous breakdown. I'd give anything to be able to take it back.

"Maybe if your email works, I'll consider forgiving you," Emma says, blowing on her steaming espresso to hide her twitching smile. "You never know. You might have saved yourself from my eternal shit list yet."

"I thought I was already a permanent fixture?"

Emma shakes her head, quietly laughing as she picks up the spoon in the sugar pot beside the coffee machine.

Crap. Damn Emma and her sweet tooth.

"Wait!" I shout, darting forward to grab the contaminated supply. Emma stares at me like I've lost my mind until she realises what I've done.

"You messed with the sugar again, didn't you?" she asks in disbelief.

"Maybe," I mumble, not so subtly pouring the doctored contents into the bin.

No one wants a salty espresso.

"Bloody hell, Jamie." Emma sighs irritably, opening the overhead cupboard to find a new bag of sugar.

"I'm sorry," I groan. "It won't happen again. I promise."

And I mean it. Starting from now, I'm going to be the best roommate ever.

Peace and quiet, that's what Emma needs.

I can do that, right?

Chapter Seventeen

Emma

Have you ever tried to sneak into a quiet house at night? If so, you'll know everything suddenly sounds ten times louder. Every floorboard creaks, your bedroom door needs oiling, and your nose has spontaneously blocked, meaning you sound like a pug that's swallowed a harmonica.

That is what I have been living with for the past three days. Jamie has been creeping around my flat like a mouse. A terrified, intrusive—and still incredibly noisy—mouse.

Yesterday morning, I ended up screaming into my pillow when Jamie tried to open the bathroom door. The hinges groaned for well over thirty seconds while he gingerly inched it open. The endeavour was rendered even more pointless when he turned on the bathroom light, and the extractor fan blasted to life.

Jamie is walking on eggshells, and I fucking hate it. I thought this subdued version of my husband would be an improvement on the boy who'd once made it his mission in life to cast mine into chaos.

But it's not. His tension is contagious. I've found myself

tiptoeing around my own hallways just so I don't spook Jamie even more than he already is.

After Vegas, I'd hoped his knight-in-shining-armour days were over. I am beyond mortified that he had to talk me out of another panic attack. I thought my heart was going to burst out of my chest and my lungs would run out of oxygen. I don't know what would have happened if Jamie wasn't there.

Why didn't I check if my scheduled email had been sent? I'm never that careless. Usually, I obsess over something so important, religiously checking and rechecking whatever's needed until I'm satisfied. Instead, I was sloppy, and it's becoming more of a habit than I'd like to admit.

It's tempting to blame everything on Jamie. Maybe if I hadn't been so distracted by his pranks, or maybe if he hadn't disabled my Wi-Fi, I would have had more mental space to dedicate to my application.

But that's not fair. Even without Jamie's antics, there's just too much on my plate. The email would have been forgotten regardless, pushed out of my mind by the next looming task on my never-ending list.

Besides, it's hard to blame Jamie when the damage control email he wrote actually *worked*. I don't know why I'm surprised. He spent his formative years perfecting the art of bullshittery—and I don't think I've ever been more grateful for that.

I take back all the times I cursed him for sweet-talking our teachers into another homework extension. Without Jamie, my job would have been on the line. Instead, my bid was accepted without issue, and my boss is none the wiser. I dodged a metaphorical bullet, leaving me standing to deal with my next pressing contract.

I've turned my attention to a software company about to

start a huge international expansion. They want a rebrand that will appeal more to overseas consumers.

My boss managed to talk the client into delaying the project whilst I was in the midst of the bid. But now that shitshow's been dealt with, the client's been promised utter perfection in a quicker turnaround than we'd usually offer.

No sweat. I've got this.

I'm just getting to the heart of their new branding document, harnessing the details currently floating around untethered in my mind, when—

Tap, tap, tap, tap.

Considering I'm working from home, it's not hard to discern who has dared to interrupt my train of thought, albeit very quietly.

Jamie doesn't wait for me to invite him in or, more aptly, to tell him to bugger off. Instead, he slinks into my office, his shoulders hunched as if trying to make himself as insignificant and non-threatening as possible.

This is another novel development since my ill-timed breakdown. Jamie is *constantly* checking on me, reassuring himself that I'm okay under the pretence of bringing me tea. Or coffee. Or biscuits. One time, it was a strawberry 'smoothie' that turned out to be a ready-made cocktail mix he found at the back of my freezer.

This evening, we've circled back to tea again. He carefully sets the steaming cup down next to all the other half-empty cups I've accumulated since lunch.

"I was just brewing up to celebrate the end of the day," Jamie lies pathetically.

I continue typing, hoping he'll leave me alone if I ignore him long enough. Not that it's worked the last three times.

As expected, Jamie doesn't take the hint. He leans against my desk and gives me an awful, sympathetic smile that just seems plain wrong on his face. "It's after five, Emma."

Give me strength.

"Thanks for the time check," I reply through gritted teeth. I know he's not trying to be annoying, but dear lord, his patronising concern is insufferable. I've always had his attention, but I've never before had his pity. It's horrible.

I never thought I'd say this, but... bring back fuck boy!

"Why don't you hit save and come back to it tomorrow? Whatever you're doing will still be there in the morning."

It's, like, one minute past five. At this point, I have worked a whole sixty seconds of overtime.

"I'm quite capable of managing my own work hours," I remind him tersely.

"I know. I just don't want you to burn out again," Jamie says with more sickening sympathy. "Your boss is clearly taking advantage of you. It's not right that your reaction to an unsent email was worse than it was to those assholes in Vegas."

Heat spreads across my cheeks, my whole body tightening with pent-up frustration. I close my eyes in a desperate attempt to calm myself down. I don't want my growing anger to spill out all over Jamie... Again.

I don't know what I resent more. Jamie thinking I'm some fragile doll or that he's hit the nail on the head. Still...

"Believe it or not, Jamie, I don't need you to mansplain working hours to me." I've set my desk to sitting height today, a choice I'm now regretting as I try to throw daggers up at Jamie.

"I'm not mansplaining shit," Jamie snaps, his shoulders straightening for the first time in days. He suddenly seems impossibly big in my tiny office. "You're just pissed because I'm right, and you know it."

Damn.

"I don't get it, Emma," Jamie vents, throwing his hands in the air. "You're mad at me no matter what I do. It doesn't matter if I'm trying to help you or piss you off; it's all the same. I can't win!"

Sick of Jamie having the upper hand, I push out of my chair and try to match his lofty height. It barely helps, but at least I'm standing my ground. Why does he have to be such a giant?

"Jamie, I'm not some damsel that needs saving from the big, bad world. I don't need you to rescue me, okay?"

"That's funny. Because I'm pretty sure we're in this situation because I rescued your ass in Vegas."

"We're in this situation because you got me drunk and married me!" I yell, poking Jamie accusingly in his chest.

"I got you drunk?" Jamie laughs sardonically, grabbing onto my wrist to stop my furious prodding. "That's rich coming from you, *Mrs We'll-Take-The-Bottle.*"

"Oh, so this is my fault?"

"I'm glad we finally agree on something."

"In your dreams," I scoff.

Jamie's eyes darken, his grip on my wrist tightening as he looms over me. "Princess," he growls. "You know nothing about my dreams."

Before I can conjure any kind of response, Jamie tugs on my wrist, throwing his arm around my waist and dragging me into his hard chest.

I immediately freeze. I can feel him everywhere. My senses are rendered useless, so full of Jamie that all I can see, feel, or hear is him. The heat from his hard muscles burns through his thin, black T-shirt, and his thick, jean-clad thighs rub against mine as he leans ever closer, bathing me in his spicy musk.

But it's the darkness in his eyes that has me rooted to the spot. A threat of what's to come if I only let him drag me under. He's giving me a chance, waiting for me to tap out or take the bait and join him in the abyss.

I'm a helpless victim of his magnetic force, drawn to him whether I like it or not. My chest heaves, and my nipples harden, brushing against him as I rise onto my toes. His breath skims across my lips, a teasing brush that makes me want to squirm away.

But still, neither of us moves.

We both know what's coming. We both know how this will end. The question is, which of us has the courage to take that first reckless leap?

Nothing will ever be the same again. Any pretence of normality will soon be a distant memory. But hey, is our normality even worth clinging to? Hasn't the last week shown us we don't work as friends?

Hell, what's one more mistake between enemies?

All at once, the frustration that's been blistering in my heart for days, months, decades, detonates in my chest. A lifetime's worth of unspent energy bursts out of me, desperately latching on to the first vessel it can find. I yank my wrist from Jamie's hold, tangle my fingers in his hair, and slam his smart mouth against mine.

It's only a second. Just one. A single flash of madness that changes the essence of my soul. Because the moment his lips touch mine, I'm done. The moment his lips touch mine, I'm *his*.

And Jamie knows it.

He doesn't seek entry. No, he demands it with all the confidence of someone who knows there's not a chance in hell he'll be denied.

His tongue sweeps teasingly along the seam of my lips, and I surrender to him instantly. The groan he pushes into my mouth is sinful, lighting up my every nerve as it reverberates down my spine.

Jamie deepens our kiss, and I match him stroke for stroke, right there with him as we're overcome with lust and want. My skin is burning with need, and he is the only salve.

I twist my fingers in his messy hair and tug hard, bringing him even closer so he can devour me all the more.

And Jamie doesn't disappoint. His strong hands, calloused from hours in the gym, roam every part of me, grazing my oversensitive skin and igniting my desire.

He palms over my ass and encircles my waist before inching his way to my breasts. It's a painfully slow trail that has my heart skipping in anticipation and my nipples pushing maddeningly against my bra.

I melt against him, my body arching into his sculpted chest, wordlessly pleading with him to touch me. To put me out of my misery and take what we both want.

Whether feeling my desperation or his own, Jamie's fingers dip under the flimsy material of my tank top, seeking the swollen flesh of my breasts.

I rip my mouth from his, a moan tumbling out of me as his fingers slip higher and higher, teasing me to distraction. My whole world revolves around his torturous, wandering fingers. At least, until Jamie pushes his knee between my thighs, grinding against my pulsing centre at the same time as he finally sweeps over my stiff peaks.

I can't take it. I need more, so much more. My mind is going to snap if he doesn't release me from this delicious torment.

I may be at Jamie's mercy, but I won't go down without a fight. I surge forward, taking his mouth and biting hard at the soft flesh.

Jamie instinctively pulls away from me, his eyes dark and his mouth curved into a manic grin. Tentatively, he lifts his hand to swipe his fingertips across his kiss-swollen lips.

The feral rumble in his chest is the only warning I get before he lunges for me, grabbing me around the waist with one arm while knocking the contents of my desk to the floor with the other. His path clear, he grips the backs of my thighs and lifts me onto the cold, hard surface.

If I wasn't so high on lust, I would be ashamed of how easily my legs fall open for Jamie. He doesn't wait for an official invitation, stepping between my parted thighs and running his hands up the length of my jeans as if he has every right to be there.

I throw my head back, willing to submit to the predator before me. Jamie wastes no time in claiming his prey, nipping at the curve of my neck and branding my skin with the friction of his stubble.

I stretch my palms out behind me and brace myself on the surface of my desk. My back arches to push my body into Jamie's intimidating torso, and I grind my hips forward, desperately seeking relief from the heat throbbing in my pelvis.

Jamie immediately releases my neck, his hands flying to the buttons on my jeans. Mercifully, I don't have time to worry about what mismatched underwear I pulled from my draw this morning because Jamie hooks his fingers into every piece of material standing in his way and rips it from my body with one impatient tug. The dull thud of my jeans hitting the floor is surpassed only by the sharp zing of Jamie's own zip coming undone.

My cheeks flush when I realise I'm naked from the waist down, my legs spread wide to bare myself to my adversary. I feel obscene. Jamie's black eyes fixate on my wet core, his urgency setting my flesh ablaze.

Then, just as I'm about to give in to the maddening lust and reach for Jamie's impressive bulge... he tears himself away.

I'm not proud of the desperate whine that falls from my lips, and we shall *never* speak of it again.

"Fuck..." Jamie pants, his eyes squeezed tight as if he's only just holding on to his control. "Condom. Don't move."

Before I can blink, Jamie skids out of my office. The porcelain bowl by my front door clangs as he clumsily disturbs its contents. *Shit.* How is Jamie the most level-headed of the two of us? Protection hasn't even crossed my mind, conclusive evidence that Jamie is bad for my health.

He flies back into the room, his eyes possessed as he throws his wallet into the corner and tears into the foil packet with his teeth.

I nearly cry with relief as I watch Jamie free himself from the confines of his jeans and deftly roll on the condom.

I could wax lyrical about the perfect, thick cock jutting obscenely from his boxers, but that would take brain power I don't have right now. My every thought, my every sensation, all are focussed on the incessant pulse between my thighs. And the cause and the cure of my desire is stalking menacingly towards me.

Neither of us speaks, too scared to break the heady spell that's fallen over us. But the challenge is there in Jamie's dark eyes.

You ready for me, Princess?

I bite my lip as another wave of lust crests over me, and Jamie strikes. He sucks my lip free, consuming me like a man starved as he grips my hips and drags me into position at the edge of my desk.

This is not soft. It's not gentle. There's no need for foreplay, not when we've spent our entire lives teasing and provoking each other to insanity. This is the crescendo of an infatuation that's been mounting for decades.

Jamie nips down my jaw to suck at the sensitive skin behind my ear, the scrape of his teeth distracting me from the blunt head of his cock nudging against my ready heat. I can only urge him on, wrapping my legs around his waist and pulling him into me.

If his first thrust steals my breath, the second steals my soul. On his third thrust, he bottoms out, filling me so completely that I wonder how I'll ever feel whole again.

I clench around the intrusion, eager to commit every inch of Jamie's powerful girth to memory. His answering groan stirs the embers smouldering in my stomach, and I clench again, needing to hear him lose control.

Jamie growls through gritted teeth, his heavy eyes boring into mine.

Is it a warning or a dare? I decide I don't care.

I dig my heels into his back to push his cock deeper inside of me, and... he snaps.

Jamie pulls out so only the head of his cock remains inside me, circling his hips before slamming back in, his brutal thrust shunting me across the desk.

His fingers bruise into my hips, dragging me back down so he can thrust into me again. I brace one hand behind me so I can match his relentless pace, throwing one arm around his neck and pulling him in for a messy kiss.

Every time he slams into my ready body, his thick cock pushes against that sweet spot inside of me, working me higher and higher until the room is filled with my keening cries.

Jamie rests his forehead against mine, his eyes fluttering closed as he pounds into me again and again. And again.

The burning heat inside me spirals, tightening into one heavenly bundle of nerves that pulses persistently at my centre. My orgasm crashes over me, one so powerful I can do nothing but chant Jamie's name as he fucks me through the blessed release.

I feel myself milking Jamie's cock, and he dutifully

follows me over the edge, his mouth dropping into a pained moan as he unloads himself into the condom.

We fly together, our gasped breaths joined as intimately as our bodies while we push each other through our peak. Jamie's pulse is racing in his neck, his heartbeat matching mine as we both crash back down to earth on the other side of our shattering orgasms.

As the trembles that wrack my body dissipate, there's room for my conscience to rear its judgemental head. My nails bite into Jamie's shoulders, and his own dig into the soft flesh around my hips. Both of us will be wearing the proof of our transgressions tomorrow. And, as much as I like the thought of every woman in London seeing my marks on Jamie, the fact that I'll be carrying my own reminder is horrifying.

We stare at each other in silence, our heavy breathing the only sound penetrating the room. Jamie recovers more quickly than I do, a testament to his strict gym regime. A regime I will never make fun of again now I've sampled both the visual and physical benefits.

The awkward moment stretches painfully, the magnitude of what we've done settling over me.

I had sex. With Jamie—*my husband*. On my bloody desk.

This will change everything. How we hate each other, how we tolerate each other, all of it will be corrupted by this one act.

We're struggling to function as roommates as it is. There's no way adding sex into our dysfunctional relationship is going to make things *less* volatile. Now, I'll have to live with the memory of how he sounds when he comes, of how his sculpted muscles flex when he fucks, and of how incredible his heavy cock feels as it bursts inside of me. The invasive scent of his aftershave is a fond, innocuous memory compared to this.

Shit, in what world was letting Jamie into my pants a good idea? What if he thinks this is more than it is? Something more than just an inevitable collision after twenty years of escalating hatred? I don't have time to commit to a goldfish, let alone a whole-ass human.

Or maybe he won't want to do this again at all. That's more likely. I'm probably just the last in a long line of women who have willingly fallen onto Jamie Payne's dick.

But what if he does want a repeat? The ghost of the orgasm haunting my body whispers that worse things have happened. What if I start to get attached? What if this starts to *mean* something to me, and I have to watch him move on to someone more exciting? Someone fun and happy. Someone more like him.

I can't do that. I can't watch him leave me behind as if I'm nothing. It's better we end this now before one of us gets hurt.

"This never happened," I whisper. Of course, that statement would be more convincing if Jamie's dick wasn't still inside me.

It's a tense moment before Jamie nods, his eyes narrowing at me as he pulls out and tucks himself back into his jeans.

Without a word, he spins on his heel and leaves. One slammed door later, and I'm alone again, safe to collect all the pieces of myself that Jamie shattered into oblivion.

Chapter Eighteen

Jamie

If Emma wants to pretend we didn't fuck on her desk like a couple of horny teenagers, that's fine.

Stupid, but totally fine.

I just don't see what the big deal is. It's not like having sex could have made our relationship *worse*. That would be like adding sprinkles to a cheese and banana sandwich and calling it ruined. Emma and I never worked to begin with, no matter what frills we added.

Does it hurt that she refuses to acknowledge it ever happened? Sure. Having Emma regret it before I'd even pulled out certainly wasn't an ego boost. But if she wants to act like nothing has changed between us, I'll give her that.

I'll pretend my entire life didn't change the moment I sank into her perfect body. I'll pretend my every waking second isn't spent replaying that afternoon over and over in my mind. I'll even pretend her soft moans aren't all I hear when I close my eyes or that the biggest regret of *my* life isn't taking the time to savour every inch of her.

I can't get Emma out of my head. No matter how much I throw myself into work or how many hours I spend at the gym, I can't outrun my memories.

I even offered to go cummerbund shopping with Anthony, only to spend the entire time brushing the crescent-shaped cuts on my shoulders, reliving the way Emma clung to me while I lost myself inside her.

Like I said, I'm fine.

Okay... actually, I'm fucked. But I have no one to blame but myself.

Of course, Emma has mastered acting normal. She's just as detached and pedantic as ever. I, however, have no idea how to act.

Since her panic attack, I know I can't mess with her. I can't tiptoe around her either because that pissed her off so much we ended up fucking out our frustration. I'm so confused about how I should behave that I've chosen not to deal with it at all.

In short, I'm avoiding Emma.

It's been a torturous weekend of gruelling morning runs, extended solo lunch dates, and, when all else fails, hiding out in Emma's bathroom.

I almost cried with relief when I got back from my workout this morning to find Emma had already left for work. I have a whole day stretched before me where I don't have to worry about anyone else.

Well, except for the hundreds of people on social media demanding an explanation for the glitch in our new online banking app. But even that pitchforked mob is blessed relief compared to the relentless memory of Emma writhing beneath me.

I'm so lost in my work that I don't notice how time flies. Before I know it, the front door bursts open, the air freezing around me as the ice queen sweeps back into her lair.

Damn. I'd planned to be halfway to the gym before Emma made it home tonight. What do I do now? Do I welcome her back? Do I pack up my stuff and leave? Or do I continue to sit here, my hands suspended above my keyboard like a child caught stealing from the biscuit barrel?

I'm just plotting my escape when I realise it doesn't matter. Emma hasn't even noticed I'm here despite me taking up half of her dining table.

She's clattering around the kitchen, throwing open cupboards to grab everything she needs to pour herself the largest glass of wine I've ever seen.

Or at least it *was* the largest glass I've ever seen. It didn't last long.

After topping herself up, she sets her drink aside in favour of gripping the countertop and groaning at the ceiling.

"You okay, Emma?" I finally croak, bracing myself for impact.

Emma spins towards me, her hand flying to her chest as her soft summer dress wraps itself around her slender legs. "Bloody hell," she gasps. "You need to wear a bell."

I'm not going to point out that she literally walked right past me.

I don't have a death wish.

"Rough day?" I ask politely, trying like hell to avoid another slanging match.

I fail. Emma clenches her teeth so hard I can see the strain in her temples. "Everything is fine," she snaps.

That's blatantly a lie. Emma is *worked up*. Not for the first time, I consider the benefits of paying Emma's boss a visit and punching him in the face.

It's obvious to anyone with eyes that he's taking advantage of her. No one should be burdened with the workload Emma has. I'd bet my inheritance her boss clocked how desperate she was to impress the moment he met her.

Emma's eyes dart around her kitchen, cataloguing every surface and speck of dust.

I glance nervously at the plate I washed at lunch. Did I leave a grain of rice stuck to the underside? Has the sponge dripped murky water onto the pristine countertops?

Crap! Did I use her favourite frying pan again? I accidentally scratched it once and nearly ended up homeless.

No. I'm sure I've left the flat exactly as I found it this morning. And, unable to find fault with anything, Emma narrows her eyes at me accusingly. How dare I fail to provide a reason for her to yell at me?

"Clean up your shit," she eventually spits, throwing her hand at my open laptop. "I have an office for a reason."

With that, she storms out of the kitchen, leaving a trail of ice behind her. I hold my breath, not brave enough to move, until I hear the roar of the shower echoing down the hallway.

Wow.

I'm trying not to take it personally. For once, I don't think I'm the cause of her anger. Not that it matters. I'm still the one in the firing line. Like I said before, I'm a live-in punching bag.

I consider messing up her flat to really give her something to shout about. I'd unload my laundry all over the lounge and unbox every single bloody cable I own. But I've walked that path before, and it only made things worse.

No, if she's going to take it out on me regardless, I have a better way to release her anger.

Time to take back control of this fiasco.

Calmly, I shut my laptop and store it on the counter behind me. I clear up the remnants of Emma's wine and rinse the glass before carefully balancing it on the drying rack.

I smirk the moment I hear the water shut off. Poor Emma. She has no idea what she's done.

I stalk towards the bathroom, dragging my hand along

the wall beside me. Gone is the man who walks on eggshells. Emma's unwittingly cast me as her solace when things get too much, and I'm all too happy to be the best bad idea she's ever had.

I lean against the wall opposite the bathroom, crossing my legs at the ankle while I wait. My body hums with anticipation, my fingers itching to reclaim the body I've already branded as *mine*.

Emma doesn't keep me waiting long. Within minutes, the bathroom door opens, spitting her out in a billowing cloud of steam. Her hair is still pinned haphazardly atop her head, a crisp, white towel the only thing standing between me and what I want.

Emma stops short, clinging to the linen for dear life. "What the fuck, Jamie?!"

I don't say a word. Instead, I step forward, wrapping my hand around her arm and dragging her into me.

Emma's chest skims against mine, and I hear the gasp catch in her throat when I lower my mouth to her ear, leaning in close enough for my lips to brush against the tender flesh.

"Do you need me, Emma?"

She says nothing, but she doesn't need to. Her body gives her away. A shiver travels over her still-damp skin, and I hold my breath, waiting to see if she'll pull away from me or finally give in to the inevitable.

The second I feel her weight shift closer, a feral grin spreads across my lips. It's the only solicitation I need.

"Are you stressed, Princess?" I nibble at her sensitive lobe, relishing the way she trembles against me. "Do you need to work out some tension?"

"Jamie," Emma moans. "This is a bad idea." But her protests are half-hearted at best.

I trail my lips down her throat, and she throws her head

back, her hips melting deliciously into mine as her fingers knot into my T-shirt.

"A bad idea is pretending nothing's changed between us," I murmur into her collarbone, peppering kisses over her heated skin. "A bad idea is denying how good I can make you feel."

I push my hands under the hem of her towel and bunch the material over her smooth thighs. "Don't act like this isn't exactly what you hoped would happen when you tried to goad me into an argument. Tell me, did you want me to fuck you on your pristine kitchen worktop?"

Emma's soft whimper is the only subtle sign that she can hear me.

"It's okay, Princess." I lift my lips to hers to whisper my tempting challenge. "Use me. I dare you."

I see the moment Emma's mind loses the war with her body. Her eyes sharpen, determination taking over as she tugs me forward and slants her lips over mine.

It's every unsaid word and averted gaze, all crashing down into one explosive kiss. We duel for dominance, neither willing to yield to the other.

Emma's fingers claw over my chest, the material of my shirt hitching as her hands trail down to my sweatpants.

Now that my Princess has her sights set on something, nothing will get in her way.

Except that's not the way we're going to play it tonight.

"Nuh-uh," I taunt, unhooking her fingers from my waistband. "This time, I want you in a bed. This time I want you trembling beneath me, so desperate for my cock that you'll beg for it."

For once, Emma doesn't argue. Not even a huff of indignation. Instead, she follows me obediently down the hall, her quiet 'okay' following behind as we burst into her bedroom.

The last time we walked this path, we both took what we needed. It was desperate. Impatient. We sated the ache that's been building and burning for years. It was the best sex of my life.

Now, I want more. I want to savour her, to learn every inch of her body and taste every morsel I can reach. I'm going to drive us both to insanity so we can do nothing but surrender to our frantic need. I will force us to the edge and then push us even further.

Like Emma, her towel is barely holding itself together. There's really no point to it at all. So, I push her back against her bedroom door and flick the precarious knot at her chest.

The linen drops to the ground with a heavy slump, and I take a step back to relish the moment that Emma's bared to me for the first time. Every curve, every dip, every inch of her body, all of it mine.

Fucking hell.

She's utter perfection—and a complete paradox. She's soft lines and gentle arches, her smooth, lithe body enticing you in and promising bliss.

But when you stir closer, you realise your mistake. She's lured you in, and now you're trapped in her hypnotic snare. A web of fierce passion that captivates and enslaves you. She may be the one who's naked, but I'm the one who will submit tonight.

Emma's everything her bedroom is not. We're surrounded by nondescript white walls and neat white furniture. The only splash of colour is from the duck egg sheets on her bed. Everything has its place, pristinely positioned, so no particular thing stands out.

I hate everything about it. Emma is sultry temptation. Volatile desire. She demands attention with a single look.

This pretty and inoffensive space is an affront, and I can't wait to sully every fucking inch of it.

Well, there's no time like the present.

I sink to my knees, ready to worship at her feet. I run my hands over her smooth stomach, her muscles twitching under the roughness of my palms as I trace my way to her pert breasts.

The moan when I ascend her soft mounds is heavenly, but the groan when I brush over her hardened nipples is pure sin.

I gently pinch down, my cock throbbing as Emma's hands scramble for purchase on the door behind her.

Her unbridled lust is bewitching. She's so responsive that I want to see how much she can take before she falls apart completely.

Gripping her knee, I lift her leg over my shoulder, turning my head to drag my nose along the length of her thigh.

Her panted breaths reach my ears just as her fingers tangle into my messy hair. I ghost my lips over her inner thigh, her hipbone, the skittish flesh above her neatly trimmed pubic hair. Everywhere except for the one place she so desperately needs me.

Emma rocks her body forward and back, not knowing whether she's advancing to pleasure or retreating from torment.

Little does she know, I'm just as desperate. The intoxicating scent of her arousal is sending my blood rushing south, my cock heavy against my leg.

Finally, as I kiss along the delicate crease of her thigh, my resolve crumbles. I lower my head and dip my tongue into the nectar at her quaking centre.

Emma's strangled cry sets my blood aflame, every part of me captivated by her erotic abandon. I swipe over her sweet core again, catching her hips in my hands when her knees buckle beneath her.

"Jamie," Emma breathes, her head banging against the solid door behind her.

I push in deeper, spearing her open and then pulling back to tease her swollen nub.

Shit. I'll crave this taste for years to come. The sound of her moans, her stinging grip on my hair, and the tremble of her thighs will forever be a part of me.

My name is the only word she can find. By the night's end, it will be embossed on her lips.

"Jamie," she pants breathlessly. "Need you..."

Oh, I'll never tire of hearing that.

I sink back onto my heels and drink in her debauched body. She's wrecked. Her breasts rise and fall in time with her panted breath, and a delicate flush spreads from her taut nipples all the way to her cheekbones.

This is Emma. Wild and untamed. Veiled in a haze of lust and completely at my mercy.

It's stunning.

Slowly, I rise to my feet and slip my T-shirt over my head. I push down my sweatpants, and I can't help but flex when Emma's hungry eyes snag on my erect dick.

I don't think I've ever been so devastatingly hard. Not even the last time I sank into her perfect centre. I grab hold of my shaft, slowly pulling my hand along its length to circle my sensitive crown.

What will Emma do now? Will she watch me? Wait for me to make the first move? Or will she demand more? Will she take from me what she so clearly needs?

Of course, Emma doesn't let me have the upper hand for long. My fist tightens around my cock, and her face darkens. Determination sparks in her eyes, burning brighter with every step she takes towards me. She reaches out and pushes at my chest, so I have no choice but to fall back across her immaculate bed.

I've barely bounced against the mattress when she climbs over my waist, taking my mouth in a demanding kiss. Emma grinds her most intimate flesh over mine, and I steady her hips to stop us from taking this too far, too soon.

Only, I won't be able to hold back for much longer. Every slide of her hot body over my throbbing cock sends my desperation spiralling out of control.

Then, just as my mind starts to fray, Emma lunges to the side.

I reach for her, mourning the loss of her weight above me, until she flings open her nightstand and rummages in the drawer for a box of condoms.

A dark and primal part of me growls when I realise the box is already open. Enraged, I grab Emma's waist and drag her back over me, digging my fingers into her supple skin as I smash my mouth to hers.

I'm staking my claim, pure and simple. Erasing any lingering memories of men who have dared touch what belongs to me.

Emma's eyes sparkle with triumph as she pulls back and tears open a foil packet, reaching between us to sheath my length in the latex. Her touch is confident, unfailing, even when I thrust my cock through her firm grip.

"And you thought I'd be the one begging," she tuts against my lips. Emma rises to her knees and positions my aching cock against her slick heat.

And then stops.

Her hips are poised to take all of me, my member notched against her tightness. And yet, the only move she makes is the smug smile that tugs at her wicked lips.

It's clear she thinks she's won this round.

Doesn't she know me at all?

I wrap my arm around her back and then slam into her hard from below, taking what's mine in one brutal thrust.

Emma cries out, steadying herself on my straining chest as I lift her off my length and then force her back down. Again. And again.

And again.

Emma looks desperate. Wanton. Taking my cock as if she was made for it. As if it's everything she's ever dreamed of. I'm addicted. I throw one hand behind me and push myself up to steal a clumsy kiss from her lips.

It's laughable that I thought I could take this slow.

She feels so good. So fucking, fucking good.

We work each other higher, our combined moans an erotic symphony scored by our pursuit of pleasure. My release is already threatening, building in my spine and working its way down to my heavy balls. I'm ready to burst.

I thrust harder, aiming for that sweet spot I know will make her scream.

And she doesn't disappoint. Emma rips her mouth from mine, my name falling from her lips as she pulses around me in a violent orgasm.

She tightens relentlessly, her carnal pleasure triggering my own release. My high crashes over me, firing so hard it steals every thought from my head.

I'm floating. Flooded with endorphins, a tingling warmth that spreads from my pelvis and takes over my entire body.

I hope I never come down.

It may have been raw, fierce sex, but it feels like home. It feels like comfort and peace and pure fucking bliss.

Emma drops her head to my shoulder, her breath cooling a path down my sweat-slick back. When she purrs contentedly into my neck, my heart stumbles, struggling to remember the rhythm it's meant to keep.

Shit, I'm so gone for this girl.

We sit joined for hours—or maybe minutes—I don't know. Time has lost all meaning now that I have her in my arms, and I'm loath to let her go.

"So, Princess," I say, pulling her closer, "you had a rough day?"

Chapter Nineteen

Emma

"*So, Princess, you had a rough day?*"

Well, you could say that. Although 'day straight from the fiery pits of hell' would be a more apt description. If Jamie hadn't cornered me outside the bathroom, I'd either be buried in my laptop or crying tragically into a glass of red.

But instead, my body is glowing from earth-shattering sex and a mind-numbing orgasm. The chaos that's been colliding in my brain has cleared, and the headache plaguing me for days has finally dissipated.

"You don't have to talk about it if you don't want to," Jamie says when I don't answer his question.

My natural instinct is to shrug it off. To hide any weakness from the world and pretend I'm not drowning. Besides, Jamie just suffered an incredible loss. My problems will only sound trivial in comparison.

But he looks so earnest. As if he really does want to know what's on my mind.

And what could it hurt? Jamie's the only one who's been there for me in the past few weeks. He swooped in like some gallant superhero in Vegas and again when I thought

I'd tanked my entire career. He's the only person in years who has managed to scale the walls I've built to hide how much I'm struggling.

The question is, did I throw him the rope? Jamie said I intentionally goaded him tonight. Is that true? Did I want him to snap in the hope that we'd end up tearing into each other before falling into bed?

Maybe.

It's taken every ounce of my mental energy to stop myself from fantasising about Jamie this week. Ever since I discovered how it feels to have him work me up and pull me back down, I've been yearning for that release.

So, I iced him out, determined to give myself a chance of surviving this with my pride intact. Jamie will soon move on with his life, and I need to be able to do the same.

And yet, here we are. Again.

If tonight's shown me anything, it's that no matter what we do, the way Jamie and I come together is inevitable. I might as well milk it for all the comfort I can. Future Emma can worry about what happens when this falls apart.

"Yeah, my day was pretty bad," I finally admit, nestling further into Jamie's arms.

"Want to talk about it?"

"Want to remove your dick from me first?"

Jamie sighs as if I've asked him to do the dishes rather than remove a part of his body from mine. "If I must."

He lifts me up like I weigh nothing, his biceps rippling as he carefully lowers me onto my plush duvet. "Be right back," he says.

While my legs still have the structural integrity of jelly, Jamie can somehow jump from my bed and slip from my room without a single stumble.

The smug bastard.

My own dismount is far more hesitant. I have to lean

against my dresser to have any hope of remaining upright while I hunt down a tank top and pyjama pants.

When Jamie returns, I'm still propped up by my bedroom furniture. He's 'dressed' in a pair of tight black boxers, proudly showcasing every tanned and sculpted muscle on his body. If it wasn't for the sated ache between my thighs, I'd happily spend the evening with my tongue attached to his skin.

"So," Jamie says, flopping onto my bed and patting the spot next to him. Apparently, this is some kind of slumber party. "What's up?"

I slide in beside him, making a show of rolling my eyes to disguise how much my heart is racing at the sight of Jamie sprawled out on my duvet.

"You remember that bid I was late submitting?" I don't know why I'm phrasing it as a question. He's hardly going to forget the spectacular meltdown I spewed all over him.

"You didn't get it?" he asks, his face falling like someone kicked his puppy.

"No, we did."

"But... that's good, right?"

"Yeah, it's good," I say, picking absentmindedly at my shorts. "If there were a hundred more hours in the week. Little did I know my boss wasn't planning to cover my other clients. He'd hinted that we'd take on a couple of new hires if we got the work, and I stupidly took that as gospel.

"Now I'm stuck with a thousand more things to do and no time to actually do them. When my boss invited everyone to come together and toast *our* success, all I could think about was how the hell I'm going to manage."

"Urgh," I groan defeatedly, "I'm such an idiot."

"You're not an idiot. Your boss is a dick," Jamie says, darkness clouding his sharp features. "He knows you'll do anything to make this work for him, even if that means burning yourself to the ground in the process."

"You think I'll make this work?" I ask hopefully.

"That's what you took from what I just said?"

"Well, it's probably one of the only compliments you've ever given me."

"Fine," Jamie huffs, throwing his arm around my shoulders. "Yes, I think you'll make it work, even if it kills you. You're the most stubborn person I've ever met. It just sucks your boss is taking that to the bank."

It's true. These next few months will be agony. But still, I can't pluck up the courage to tell Howard he's asking for the impossible.

I've spent years carving out my reputation as the person who will never let you down, the one who will go above and beyond to achieve miracles. And I have the non-existent social life and frayed nerves to prove it.

If I shatter that illusion, what do I have? I've poured everything into my job. Everything. Without it, all that's left is a flat I won't be able to afford and a husband who sleeps on my sofa.

All at once, the weight Jamie had lifted from me tonight crashes back down. I rub at my chest, hoping to ease the tightness that's taken hold.

"You can always talk to me, Princess, about anything." Jamie reaches up and strokes his fingers across my cheek, the tender caress dulling the dread that's settled in my heart. "And if you need more, I'll be here. Just know I am always an option if things get too much."

It takes me a moment to decode his cryptic offer. "Jamie, are you suggesting we become friends-with-benefits?"

"Yes?" he asks. The way he's steeling himself for my reaction is adorable.

"Are you insane?" I laugh.

"No. No, you're totally right. Bad idea. Just forget I said anything," he mumbles, leaping from the bed and motioning frantically towards the door. "I'm just going to go."

I pull him back down before he can make his getaway, a playful smirk on my face.

"I can't believe you think we're friends."

As it happens, Jamie is skilled at both being a friend and our agreed-upon benefits. It's been a week since Jamie *selflessly* offered up his body for the purpose of stress relief, and one thing's become abundantly clear...

I'm a lot more stressed than I thought.

If I had any shame, I'd be embarrassed at how many times I've sought comfort in Jamie's arms. Or rather, on his rather sizeable package. But, alas, I have *no* shame. Sex with Jamie is all-consuming. Cataclysmic and completely addictive.

And considering all I have to do is raise my eyebrow in his direction before he's catapulting himself into my bed, I can't imagine our arrangement is a hardship for him, either.

Jamie's really onto something. Sure, work is still dire. I've spent more hours working overtime in the past week than ever before. But that's been so much easier to deal with knowing what's waiting for me when I close my laptop for the day. Or rather, the night.

I've even been sleeping better. Which is weird since Jamie's taken to crashing in my room after our mutual orgasms. There was never an official invitation. It's just that he has a ten-minute grace period between when he comes and when he collapses into a deep sleep.

I thought I'd hate having Jamie in my bed. My room is where I let down my guard, and I've never felt comfortable sharing that with anyone. But Jamie somehow adds to the sanctity of the space. It's as if our shared secret has been given a place to rest while we face our other problems.

I can't believe I ever thought sex would make our relationship worse. Our home life is unrecognisable. We've been arguing less, with any residual tension burned off during our nocturnal activities. I've even started to find him... endearing.

This afternoon, when I was in a particularly fraught video call, Jamie crept up behind my laptop and slapped a sticky note right beside my boss's puce face.

How I managed to hide my laughter while Howard unwittingly talked into an incredibly detailed—and anatomically correct—sketch of an asshole, I'll never know.

Of course, I pretended to be furious with Jamie, which had the desired effect of winding him up enough to tear open my shirt and push me to my knees.

By the time we both reached our climax, I was bent over the sofa, our clothes nowhere in sight, and a set of bite marks ruining my upholstery.

But I can't bring myself to care, not now I'm sprawled across Jamie's chest, his fingers leading a tingling trail up and down my arm.

"Do you want to go out tonight?" Jamie asks, breaking our easy silence.

"What? Where to?" I push myself up on his chest.

"I was thinking that new wine bar down the street." Jamie shrugs beneath me, the measured move *almost* passing as nonchalant.

"It's a Tuesday," I say stupidly.

"I know. But you deserve a break."

Remembering that Jamie dragged me away from my laptop at gone ten last night, I admit he might have a point. Still, I'm hesitant. We've only just found the delicate balance in our friendship. What if testing it out in the real world ruins that?

It might sound melodramatic, but it's not outside the realm of possibility. The last time I went to a bar with Jamie, I ended up heavily involved in a wedding I have no recollection of!

"Come on, Princess. Let me take you out?" he pleads. Jamie's hanging on my next words as if they'll make his day or break his heart.

"You want to go on a date?"

"We've done everything else, so why not?"

"Doesn't that kind of defeat the point of friends-with-benefits?" I ask.

"Why don't we be *friends-who-date* for tonight? What could it hurt?"

One look at the eagerness shining in Jamie's eyes, and I crumble. He's right. What could it hurt?

"Okay," I agree, sealing the deal with a kiss. "It's a date."

I've found that getting ready for a first date is a ritual. You shower, you shave, you buff, you try on fifty different outfits, each sluttier than the last, before settling on the first one you tried. Your hair volume defies the laws of physics, and your feet are numb from shoes that might as well be torture devices.

It takes hours.

I've also found achieving that effortless illusion is impossible when you happen to live with the man you're dating.

Tonight, I have to create perfection in the same amount of time it takes me to get ready for work. Otherwise, the deception will be ruined forever. My only consolation is the dense cloud of woody aftershave flowing from my bathroom. It's not just me who's pulling out all the stops.

After flinging my entire wardrobe onto the floor and cursing everything I've ever bought, I've settled on blue bootleg jeans and a burnt orange silk top. The spaghetti-thin straps make the material skim enticingly down my curves, and I've even got a pair of stilettos that match the colour exactly.

Now I'm ready, I'm not sure what to do. Do I leave the safety of my room and wait for Jamie in the lounge? Or do I linger awkwardly and wait for him to 'pick me up'?

Thankfully, the decision is made for me when Jamie knocks on my bedroom door.

He's wearing black jeans and a relaxed cream button-down shirt. The rolled-up sleeves not only serve to expose his muscled forearms but also conjure salacious memories of him gripping my thighs and lifting me into the air.

Even his hair is behaving, neatly coiled into a knot at the back of his head. He's every dirty dream I've ever had. It'll be a bloody miracle if I keep my pants on tonight. And based on the hungry look in Jamie's eyes as he drags his gaze down my body, I'd say the feeling is mutual.

"You look beautiful," Jamie says, offering me his hand.

I place my palm in his and barely stop myself from giggling when he leans down to brush a kiss across my knuckles.

Who am I?

"Are you ready?" he asks. I presume the question is rhetorical since he's tugging me to my front door regardless.

Our short summer walk along the balmy street follows in much the same fashion. Jamie's like a springer spaniel, bouncing along and drawing me in with his infectious excitement.

Even when we have to wait for a table at the stylish new

wine bar, Jamie's rocking back and forth on his heels, his fingers entwined with mine as he tells me about all the questionable venues he and Anthony have frequented over the years.

The whole effect is incredibly charming. *Damn it.*

It's hard to square this carefree, animated man with the person I've watched working from my home office. It's not just Jamie's body I've become obsessed with over the past week. I've also started to notice other little things about him. Like how he scrunches up his nose when he's deep in thought or the way his tongue pokes out when dealing with a particularly aggressive social media post.

Jamie's work voice is a wonder to behold. It's deep and powerful. Authoritative and demanding. Suddenly, my response to his bedroom voice makes more sense. It could bring anyone to their knees. Really, I'm just a victim of his commands—a very willing, completely fanatical victim.

After shamelessly eavesdropping on a few of his work calls, I discovered Jamie's been seriously downplaying his job. It's high stakes and high pressure. A whole team reports to him, including a batch of interns who frequently fall over themselves to catch his attention. He holds his own with suited bankers who don't see the point of social media—or even the need to interact with us lesser mortals at all. He's a force to be reckoned with.

"How do you do it?" The question tumbles out of me, surprising an approaching waitress so much that our lychee martinis wobble on her little tray.

"How do I do what?" Jamie asks, carefully claiming our drinks before they end up on his lap.

"How do you have a job just as pressured as mine and still have a life?"

"Work hard, play hard," Jamie jokes, sipping his cocktail with a mischievous grin.

"No, I'm serious. Why am I a mess, and you're... you?" I gesture in his direction as if that makes my words any clearer.

Jamie takes a moment to mull it over, casually leaning in to rest his elbows on our high-top table. "What's your goal in life? The thing you've been working for since you were a little girl with pigtails, running around the school and getting me in trouble?"

I don't even have to think about it. "To be successful. To make my own money and never have to rely on anyone else."

It's hardly a surprising admission. I imagine half the people in London would say the same thing. "And I never had pigtails," I add hurriedly.

"See. That's the difference between you and me. I want to be successful too, but I want to be happy more. If there's no joy in life, what's the point?"

"You make it sound so simple," I sulk. "But happiness doesn't pay the bills or fill the fridge."

"I know. I'm just saying I try to have balance. If I have a bad day, I make sure I go to the gym or hang out with Anthony. I play stupid games or find something to give me an adrenaline rush.

"Life's too short to be miserable. My nan drilled that into me. I know it's a privileged way of thinking. My family is great, and I've never known what it means to go without. But that's how I look at life. If I'm not happy, then why am I here, you know?"

"Sometimes I went without," I say quietly, spinning my martini glass on the glossy table. "We weren't really poor, but things were tight. My mum raised me on her own, and I could see how stressed she was at the end of every month. I knew when I grew up I didn't want that. I wanted the freedom and nice things that come with money. And I wanted to earn it all myself."

"And do you have that?" Jamie asks.

"Well, I do have a pretty good shoe collection," I laugh.

"I've noticed." Jamie's eyes twinkle as he bumps his foot against mine. "But other than shoe shopping and jumping on my dick at any chance you get, what do you do for fun?"

"I read," I admit, sipping my overly sweet cocktail and praying Jamie doesn't ask me to elaborate.

Jamie rolls his eyes. "I'd gathered that, given the hundreds of books lying around your flat. No offence, but none of them look like your thing."

"What do you mean?"

"Well," Jamie says cautiously, "they all look kind of trashy."

I gasp dramatically. "You take that back."

"Princess, I pulled one out yesterday to find two naked men wrapped in a towel on the cover. Towel singular. There was one towel!"

"Oh, I loved that one," I sigh. Though Jamie has a point. That was definitely one of my trashier reads. "What's the matter, Jamie? Did my book offend your delicate sensibilities?"

"Not at all, I loved it. I even skimmed through the best bits. I just thought you'd be a stuffy classic sort of girl, that's all."

"Urgh, no thanks. I think too much at work. I don't want to do it at home as well. I want a book that gets to where it's going, and if there's some smutty sex along the way, then all the better."

Hmm, how strong is this martini?

"That reminds me." I point at Jamie accusingly. "You still owe me a book."

Jamie flings his head back and groans. "I thought I'd gotten away with that."

"Not a chance. I will accept a book voucher or something from my TBR list as payment."

"What the hell is a TBR list?"

"To Be Read, and don't change the subject. Why were you such an asshole in Vegas, anyway? I mean, you were hardly Prince Charming before, but there, you were downright mean to me."

"I think you'll find that was you changing the subject," Jamie chuckles.

"See! You did it again!"

"What the hell is in these martinis?" Jamie looks into his glass as if it might hold the answer.

"Nuh-uh, spill," I say, tapping him on his forearm. Well, if he will flaunt them...

Jamie huffs, draining the rest of his drink. "Okay, I might have been a bit pissed off with you in Vegas."

I raise my eyebrows when he doesn't expand, staring him down until he's forced to continue.

"I was late to the airport that day because I'd spent the evening with Nan. I'd got home late from the hospice and then couldn't sleep because I felt guilty about leaving her. When I finally did drop off, I overslept. So, when I got all your texts calling me every name under the sun, it just grated on me.

"I know it was juvenile, but I wanted to make you feel as bad as I did that morning. And I am sorry. I should have just told you what was going on instead of trying to ruin your trip."

Oof, that's hard to hear. Jamie must have found it so hard to leave Maggie, and I inadvertently went out of my way to make things worse.

"I'm so sorry," I say, covering his hand with mine. "I

never should have treated you like that. I know it's the worst excuse in the world, but if I'd known what you were going through, I'd have left you alone."

"That's okay. I'm kind of glad you didn't leave me alone. It felt good to have your undivided attention all weekend," Jamie says, smiling roguishly.

"Cut it out," I laugh, kicking Jamie under the table. He kicks me right back, and the girlish giggle that's been threatening to escape all evening finally breaks free.

Oh my God, I'm flirting with Jamie.

"Can I get you two another drink?" Now, it's our turn to jump when our waitress appears out of nowhere.

"No thanks," we both reply in tandem. I wonder if Jamie's thinking the same thing I am. If we ended up married the last time we drank together, what damage could we do now that we actually *like* each other?

"Tell me, Princess. Why do you think we did it?"

"Did what?"

"Why do you think we got married?" So, he *was* thinking about our Vegas mishap.

"Er, tequila?" Is there really any other reason?

"You think that's all it was?" Jamie asks, his voice smug. "Interesting."

"Do you have any other theories?"

"After the last few days, I've started to think we were inevitable."

"In what world was us getting married inevitable?" Maybe we should have ordered another drink. Where is that waitress?

"Not married exactly. But you have to admit it feels right when we're together. I think giving in to the tension between us was bound to happen, even when neither of us could admit it. The alcohol gave us a nudge, and we veered off in the wrong direction. Instead of falling into bed, we ended up at the altar."

Hope blooms in my chest, a foreign feeling that soaks through my body, lighting up every cell it touches. Jamie's right. We fit together. No one has ever made me feel so good.

But still, Jamie's words can't drown out that snide whisper telling me he'll tire of us eventually. That I'm not exciting enough to hold his attention. Not in the long run.

"Or," I counter, locking up that hope to protect my tender heart, "you had an impulsive thought, and my brain was too soaked in tequila to question it."

"You still think this was my fault? Interesting," he repeats.

I'm going to strangle him. "Of course, this was your fault. You think I came up with the idea?"

"You tell me, Mrs Trashy-Romance-Novel."

"Oh, I'm sorry, Mr I-Accidentally-Lost-My-Flat. I forgot you were the patron saint of good decisions."

"You wanna go home and work this out once and for all?"

"Yes." I grab my handbag, heat already simmering in the pit of my stomach as I glare at him. "What are you waiting for? Let's go."

And if my heart danced when Jamie called my flat 'home'? Well, that's beside the point.

Friends-who-date, my ass.

Chapter Twenty

Jamie

It has become abundantly clear that Emma doesn't do anything for fun.

Well, except for me. Wink.

My newest resolution is to push Emma out of her comfort zone. And considering her comfort zone extends to... reading... it's not as if I need to push that hard.

Persuading her to join me on one of my morning runs was a flop. I won't elaborate on all the promises I had to make to get her out of the door. Let's just say my jaw was pretty sore the next day. But my logic was sound. I thought if she could start her day with a hit of exercise endorphins, perhaps her boss's grating nasal voice would be easier to deal with.

However, half a mile in, Emma was cursing me to hell. Apparently, my legs are too long, my strides are too big, my breathing's too loud, and if I have the gall to invite her on a run, I should at least make sure it isn't raining first.

All in all, a complete bust. Note to self: Emma only enjoys one activity that involves breaking a sweat. Armed with that knowledge, today, I'm trying a different tactic.

It's Saturday, and Emma is free. How do I know she's

free? Because there's no work on Saturday. Also, Anthony and Cindy are away visiting family. That means when I do eventually roll myself out of bed and join Emma in the kitchen, she'll have no plausible excuse to wriggle out of my plans.

I'm not usually one for lying around in bed. Once I'm awake, I'm more of a get-up-and-go sort of guy. But since spending a few weeks on a hard sofa bed, I'm relishing every moment with a mattress that isn't the depth of a hamburger.

Emma's side of the bed is still warm, so she can't have been up long. I give my body one more luxurious stretch and follow the alluring smell of coffee emanating from the kitchen.

For where there is coffee, you will find my wife.

Emma's leaning against the countertop, still deliciously sex rumpled after last night. Her long, tanned legs are crossed lazily at the ankle, accentuated by a pair of tiny pink pyjama pants.

It's not until Emma clears her throat that I realise I'm staring. I tear my eyes away from her tempting legs to focus on a more appropriate target. Like her breasts, which are spilling out over her matching laced camisole.

Wait! Her face, I focus on her face.

"Morning, Jamie," Emma teases, one eyebrow arched accusingly.

I lean in to brush a soft kiss across her cheek, obsessed with the way Emma blushes whenever I do something charming. I don't know how long I have left before she gets sick of me, so I'm going to kiss her as much as I can for as long as she'll let me.

"Get dressed. We're going out," I tell her, pulling away before I'm tempted to hoist her onto the counter and do something very *un-charming* to her body.

"What? Where?"

"It's a surprise. You'll find out when we get there."

"What if I'm busy?"

It's my turn to raise an eyebrow. "Are you busy?"

"Well, I could have been," Emma sulks.

"But you're not. So, get moving. We've got about an hour before we need to leave."

"To do what?"

"I told you, it's a surprise!"

"But why?"

Oh my God, why is everything such a battle with Emma?

"Because you need to have some fun. Don't forget, I watched you snap a ballpoint pen in half with your bare hands yesterday."

She didn't even notice. It was terrifying.

"And your solution to that is to ambush me into a mystery outing?"

"That's a very dramatic interpretation of what's happening here."

Emma shakes her head, but I can see she's trying not to laugh. "You're an idiot."

"A loveable idiot?"

"Not even close," Emma purrs, finishing her coffee and dropping the empty cup into the sink.

"Look, I know you're not busy today. So, suck it up. We're going out, and we're spending the day together."

"You're not going to let this go, are you?"

"Nope," I pop.

"Fine," Emma finally relents. "What do I need to wear? We're not going skydiving or anything, right?"

"What? No. Just wear something normal. Jeez, whatever we do now will be boring if your expectations are that high."

Emma pushes away from the countertop, stalking out of

the kitchen and muttering under her breath, "Some of us like boring."

Clearly not you, Emma. Or you wouldn't have married me.

Once Emma was on board with my plan, or rather lack thereof, it didn't take long to shepherd her out of the flat.

I'm pleased she's not dressed for skydiving, although her short denim playsuit makes her look like a naughty fighter pilot. I've kept it simple today in a pair of black jeans and a tight, white T-shirt. If it so happens that said T-shirt shrunk in the wash and now hugs my chest indecently, then that's purely a coincidence.

It's a gorgeous day in London. Summer has truly arrived. The sun is beating down mercilessly, and the city's swarming with excited tourists. Unfortunately, that also means the underground has started to resemble the underworld. But it's only a short journey to Waterloo, and I'd contend with the thousand-degree heat any day to feel Emma's body rock into mine whenever we pull into a station.

The moment we ascend the escalators into central London, I think the jig is up. We're in the city's tourist haven, each sight and spectacle shouting louder than the last. But still, Emma looks confused.

It's not uncommon for people in London to have lived here for years but never visited a single attraction. It's almost an unwritten rule. A real Londoner leaves *all that* for the sightseers.

But not today.

I grab Emma's hand and drag her through the crowded streets towards the river. Our destination is only a brisk five-minute walk away, but based on Emma's scowl, perhaps a romantic stroll would have set a better pace.

Glossing over her annoyance, I gesture up at our first stop, too excited to hold it in any longer.

"Ta-da!" I exclaim.

Emma looks up at the imposing stone building, a black and green gothic sign daring us to step inside its creepy walls. I watch as realisation dawns on her face.

"We're going to the City Crypts?" she asks, her eyes wide. I can't tell if she's surprised or horrified. Either way, this is going to be a blast.

"You bet. Welcome to destination one. Today, we're going to be tourists."

"I've never been here," she says with awe, or maybe disbelief.

"I didn't think you would have. I went years ago with the university's football team. My friend Lars had to bail out halfway through because he nearly wet himself."

"What?" Now, I can definitely identify that expression as horror.

"Don't worry. It was mostly due to all the beer he'd drunk the night before."

Emma doesn't look reassured, so I keep to myself that Sweeny Todd had tried to wrangle Lars into his barber chair. Instead, I tug her towards the stone steps and through the jarringly modern automatic doors.

I'd had the foresight to pre-book tickets on the train. It feels strange to flash my phone at a Victorian peasant, but nonetheless, the historical woman prints off my receipt and waves us on.

"What? Not going to fight me on the price of the tickets?" I ask Emma, pocketing the piece of paper as we move through reception.

As with everything, we'd argued about splitting the

drinks bill on Tuesday. Emma finally relented and let me pay, but only after I'd agreed she could foot the next bill.

"This is all on you," Emma laughs. "It's your hair-brained idea, after all."

There's a huddle of people in the dark foyer beyond reception, the atmosphere thick with nervous apprehension and childlike glee. We join the back of the tour and wait for our descent into London's sinister past.

"Who paid for our wedding?" I ask. Though I don't remember anything about that night, I'm certain it wasn't me. There was nothing on my bank statement, and no dollar bills were missing from my wallet.

"I did," Emma admits reluctantly.

I knew it! My idea, my ass.

"Interesting," I hum.

"Oh God, don't start that again," Emma groans. She looks so cute when she's annoyed.

I grab her hand and pull her into me, wiping the pout off her lips with a steamy kiss.

Emma sighs, my blood ignited by her desperate keen. Then, just as I run my hand down the small of her back, we're interrupted by an honest-to-God dungeon master.

Fucking creepy cockblock.

The medieval oddball ushers us into an ancient elevator, cackling as we edge into the iron cage one by one. I'm not sure whether the guy has drunk too much caffeine or whether his unsettling energy is all part of the act. Either way, I don't hear a single rule he's throwing at us because I'm haunted by the heavy chains rattling around his waist.

The lift clunks to life, juddering downward in what I hope is a dramatic effect rather than a symptom of the ageing mechanics. After a particularly violent jolt, Emma tucks herself into my side, and I feel like the tallest man in the world when I wrap my arms around her shoulders, a promise to protect her from spooky elevators and Mr McCreepy in the corner.

I knew this was a good idea.

When we finally grind to a halt, our small, bewildered crew exits the elevator with a collective sigh of relief. Not that the dungeon master cares. He closes the elevator gate, laughing manically as he ascends to find his next victims.

What's that saying? Find a job you love, and you'll never work a day in your life. If my career in social media relations doesn't work out, I reckon I'd have a future here.

We've stepped straight onto the set of an old, dingy alleyway. The sun might be blazing outside, but it's cold enough for goosebumps to lift on my bare arms down here. I take this as an excuse to tug Emma close and rub my hands up and down her chilled skin.

The City Crypts is just as awesome as I remember. The grim sights and eerie sounds, even the damp, smoky air, all of it mixes together to give the impression that you've jumped into the pages of a history book.

We wind down cobbled streets, passing gas lanterns and crooked shopfronts. Every now and then, someone from London's past knocks us off course, luring us into their lair to act out the horrors woven into the city's rich tapestry.

Guy Fawkes takes us under the Houses of Parliament, a man with a sloshing bucket paints the picture of the Great Fire of London, and a vampire tells us about his resting place in Highgate Cemetery.

Jack the Ripper even tries to entice Emma down a dark alley until she swings me around to use as a human shield.

At least I know where I stand. And apparently, that's between Emma and London's most notorious serial killer.

The final stop on our dark tour is a torture chamber. An actual torture chamber. There's a rack, an iron maiden, and an array of terrifying contraptions lining the walls. The spikes and bolts and *fucking clamps* make me cringe.

I turn to Emma, intending to offer my support during this difficult time.

Imagine my surprise when her eyes are shining, enthralled by the display like a kid in a candy shop. If I didn't know better, I'd say she's about five seconds away from stealing something as a keepsake.

"You know, I just finished a book where the guy kidnapped someone and kept them in a dungeon just like this."

"I thought you only read romance?" I ask, subtly pulling her back from a dusty cabinet in the corner. God knows what they keep in there. Why the hell did they make this place so realistic? Half of these things look like they might *work*.

"I do," Emma says matter-of-factly before walking up to the grim reaper himself and pointing to something on the wall. She lights up when the robe-clad man takes what appears to be a spiked gag from the wall.

I think I need to take a closer look at Emma's bookshelf. Because what the fuck?

Okay, so I might, *might,* have got us thrown out of the City Crypts.

And banned.

For life.

But it wasn't my fault. Honest!

What was I supposed to do when the dungeon master jumped out at me from a bathroom stall? Apparently, it's all part of the immersive experience. But how was I to know that? I was already jittery after watching Emma salivate over instruments of torture and having a madman come for me while peeing was the last straw.

Okay, I may have punched a bit too hard. But I didn't do any lasting damage. And, if you scare a guy when his back's turned, you've got to expect some kind of knee-jerk reaction.

I thought Emma would be mortified, escorted off the premises with a real troublemaker.

Emma Drayton would never!

My saving grace was that she'd been the victim of her own jump scare. Let's just say she was sympathetic to my plight after a chimney sweep had pounced on her while she was browsing the gift shop.

In fact, I've not been able to get a coherent word out of her for about ten minutes. Even when we visited a little coffee stand along the Thames, she snorted in the vendor's face, unable to hold her giggles long enough to order our iced mochas.

"I–I can't believe you pun–punched the dungeon guy," Emma laughs around her straw.

"He was scary!"

"Aw, Jamie," Emma coos, rubbing my arm patronisingly. "I'm sorry I wasn't there to save you."

"So you should be," I huff. "What were you doing in the gift shop, anyway? Looking for torture devices to add to your collection?"

"They didn't sell any," Emma pouts.

"We'll be returning to your fascination with medieval punishment later."

"Is that a promise?" Emma purrs.

"Hell no! I like my sex pain-free, thank you."

"Spoilsport," she says, nudging me with her shoulder.

I've never seen Emma so free, so playful, so absolutely happy. She's practically glowing, and I can't help but feel responsible. I want to climb Big Ben and shout it to all of London.

See that smile? I did that!

Instead, I sling my arm around her and bury my nose in her floral hair. We're the very picture of disgusting young love, walking the city's streets with eyes only for each other.

Part of me wishes we'd put on our wedding rings. I want everyone to know Emma is mine. That she belongs to me just as much as I belong to her.

Being with someone has never felt so right. But I'm too much of a coward to ask Emma if she feels the same.

So, for now, I'll settle for this day.

And hope it never ends.

Chapter Twenty-One

Emma

"**A**h, Emma. Just the girl I wanted to see."

Bugger. I was so close to making it through the morning without crossing paths with my boss. Why did I think the extra-large frappé was a sensible drink choice? Damn, my bladder!

"Hi, Howard," I say, slipping on what Jamie calls my 'suffering through idiocy' face.

"I ran into Roger Barlow on the golf course yesterday. His wife's cosmetic brand has had a bit of a bad run-in with a marketing consultant. He royally screwed up their campaign and won't do a thing about it. By all accounts, it was made by someone with the skill of a schoolboy."

I feign polite interest, praying this conversation isn't heading in the direction I think it is. "Do you know who they used?"

"Some cowboy fresh out of university, I believe," Howard says, waving it off as if it's of no consequence. "If only she'd asked Roger for *his* opinion. He would have steered her to us, and we could have avoided this whole mess.

"It's a bit of a hobby for her, you see. Something to pass

the time while Roger's travelling. But she's upset, none-theless. Roger wondered if we could knock something up for her. I said I knew just the girl. They need a proposal tomorrow morning, and we can move to a campaign for Monday."

"Next Monday?" I choke. I'd laugh in Howard's face, except I know he's serious.

Five days' time? There's no way we can get a proposal done by then, let alone pull together an entire portfolio for a brand-new client.

And—even if I could work miracles—the design team would murder me. The decapitated body with no hands or feet kind of murder.

It's impossible. Even if I re-scheduled the mountain of work on my desk, I'd have to slog through an entire weekend to be halfway close to finished. Perhaps two months ago, I'd have considered it. But now? Now I have better things to do.

It's not that I don't *want* to work. Actually, since playing tourist with Jamie, I've been coming into the office with a spring in my step. By letting loose at home, I have more mental space to dedicate to the creative thinking that made me fall in love with marketing in the first place. Jamie was right. It's all about balance.

Our trip to the City Crypts was absolute carnage. And I loved every insane minute. I gasped, screamed, and laughed myself to the point of tears. I even had Jamie convinced I had some kind of pain kink. The way his face paled when I spoke to the dungeon master will live rent-free in my mind for years.

And when we looked over the city skyline from the top of the London Eye, I had never felt such peace. My head was quiet for the first time in as long as I can remember. But my heart? My heart was full. We stood in perfect silence, my back to Jamie's chest, wrapped in his possessive arms.

We sank into the moment, finally letting the shattered fragments of ourselves settle. We each reshaped the pieces of our being and made room for the other.

It was everything.

I want more moments like that. So many more. I don't know how long I have with Jamie, so I'm stealing every second while I can. Starting now.

"I'm sorry, Howard." My voice cracks around the foreign words. "That's only going to be possible if someone else completes the Clough account deliverables this week."

Even then, a campaign by Monday is not possible. I'm banking on the fact that literally no one else can step up to the plate. Clough is by far our biggest client, the one I fought so hard to secure. Howard won't risk that for his golf buddy's wife's hobby.

My boss stares at me, his tightened eyes daring me to change my mind and find a forgotten pocket of time to weave into a miracle.

I shrink under his scrutiny.

"Are you sure, Emma? If it's overtime you're after, log the hours, and you'll be compensated." He scrunches his nose as if the idea repulses him. Not the thought of paying overtime, but that I might be motivated by something other than an altruistic team spirit.

Right now, I *am* the bloody team.

"I'm sorry, it's not the overtime." *Oh God, why do I keep apologising?* "I'm already working late nights on the Clough account. There's literally no more time. I'd be happy to speak to your friend's wife about her next campaign when our current projects calm down. Or perhaps someone else can take a look for her?"

Ha. Someone else.

220

A sinister silence stretches between us, Howard's jaw ticking as I stand firm in my resolve. At least, I hope that's the impression I'm giving because inside, I'm wilting.

"If you're sure there's nothing you can do," Howard drawls, eyeing me suspiciously, "could you let Roger know you won't take the campaign? Get his number from Silvia."

And with that, Howard turns on his well-heeled shoes and marches off down the corridor.

Cowering in his wake, all I can do is breathe. I suck in air as adrenaline works its way out of my system. Lights spot my vision, and every humiliating way Howard could fire me plays on a loop through my mind.

I scramble back to my desk, my frappé bladder forgotten. Realistically, I know my job is safe. My work is impeccable, and thankfully, no one but Jamie knows about my late email fiasco. But that doesn't stop my brain from picking me up and throwing me into panicked waters.

I don't know how long I stare at the blurry words on my laptop, but I estimate *it's too long* based on Silvia's concerned expression when she hands me Roger's phone number.

I'm about to call Roger and let him down when my own phone vibrates across the desk. My stupid heart skips a beat when I see the name on the screen.

Jamie: I'm outside.

Me: What? Why?

Jamie: Can you take your lunch break? I'm sat on the steps.

I glance at the time on my laptop. It's just after midday. I guess I could take a lunch break? At least it would give me a chance to get my nerves back under control. Besides, it's a beautiful day, and every atom of my being wants to spend it with Jamie.

Me: I'll be right down X

It takes me a few minutes to figure out how to set my online status to '*on break*' and lock my laptop. I finally get to visit the ladies' room, and then I'm flying down the grand staircase and out of the heavy front door.

I find Jamie leaning against the intricate iron railing of my office. He's taken the day off to help Anthony paint some old chairs for the wedding, and he looks the part in paint-splattered jeans and a ratty grey T-shirt. Even his baseball cap sports chalky white spots. It's cruel of him to flaunt how delicious he looks when it's at least six hours until I can do something about it.

His head turns as soon as he hears me click down the stone steps, and I hurry towards him until his soft smile is all I can see.

"Hey. What are you doing here?"

Timidly, Jamie holds out a plastic tub. "You forgot your lunch. I thought I'd bring it over."

"Thank you," I breathe, a flutter of nerves scattering through my chest.

I peek through the lid and see a fresh, homemade salad on top of yesterday's pasta. It certainly wasn't there last night, which means Jamie took the time to make it this morning.

I swallow around the lump in my throat, touched that Jamie would put so much effort into this one small act. It's been years since someone's cared about me like this. I'd almost forgotten how it feels to be a priority.

Christ, I'm getting emotional over some lettuce leaves and chopped tomatoes. What's happened to me? And what's happened to Jamie, for that matter? The man who once sat back and watched me drink a salty espresso.

"Can you take a break, or do you have to get back to work?" Jamie shoves his hands in his jeans as if he's easy either way. But there's no mistaking the hope in his eyes.

I've already pissed off my boss once today, so I might as well go the whole hog and take my entire lunch break. In for a penny, in for a pound, right?

"Sure. Want to go grab a coffee?"

"As long as it's iced," Jamie sighs. "It's the hottest day of the year, and Anthony had me painting fifty chairs. I wouldn't mind, but he only did six!"

"Aw, poor Jamie," I mock, rubbing his arm in consolation. A lame excuse to feel up his taut muscles? You'd be correct. "Let me just run this inside, and we can go."

Luckily, our office kitchen is on the ground floor. I dart in, stash my precious pasta in the fridge, pray no one else eats it (I'm looking at you, Silvia), and race back out to Jamie.

"There's a nice place down the street. Have you heard of Molten Toffee?"

"If it has air conditioning, lead the way," Jamie says, fanning his T-shirt.

The August heat *is* stifling. By the time we collapse through the door of the coffee shop, Jamie's paint-splattered skin is glistening, and my silk blouse is clinging to my stomach. Iced coffee is definitely the order of the day.

We patiently join the queue, the other patrons a fascinating mix of harried office workers and ambling visitors, all taking a well-earned break from the sun.

The line moves slowly, Jamie's hand pressing on my lower back whenever it's our turn to move forward. I lean into his touch, barely fighting the urge to rest my head back against his chest while we wait.

"Anthony invited me for drinks after our tux fitting this weekend," Jamie says, his thumb tracing delicate circles at the base of my spine. "You should expect a similar offer from Cindy."

"What? Just the four of us?" Anthony and Cindy know better than that.

"Yeah, subtlety is not Anthony's strong suit. He asked if I'd seen you since the stag do and then casually dropped in the idea of drinks. I think it's their last attempt at getting us to play nice before the big day."

I sigh. "Doesn't Anthony know a lost cause when he sees one?"

"Oh, I'm a lost cause, am I?" Jamie wraps his arms around my stomach, pulling me in to nip playfully at my neck. "We'll see about that."

I squirm in his hold, breathless and completely oblivious to everything around us, until...

"Ahem." A knotted hand taps Jamie on the shoulder. We both turn slowly, coming face to face with a very unamused old woman. She nods her head forward, silently telling us to cut it out and move our asses to the front of the queue.

We scamper up to the register, placing our order before moving as far away from the scary, scowling lady as possible.

"So, how are we going to play it?" Jamie asks, his hands in his pockets to keep them out of trouble.

"What do you mean?"

"Drinks this weekend. Are we going to pretend we're still mortal enemies, or do we come up with a story about how we're friends now?"

"What did you tell Anthony when he mentioned me earlier?"

"I tried to change the subject as quickly as possible," Jamie laughs, grabbing our two iced coffees from the barista.

I scoff, heading towards a small table in the window. "Well, that's not at all suspicious."

"What did you want me to say? Emma and I are good now. We had a little talk, and it turns out she's not so bad when she's stuffed full of my dick." Jamie takes an obnoxious slurp of his coffee. "Oh, and by the way, we're secretly married."

"Well, obviously not," I say, rolling my eyes at him. "I'm just thinking it's safer to act like nothing's changed. Then we don't have to worry about our stories matching up."

Plus, pretending to hate each other all night is our kind of foreplay.

"That actually might be fun," Jamie agrees, smirking at me across the table. "I miss hearing how despicable I am on an hourly basis."

"I can start reminding you again if you want?"

Jamie lobs his screwed-up napkin at me. It lands with a thump, heavy from the condensation around his cup. I pick it up and throw it straight back, overshooting to hit him right on the nose.

One look at the pure shock on Jamie's face has me dissolving into a fit of laughter. I can't stop, not until the violent scrape of a chair pierces my periphery.

We were already in the stone-faced lady's bad books, and given her disapproving glare as she takes her seat at the adjacent table, we've not achieved redemption.

225

Before we can disgrace ourselves further, we hightail it out of the café.

By the time I'm back at work, all that remains in my cup is a pale, watery imitation of coffee. Still, caffeine is caffeine. I quickly slurp at the dregs, hoping Jamie doesn't notice my faux pas. Though, given Jamie's grin, I've not been as subtle as I'd like.

Unperturbed, he bends down to press a kiss to my lips. It's a gentle brush that warms every cell in my body, pooling in my chest and the depths of my stomach.

"Bye, Emma," he whispers, slowly pulling away from me.

"Bye."

Jamie shoots me one last devastating smile before turning around and jogging in the direction of the underground.

I float up the steps of my office with my heart bursting out of my chest. Jamie wanted to spend today with *me*. Of all the things he could have done with his precious time off, he chose to make sure I had a proper lunch.

Holy shit, I like a boy. And, against all odds, I think he likes me back!

Of course, our situation is complicated somewhat by the marriage certificate hidden on top of my bookcase. We're both skirting around the subject, studiously avoiding the elephant in the room.

The list of suitable solicitors in my inbox is gathering internet dust. Has Jamie forgotten I have it? Or does he think I'm still working on the annulment? Another possibility is that Jamie wants to ignore the list as much as I do. Perhaps he's not ready to permanently end what we started in Vegas, either.

God, I hope that's the case.

I think I want to see where this can go. The fear Jamie

will get bored of me, that I'm too strait-laced for him, it's still there. But I'm starting to see that's a *me* problem. I think of my meticulously prepared salad and consider that I might be more than just a convenient hook-up for him.

Still giddy, I grab my lunch from the communal kitchen and make for the stairs. My mind is stuck on Jamie—how his muscles moved in that poor excuse for a T-shirt and the specks of paint still in his hair. That's how I almost run headfirst into Howard.

For a moment, I'm taken aback by the hostility on his face. There's a stiffness to his body that has my own jumping to attention. Whatever's happened, Howard is furious.

"I can't believe how hot it is out there," I laugh nervously, stating the bleeding obvious.

Howard merely hums, his eyes narrowing at me. I can't stand the awkwardness, so I dart around him, running up the stairs as fast as my heels and shoddy cardiovascular fitness will take me.

I'm nearly in the clear when Howard's nasal voice stops me in my tracks.

"I'm surprised at you, Emma."

I turn slowly, my stomach sinking when it dawns on me that *I* am the reason for Howard's foul mood. Oh God, did Clough contact him? Did he somehow find out I missed the application by three whole days?

"I'm sorry?" I gulp, unwilling to incriminate myself just yet.

"He's not who I pictured you with." *Wait, what?* "If you're throwing away career opportunities for a guy, I at least thought you'd steer clear of *that* type."

Wow. There's so much wrong with his statement that unpacking its toxicity will take me a minute.

Throwing away career opportunities? Because I'm

227

refusing an impossible project that'll derail everything our firm has been working on for months? And *that type*? Are you kidding me? I'd cringe if I weren't in such shock.

It's on the tip of my tongue to correct Howard. To tell him that Jamie heads up media relations for one of the biggest banks in the country. Hell, probably the world. But why should I? Why the fuck does it matter? It doesn't make Jamie anymore 'my type'. Howard has made a snap judgement based on Jamie's old clothes and got it wrong. That's his problem, not mine. It's not on me to change his shitty behaviour.

The absolute hypocrisy. Need I mention he has a wife? How is that any different from whatever he thinks is going on here? Am I meant to be a celibate little worker bee while he has a life with his family and his golfing buddies?

I bet he has mistresses, too. He seems the slimy type. Maybe I'm wrong. But I'm too mad to consider any other narrative right now.

I take a deep breath, my skin vibrating with barely concealed fury. I'm actually worried about what will come out of my mouth if I don't carefully consider every word.

"Howard, thank you for your concern. But I would appreciate it if you didn't use such inappropriate language to talk about my husband."

It sounds like I've plucked a line straight out of our HR handbook, but at least I thanked him.

I'm such a polite girl.

The look on Howard's face almost makes this painful conversation worth it. He can't find the words to say, so instead, he gives an excellent impression of a fish.

"Why didn't I know you were married?" he finally splutters.

I level him with my deadliest glare, one Jamie himself has cowered away from over the years.

"As my personal life has *never* interfered with my work, I didn't think my marital status was of any interest to you. Clearly, I was wrong." I spin on my heel, unwilling to waste another second on this prick today. "Now, if you'll excuse me, Clough wants an update on *my* progress. I wouldn't want to keep our biggest client waiting."

I hold my head high as I settle back at my desk. My first task? Changing my email signature to boast *Mrs Emma Drayton-Payne*.

Suck it, Howard.

I can't wait to tell Jamie.

Chapter Twenty-Two

Emma

In my opinion, there are very few scenarios in which drinking before lunch is acceptable. Luckily, watching my best friend try on her wedding dress is one of them.

I don't know if the champagne bubbles have gone to my head, but the second Cindy steps out from behind the heavy cream drapes, I burst into tears.

She's stunning. There are simply no other words to describe how beautiful she looks. The dress is exactly what I would have chosen for her. Simple and effortlessly chic. The entire dress is held up by the thinnest straps I've ever seen. Yet, it's been so perfectly engineered that the silk hugs every curve of her body while leaving her back completely bare.

"You look so gorgeous," I hiccup embarrassingly.

To her credit, Cindy lasts a good five seconds before her face crumples, and she starts to sob a stream of happy tears. We're both a wet, slopping mess, hooked in a weird embrace, with our faces leaning outwards to ensure no stray moisture risks falling onto Cindy's dream dress.

Thank goodness there's no one else here to witness our

downfall except one completely unfazed sales assistant. In a practised move, the middle-aged woman reaches back into the changing room to pull out a gold-plated box of tissues. I gratefully accept the offering and try my hardest to stem the happiness leaking from my eyes.

"Bloody hell," Cindy snorts around another sob. "Do you think Anthony and Jamie are getting this sappy at their fitting?"

"Are you joking? I bet Anthony is ten times more emotional than us. A part of me almost feels sorry for Jamie."

Cindy gasps dramatically. "You feel sorry for Jamie?"

I roll my eyes around my soggy tissue. "Calm down. I said I *almost* feel sorry for him. Another, bigger part of me hopes Anthony snots all over his shoulder."

There. *Operation Status-Quo* is off the ground.

Thankfully, my own dress fitting is less tear-jerking. So much so that Cindy and the dresser have left me to change back into my clothes while they talk about headdresses.

The beautiful gold dress fits flawlessly. It's a strapless floor-length number with a slit up one side that stops just short of indecent. I love it. I twirl around in front of the changing room mirror, mesmerised by the way the weight-less material shimmers under the spotlights.

Struck by a bolt of inspiration, I strike a pose I hope is equal parts seductive and blasé. Then, I flick back the iridescent material so that my thigh is peeking through and take a quick selfie.

Pulling up my message thread with Jamie, I attach the photo. I consider adding a witty message, but ultimately, don't bother. There's no need. This dress does all the work for me.

"You ready, Emma?" Cindy shouts through the curtain, startling me so much I nearly drop my phone.

"Er, just a minute." I ease myself out of the dress, making sure to hang it carefully to stop it from creasing. I know it'll be steamed before the wedding, but something that pretty deserves to be handled with reverence.

Back in my baby-blue sun dress, I step out and meet Cindy by the pay desk.

"Your headband is on order," the sales assistant reassures Cindy. "We'll deliver it with the dresses before the big day."

"Thank you for everything," Cindy gushes, a blinding smile on her face as we wave goodbye and head out for our lunch reservation.

We talk of nothing but dresses and weddings on our walk to the sushi bar, and, to my surprise, I don't hate it. Usually, half my mind would have wandered elsewhere, focused on a recent project or planning for my upcoming week.

Watching Cindy fall in love with her dress makes me realise how much I've been missing. I've been here, but I've not been *present*. And I can't put my finger on when that started. Is it something Cindy's noticed? Or has it been a slow descent into self-absorption? Either way, the epiphany makes me desperate to make up for lost time.

"How was your trip home?" I ask, taking another plate of salmon rolls from the conveyor belt in front of me. "How are your parents?"

"Oh, amazing. It was so good to be away from the city. I love London, but sometimes you can't beat the peace and quiet of home, you know?"

I don't really know, but I understand the sentiment. Having spent the first eighteen years of my life in the centre of Woking, I'm no stranger to the sights and sounds of a bustling area.

Whereas Cindy grew up in a tiny village, one of those

places where the local pub is also the corner shop. Cindy and I might have met at school, but her morning commute took three times as long as mine. Moving to London was quite an adjustment for my best friend.

"It's been a few years since I've been home," I admit. "I always find it weird to go back and see how much everything's changed."

Besides, my mum and I aren't that close. I'm happy with my life here, and Mum has found a nice guy who treats her better than a queen. We want the best for each other, but our relationship can survive on a couple of texts a month.

"Everything's been the same in my village since nineteen-fifty," Cindy laughs. "The same people, the same social calendar. It's nice to know whatever happens here, I'll always have that stability to go home to. Although, I did join a puppy yoga class while I was there. That was new."

"What the hell is puppy yoga?"

"Do you remember the farmer down the road from my parents? Old Joe?"

I nod, even though I haven't a clue.

"His golden labrador just had a litter. My mum's yoga instructor persuaded him to bring them to the village hall for a class. It was the best. I wanted to sneak one home in my hoodie, but Anthony's allergic." Cindy pouts as if that's the only problem with her plan.

"It's probably for the best." I reach out to pat her knee sympathetically. "You don't want to kill off your fiancé before the big day."

"Urgh, you sound just like Anthony," Cindy huffs, signalling to a passing waiter for another round of drinks.

We're planning to make the most of our girly day before meeting the boys at the bar later. I'm even going to get ready at Cindy's house, which is a relief because my secret house-guest means we can hardly go to mine.

233

The two of us will sing obnoxiously to noughties classics while fighting over Cindy's bathroom mirror. It'll be just like old times, except the cheap bottle of vodka will be replaced by wine, and there won't be a clumsily applied eyelash in sight.

I haven't felt jitters of excitement ahead of a night out in years. I can't wait to see Jamie, which is pathetic since I was only wrapped around him a few hours ago. The idea of playing pretend and winding him up all evening is just the cherry on top of the chocolate cake.

Speak of the devil, my phone pings beside me, and I use the distraction of our prosecco arriving to glance at his message.

It's a choice I regret as soon as I unlock my screen and proceed to choke on my sushi. I should have known teasing Jamie would backfire on me.

Because how did he respond to a sneak peek of my bridesmaid dress?

A dick pic. An actual dick pic.

Jamie must still be at his tux fitting. He's wearing a pair of dress trousers, the waistband wide open, and his boxers pushed low to expose his flushed, hard cock. His hand is wrapped tightly around his length, the head glistening with a tempting bead of pre-cum.

The image is pure temptation. I'd give anything to be able to sink to my knees and tease him mercilessly until every inch of his mind is filled with *me*.

"Okay, spill it."

"What?" I say, slamming my phone down on the counter.

A slow, knowing smile spreads across Cindy's face. "Oh, Emma. Who has you so flustered?"

"Er, no one?" I squeak. "It was work. A client asking for a meeting on Monday."

"Babe, that would be so much more believable if your aura wasn't burning all sorts of red right now."

I bat the air around my head, trying to disturb whatever psychic haze is advertising my wicked thoughts. "No, it's not."

"Hmm... It was also hard to miss the giant penis on your phone."

"You saw that?!"

"How could I not? It was enormous!"

I groan as Cindy bursts into uncontrollable laughter. I can't believe Cindy's seen Jamie's dick. Fuck my fucking life. There's *another* secret I have to take to my grave.

"So, who is he?" Cindy asks, practically bouncing on her seat. "Did you meet him on an app? Was that the first time you've seen his dick? Wait! Is it serious? Oh my God, do you need a plus-one for the wedding?"

Cindy picks up her phone, her fingers stabbing quickly at the screen. "Anthony's going to throw himself into the Thames when I ask him to rearrange the seating plan. But I'll risk it for you."

"No!" I blurt out, smacking the phone out of her hand before she can ruin Anthony's life.

"Thank you, but there's no need," I correct myself, trying to sound less of a crazed banshee. "Um, it's new. We're not at the plus-one stage yet."

"You're really seeing someone?" Cindy asks, her eyes brightening.

"Sort of..."

The squeal that erupts from Cindy is so high-pitched that I'm worried our prosecco flutes will crack.

"I can't believe it! Tell me everything."

"There's not much to tell," I evade.

"Don't give me that. I saw the picture. I'd say there's *a*

235

lot to tell." She holds up her hands about eight inches apart —just in case her innuendo wasn't obvious enough.

"Oh my God, Cindy!"

"I'm just saying, good for you. I can see why you want to keep him to yourself for a bit longer."

This. Is. Torture.

"It's not that," I say cautiously. "Remember, I've not dated anyone in years. I don't want to put too much pressure on this before it's even got off the ground."

I must be getting better at lying because that actually sounds feasible. Jamie will be so proud.

"Do I get a name at least?" Cindy asks sullenly.

"And have you stalking him on every social media platform? Not likely." I give Cindy a playful wink while my brain scrambles for a diversion. "So, what's the plan this evening?" I inquire enthusiastically, leaning on the countertop and nearly upending the little stack of plates next to me.

"Nice try. We'll be circling back to this later," Cindy says, twirling her finger at me accusingly. "And to address the question you already know the answer to, I've booked us in for manicures at three, and then we're meeting the guys at *The First Trap* at eight."

"I've never been."

"Oh, you'll love it. It's kitted out to resemble an old hunting lodge. The only difference is that all the stuffed animals on the wall are wearing things like pocket watches and waistcoats."

"Stuffed animals?" Bloody hell, that sounds horrific.

"Not real ones," Cindy's quick to add. "My favourite is the badger with a top hat and a monocle. I've called him Cornelius Badgerton. I can't wait to show it to Jamie. He's going to love it."

"That does sound like something he'd appreciate," I agree wryly.

"I've really been missing him."

"What, the badger?"

"No, Jamie." Cindy reaches out to flick my arm. "I've not seen him since we've been back from Vegas."

"Oh, really?" I say, pretending I don't have firsthand knowledge of Jamie's every move since we've been home.

"No. It's been hard to find the time, especially with all the wedding preparations. And Jamie's been dealing with his own family stuff. His nan died recently, and I know they were super close."

"Yeah, it was so sad," I say gravely, taking a sip of my prosecco and sending my thoughts up to Maggie. I hope she's wreaking havoc up there.

It's only when Cindy's been quiet for far too long that I realise my mistake.

"How did you know about Jamie's nan passing away?" Cindy asks, eyeing me curiously.

How indeed? I'm so stupid, I could kick myself. Why don't I just announce I was his date to the funeral while I'm at it?

"Um... Since Vegas, we've been trying to be civil. You know, for the sake of the wedding." I quickly shove a sushi roll into my face to buy myself some more time.

It doesn't help. My mouth doesn't get the message and carries on regardless. "We've tried to keep in touch. Not all the time, just a text here and there."

And the occasional dick pic. Nothing serious.

For one painful moment, I can't read Cindy. Is she suspicious? Angry? Confused? Has she pieced it all together, or is she simply feeling queasy after so much raw fish? When she bursts into tears, I'm still none the wiser.

"You have no idea how much this means to me." Cindy

slides out of her chair and throws herself on top of me. "All I've ever wanted is for you both to get along. This is the best wedding present ever."

I pat Cindy on the back and flash an awkward smile to all the concerned customers who have stopped to watch the spectacle. An eternity seems to pass before everyone loses interest.

Cindy's still hiccupping and sniffling when we settle the bill, our waiter trying to look anywhere but directly at us. This outburst and our tears at the dress shop mean Cindy's make-up is completely ruined. She looks like the lead singer of an eighties rock band.

Once her card has cleared, she excuses herself to freshen up in the bathroom. I quickly seize the opportunity to fish out my phone, reluctantly delete Jamie's perfect cock from our thread, and then send him a quick text to warn him about our change of plan.

Operation Status-Quo is a failure.

I just hope Jamie's prepared for Plan B.

Chapter Twenty-Three

Jamie

hange of plan, Emma's text says. Change of bloody plan.

As if it's that easy when I'm halfway through a perfect performance of my *Jamie-Hates-Emma* monologue. I've spent all day harping on about how much of a drag it'll be to see her tonight. I've even gone as far as to make Anthony promise not to leave us alone together.

Although that might still be advisable, considering my dick has been half hard since she sent me that changing room selfie. Are bridesmaid dresses supposed to be that slutty? I mean, I'm here for it... mostly. There is one tiny prehistoric part of my brain that wants to stick a jumper on Emma before she wears it in public. But a bigger, hornier part of me can't wait to see every teasing seam in the flesh.

My answering dick pic was a subtle reminder of where she'll end up tonight. Twenty minutes later, when my phone vibrated in my pocket, I'd assumed Emma was responding to my masterpiece and accepting my invitation.

Wrong.

Now, I have to find a way to backtrack—and fast. How

am I supposed to convince Anthony that I don't, in fact, hate Emma, and we've been trying to be civil for *months?*

Thankfully, Anthony is too busy micromanaging the exact stitch pattern for his tuxedo to notice my inner panic. I shoot Emma a plea for help and wrack my brains for a suitable solution. She responds straight away.

And that's where my luck runs out.

> Emma: I don't know what to do! Oh my God, I'm so sorry. Just act like we've been trying to work things out.

"Who's that?" Anthony asks, nodding goodbye to the frazzled tailor.

Well, it's time to get this show on the road.

"Um, that was Emma."

Anthony stops in his tracks, spinning to face me from the doorway of the tailors. "Emma?"

My mind is working overtime, flicking through the archive of every white lie I've ever told. Of course, I've never needed a lie to cover up another lie before, so it's not exactly a fruitful search.

I usher Anthony into the street before anyone else can witness this car crash. "Yes, Emma. We've been texting here and there. Trying to mend some bridges."

"Why?" Anthony's flabbergasted. I may as well have announced I'm moving to Uranus.

"I thought you'd be pleased. After all, wasn't that your secret plan for this evening, anyway?" I sound a little more abrupt than I intend to, but perhaps reminding Anthony of his own scheme will take the heat off me.

No such luck.

"But you said you weren't looking forward to seeing Emma tonight."

"I don't think I used those exact words—"

"And not to leave you alone with her under any circumstances."

"Well, that was more of an insurance policy." I shove my sweaty hands into my jeans and pray my feet can keep me upright under all this pressure.

"Insurance against what?" Anthony asks, his face still a mask of confusion.

"Emma and I might be civil now, but who knows what might happen when we add drinks into that equation? We could say anything. It's safer if we're supervised."

At least that's not a lie. After seeing Emma in that dress, we'll be lucky to get home without a public indecency charge.

Anthony's frowning at me, his steps slow enough that agitated Londoners have to dodge around him.

"How did this even happen? Last I heard, Emma was this close to slipping arsenic into your in-flight meal." He crushes his thumb and forefinger together to demonstrate just how close I was to death.

"I ran into her on our last night in the hotel. She was heading to reception to rebook the airport transfer." *Close enough.* "It was late, so I decided to go with her. After the most awkward elevator ride in history, we thought it might be better for everyone if we tried to bury the hatchet."

Believable, right? I make a mental note to text Emma our new cover story when I get the chance.

"And then you got hammered to get rid of the taste of reconciliation?" Anthony nods as if that makes complete sense.

"Huh? What? We didn't get hammered."

241

Ahem.

"Not you and Emma. You and that girl you were with the morning we left."

Fuuuuuuuuuuck. I forgot about that...

"Oh yeah," I laugh a little too loudly. "I spotted her when I was at reception with Emma. She was sitting at the hotel bar with a group of friends, and I swear she kept looking over at me. Once I'd walked Emma back to her room, I took a chance and went back down." I shrug cockily, hoping to God it hides how much I'm flying by the seat of my pants. "The chance paid off."

Even after that brilliant yarn, Anthony still has questions. They keep coming. All day. On our walk to the pub, all through lunch, and even from beneath a towel at the barbershop. And he doesn't ask them all in one go. Oh no. Instead, his wonder strikes as unpredictably as lightning. A drip feed of curiosity... or a form of water torture.

How many times have you texted her? Have you ever called her? Are you going to meet up on your own? Did you tell her about your nan? Do you have nicknames for each other?

Princess. She will always be my Princess.

I'm a clammy, jittering mess by the time I collapse into a soft armchair at the bizarre hunting lodge inexplicably located in the centre of London. Anthony heads straight to the bar, patting a super creepy badger stuck on the wall en route.

Taking my first full breath in hours, I use the moment alone to pull myself together.

Anthony's surprised Emma and I are speaking, but I don't think he suspects there's something else going on. I've stuck as close to the truth as possible so Emma and I don't tangle ourselves in a web of our own making.

Besides, how many more questions could Anthony

242

possibly have? As long as I don't pounce on Emma the second she walks into the bar, our secret should be safe.

Tonight could even be an opportunity. We could lay the groundwork for telling Cindy and Anthony we're dating. Of course, they still can't know we stole their wedding thunder during a celebration that should have been all about them. Not for a while, at least. But this could be a step in the right direction.

I don't know why I didn't think of this before. Perhaps the best cover story for accidentally marrying the girl everyone thinks you hate is to start dating her.

Although, after having Anthony ream me out for wearing white socks to our tux fitting, I'm saving any and all bombshells for *after* their ceremony.

When Anthony returns with two overfilled beers, I resolve to relax and have fun. This will be the first night the four of us *enjoy* together, and I'm not going to spend it stewing about things I can't change without a time machine.

Anthony raises his glass in a toast to patient tailors, and we settle in to wait for Cindy and Emma.

"Did you know Patrick's girlfriend dumped him when we got back from Vegas?" Anthony says, mindlessly rearranging the coasters on the table so they're utterly straight and perfectly aligned.

"Oh really? That's a shame." It's not. Patrick's an ass. And he never really forgave me after the whole fountain incident.

Can't think why.

"Do you think he gets on with Emma?" Anthony asks. "Didn't they sit next to each other on the plane home?"

"No. Emma hates Patrick," I reply, a touch too quickly.

Or I hate Patrick. Whatever.

"What? Why?"

Fortunately, I don't have to elaborate because something

243

over my shoulder catches Anthony's attention. I turn in my seat and then nearly fall off it. Emma and Cindy have entered the building, and every male in residence has noticed.

"Damn, they didn't hold back tonight," Anthony mutters under his breath.

They certainly didn't. Cindy is really leaning into the bride-to-be aesthetic. She's wearing white lace trousers and a matching blazer, a splash of pale blue silk peeking out from underneath. She's an angel, floating through the bar with her usual air of serenity.

But it's *my* wife who has every head turning. If Cindy is virginal innocence, Emma is sin personified. From her black, patent stilettos to her red-painted lips, Emma is the essence of temptation. Her hair is styled in an artfully tussled bun, and I can't help but feel jealous of the stray strands that brush the nape of her neck whenever she moves. Yet it's her dress that has my mouth agape. She's wearing a short black number that hugs her curves beautifully, hinting at exactly where my hands will fall by the night's end.

Her hips sway seductively as she stalks closer, a knowing smile on her luscious lips as her sapphire eyes lock with mine. I'm going to be haunted by the sight for eternity.

I'm well and truly smitten. Emma and I haven't talked about where this marriage is headed, but I can't spend any longer denying I want more. I want to be her everything, not just the one dirty secret in her otherwise pristine life. I just hope Emma sees it that way, too.

I'm out of my seat before I can register what I'm doing, completely caught in Emma's spell. Thankfully, Anthony has done the same, greeting his fiancée with a kiss and guiding her into the chair next to him.

As if sensing I'm about to do something stupid, Emma

leans in for a civil peck on the cheek before sliding into the last chair at our table.

I'm itching to tell her how incredible she looks. How besotted I am. How she'll be wearing that dress around her waist the moment we get home. But I can't. So, instead, I check the time on my phone and revert back to our tried-and-tested dialogue.

"You're late," I gloat.

Emma glowers prettily. I just know she's dying to stick out her tongue at me.

"Oh, that's my fault," Cindy squeaks. "Emma's got a secret boyfriend, and she won't tell me anything about him. So, I was plying her with pre-drinks to see if I could loosen her up enough to spill his name."

"A secret boyfriend?" I ask, taking a smug sip of my drink. "Really?"

"Yep," Cindy proclaims proudly, "And I've seen the dick pic to prove it."

I spray my beer across the table. "You what?!"

Emma's eyes hold nothing but horror, pleading with me to *get it together* as I scramble for a napkin.

"Babe, you can't look at other people's penises without them knowing," Anthony explains, far too smitten for someone whose fiancée has just been caught ogling someone else's junk. "It's rude."

Thank God he hasn't worked out that Emma and I are together. Anthony would kill me!

"Can we please stop talking about penises?" Emma groans exasperatedly. "I'm sufficiently mortified, and I need a drink."

"Fine," Cindy relents, pushing out of her seat. "But only because I've seen a strawberry martini on the menu and need one immediately."

The next couple of hours fly in a heartbeat. We laugh at

all the stupid shit Anthony and I tried to pull at school, we gossip about people we grew up with and haven't seen in years, and we dream about our futures.

Cindy shares that they're going to try for a baby, and I'm beyond excited to be the fun uncle to any rugrats that might come along. Fuelled by vodka, Emma gives an uncanny impression of her nasal boss, which prompts Cindy to demand that Emma quit her 'stinking job' and go solo. If Cindy's tone's anything to go by, it's not the first time they've had this conversation. And after Emma told me about her boss's behaviour this week, I'm fully on board with Cindy's plan.

Emma is radiant tonight, carefree and effortless. Whenever she throws her head back to laugh or giggles into Cindy's shoulder, I have to remind myself that staring is bad. But it's no use. I'm a moth to a flame.

It's hopeless. Or rather, *I'm* hopeless.

My fingers have been itching to reach out to Emma for hours. I've had her all to myself for so long that sharing her again is harder than I thought it would be.

Before long, I crumble. One touch won't hurt if I'm sneaky enough, right?

Slowly, I drop my hand under the table, subtly watching for signs that anyone else has caught me in the act, and stretch out my fingers to skim over Emma's soft thigh.

I can't hear her sharp intake of breath, but that dress hides nothing. Her breasts hitch against the tight material, and I notice the almost imperceptible flutter of her eyelashes. Emboldened, I move again, this time teasing my fingers towards her sensitive core.

"So, Jamie, are you looking to take someone home tonight?" Cindy's innocent but abrupt question snaps me back to my senses, and I retreat from Emma as quickly as possible without giving away my position.

246

"I'm not looking," I answer, latching onto the sour cocktail in front of me so that my wandering hands have something else to do.

"Like, not at all?" Anthony asks.

"Nan's passing kind of changed things for me," I shrug. "I've done the hook-up thing, and now it's time to move on. The next time I date, I want it to be someone special. Someone who's in it for the long haul."

I risk a glance at Emma, and my heart stops when I find her smiling helplessly into her glass. I desperately want to tell her that she's the one, the someone special I'm holding out for.

"Naw, my Jamie's growing up." Anthony leans across the table and ruffles my hair, almost spilling his outrageously expensive drink in the process.

"Bugger off," I laugh, pushing him back onto his chair.

"I thought you had a few more years of bachelorism left in you yet. So, what kind of woman are you looking for? Someone easy-going? Adventurous? Someone who'll go thrill-seeking with you at the drop of a hat?"

More like someone fiercely headstrong and achingly beautiful, whose idea of an adventure involves indoor plumbing and keeping both feet firmly on the ground.

"I think she'll be exactly the opposite," Cindy muses, spookily astute as always. "I think Jamie would get bored with a partner who goes along with whatever he wants."

I shift awkwardly in my seat. "I just want someone to have fun with," I offer vaguely. "Someone who'll push me and won't mind when I push back."

"That sounds kind of kinky," Anthony teases, clumsily winking at me. "If you're looking for a date to test your limits, I know someone at work who'd be perfect for you."

"Absolutely not," I snort... attractively. "The last girl you set me up with spent our date listing all the reasons her ex would crawl back to her. And one of those was that she'd sent him my picture to make him jealous. I was lucky to make it out of there alive."

"That was one time," Anthony moans while Cindy and Emma fall into a fit of laughter.

"And it was so awful you permanently lost your match-making privileges."

"Fine. Cindy, do you know anyone we can set him up with?" he asks, turning to his fiancée hopefully. I know what he's doing. He wants me coupled up so we can double date.

Little does he know—

"Sorry, babe." Cindy shakes her head.

Unperturbed, he turns to my wide-eyed wife. "What about you, Emma? Do you have anyone for Jamie?"

I nearly swallow my tongue. I don't know whether I want to laugh or curl up and die of awkwardness.

"Not unless Jamie's type is married, middle-aged women," Emma says, scooting her chair away from the table and this awful conversation. "I'm going to visit the bathroom. Anyone want anything while I'm up?"

"Can you grab me a lemonade?" Cindy asks, holding up an alarmingly nuclear concoction. "I need to dilute this if I have any hope of walking tomorrow."

"I'll even ask for a slice for you," Emma says sweetly, picking up her bag and turning for the restrooms. The doors are adorned with stuffed ferrets, one wearing a top hat and the other a petticoat. I'm going to have nightmares about this place for years to come.

It takes a herculean effort to drag my eyes away from Emma. It's as if she's wound an invisible thread around my waist, rendering me powerless to do anything but follow her to the ends of the earth. If I'm not careful, our friends will notice my nauseating heart eyes.

"I'm just so happy you and Emma are working things out," Cindy says, leaning into Anthony.

"Yeah, it's great and all," he agrees, "but couldn't you have had this great epiphany before the stag do? It would have made the group activities a lot easier."

"It took how bad things got in Vegas for us to see we'd taken things too far." *That, and waking up married...*

"You're not wrong. I thought Cindy and I were going to have to act as referees," Anthony laughs. "Now, my next question is, do we think the guy Emma's talking to at the bar is her new secret boyfriend?"

It takes me a few seconds to process Anthony's great mental leap, but when I do, my blood runs cold. I twist in my chair, the move so violent that it scrapes noisily against the stone floor.

"Way to be subtle," Anthony huffs.

The bar falls quiet, the frivolity and joviality muted into thundering silence. The only sound to reach my ears is Emma's nervous laughter as Mr Tall, Dark, and Slimy skirts around the periphery of her personal space.

He's the kind of guy she should stay ten feet away from. Suited and booted, with enough gel in his hair to glaze a bakery and an air of superiority that would lap the joy out of any room.

Whatever tale he's spinning, Emma's not buying it. Her eyes keep gravitating to the barman, a desperate plea for him to serve her and end this torture.

Really? Anthony thinks *this guy* could be Emma's secret boyfriend?

I'm crawling out of my skin. I want to tear her away from that slimeball. I want to smash my lips against hers and claim her in front of this whole damn bar.

But I can't.

The only thing keeping me in my chair is Emma's

visible disinterest. That is until the sleaze leans in closer, resting on the bar and positioning himself for an unobstructed view down Emma's dress.

Nope, not happening.

I'm out of my seat quicker than you can say *'possessive husband'*. If Anthony or Cindy think it's strange, I'm not in earshot long enough to find out. I weave through the crowd, quickly reminding myself that murder is illegal, even when a guy really, really deserves it.

I see the moment Emma notices me because her lips quirk into a wicked grin. It's the same challenging smile she wears whenever she's about to put me in my place.

Sure enough, Emma's entire demeanour changes before my eyes. She moves into the intrusive man, resting her hand just a hair's width away from his.

I see. We're playing games tonight.

"That's so interesting," she lies as soon as I'm close enough to hear. Not that this guy registers the falsehood. He's clearly used to being humoured.

"I can't believe your car can drive to Edinburgh so quickly. It would take me hours longer than that on the train."

"That's the benefit of upgrading to the GT model. When time is money, you save minutes however you can." Yep, his voice is just as plummy as I'd expected. "I'm parked right outside. Why don't I take you for a spin and show you just how fast I can go?"

In the middle of London? Jog on, mate.

"I don't know anything about cars," Emma says breathily, her eyes glittering with apparent awe. "What colour is it?"

The guy moves in closer, mesmerised by her attention. "Red."

She gasps. "Oh, I love red cars."

Little minx. Well, two can play this game.

I step up behind her, snaking my arm around her waist and pressing my lips to her ear. "Make an excuse. We're leaving."

Emma turns to face me, completely unphased by my rude interruption. Which isn't surprising when this whole display has been for my benefit. "But this gentleman just offered to show me his sportscar," she purrs. "It's red."

"If this *gentleman* keeps inviting other people's wives into his car, he might find himself with a few broken fingers." I make sure my threat is clear in my eyes as I stare down this prick.

There's too much filler in his face to tell if he's disappointed or not, but he holds up his hands in surrender. "Sorry, man. I didn't know." He backs away from us in an easy retreat, already scanning the crowd for his next target.

"Well, that was uncalled for," Emma smirks. "Who knew you were such a caveman?"

I don't dignify that with an answer. She'll find out soon enough when I take her home and make her forget everything except my name.

"Meet me outside in five minutes," I growl, a sinister demand I expect Emma to follow to the letter. I leave before she can argue, pushing my way through the crowd and back to our apprehensive friends.

"Is Emma alright?" Cindy asks.

I look back at my wife and find her squirming at the bar, still waiting impatiently for that bloody lemonade.

"She's fine." I shrug smugly.

"That guy was a tool. I'm glad you stepped in."

"Yeah, he wanted to take Emma for a late-night drive in his car. I pretended we were together to get rid of him."

"See, I told you," Anthony gloats. "Cindy thought you were being territorial."

"Shut up," Cindy hisses, elbowing her fiancé in the ribs.

"What? You did! I said he was just trying to get Sleazy Steve to bugger off."

As much as I want to stick around and listen to the happy couple bicker, I have an errant wife who needs to be taken home and taught a lesson.

"Listen, I'm going to head off. I told Bridget I'd meet her for breakfast, and you know I can't touch anything with a hangover."

"No worries, man," Anthony says. "We're probably going to have another round and call it a night ourselves."

I bend down to kiss Cindy on the cheek before Anthony jumps up and tugs me into a bone-crushing hug. He's always been an affectionate drunk.

"Thanks for today, Jamie. I'd have been a mess without you."

He was a mess *with* me, but I don't mention that.

"My pleasure, man," I wheeze when Anthony sets me back down. Thank God. A cracked rib would have really put a downer on my evening plans.

With one last lame salute, I take my leave. It's hard to keep my eyes off the vixen at the bar, but I stay strong. One look at Emma, and I might be tempted to drag her out of here myself.

Outside, the warm summer night banishes the stagnant, musty air of the fake hunting lodge. The smoky breeze dances around me, stoking the embers of need in my stomach and causing the hairs on the back of my neck to stand on end.

I check the time on my phone. Her five minutes are up.

Emma's played with fire. And now, we're both going to burn.

Chapter Twenty Four

Emma

W as it a good idea to goad Jamie into cutting our night short? Probably not. Based on the sinful promise in his eyes, it was either the best or the dumbest thing I've ever done.

But I *needed* to get out of that bar. Being so close to Jamie, to his smell, to his touch, but being unable to press myself against him? That was torture.

Besides, I owed Jamie a taste of his own medicine after he flirted with everything that moved in Vegas.

He hasn't taken his eyes off me since we hailed our black cab, his stare burning hot enough to melt the icecaps. I know I'm in trouble, but I can't bring myself to care. Not when the punishment will be exquisite.

"So, what excuse did you give to leave early?" Jamie asks darkly.

"I told Cindy I was getting a headache."

Jamie smirks wickedly, stretching across the cab to whisper in my ear, "I hope that's not true because I have plans for you when we get home."

"What plans?" I breathe, his throaty vow fuelling a pulse of need in my chest.

Jamie feathers his forefinger down my arm, and I relax into his tender caress until he shatters the illusion, gripping my wrist and dragging me across the taxi. "Bad girls get what's coming to them. And you've been very bad, Princess."

I'm not proud of the way I writhe in my seat as I will the cab to hurry the fuck up. But what else can I do? Jamie's depraved snarl has turned me into a hopeless mess.

By the time we pull up in front of my building, I've neither the grace nor decorum to exit the vehicle with any kind of dignity.

Jamie and I fly up the stairs, each of us scrambling for our keys in a frenzied race. Jamie wins, shouldering his way into my flat with a destructive crash. Victorious, he tugs me over the threshold to claim his prize.

I'm pinned against my door before it's even closed, Jamie's lips on mine and his tongue demanding entry.

I open for him hungrily, pouring every ounce of wound-up frustration into the kiss. This is not a gentle reunion. This is brutal. Desperate.

I slide my hands down his chest and devour every ridge of muscle I can find. Soon enough, my fingers hit leather, and I paw clumsily at the belt, struggling with the buckle at his waist. I've barely worked the tail free when I'm hauled away from the door with so much vigour that my head spins.

Jamie turns us so my back is pressed against his front, one strong arm pinned across my chest and the other buried in my hair. Slowly, he walks us into the lounge.

"Did you forget I'm in charge, Princess?" Jamie tuts, planting a hand between my shoulder blades and pushing me so that I fall over the arm of the sofa.

I yelp, catching myself just before I crash face-first into the cushion. My brain is screaming at me to rebel, to get up and fight Jamie for control. But my traitorous body scrambles to obey, knowing the man wielding the power will make it feel so, so good.

"Look at you, bent over just for me," Jamie purrs. He runs his hands up the back of my thighs, slipping his fingers under the hem of my tight dress. In one smooth move, he pushes the material over my ass, bunching the dress up around my waist.

Next in the firing line are my panties. He quickly pulls them down and taps each of my ankles in turn, a silent command to kick off the lace.

My heels put me on tiptoe, meaning I have to arch my back to keep myself steady on the armrest. I feel exposed. Vulnerable. And utterly mindless from the desire pooling in my stomach.

Jamie palms my ass and presses his thick body to mine, rocking into my bared flesh until I sway back, seeking the perfect friction of his jeans. I can't help it. The need is too much.

"Nuh-uh." I feel Jamie's hips leave mine before *smack.* The hit isn't hard, but it leaves my flesh smarting.

"Did you just spank me?" I gasp, surprised by the blissful need that throbs between my thighs.

"You deserved it," Jamie snarls, bending down to sink his teeth into my ass.

He's driving me to madness, and he knows it. Is it possible to feel violated and worshipped at the same time?

Who fucking cares?

I love it.

With a final kiss to soothe the sting, Jamie stands up, leaving my aching body bereft.

"Bedroom," Jamie says over his shoulder, not bothering to see if I follow. That would be pointless. He knows I'll obey without question.

I hastily pull my dress back down and kick off my stilettos, the leather squealing across the floor as they fly in whichever direction they choose.

From my bedroom door, I can see Jamie standing by my nightstand, still fully clothed with his thick arms folded over his chest. The only difference is that he's let his hair loose, the thick black band now wrapped around his wrist.

"Take it off, Emma," Jamie says the moment I enter the room. His baritone timbre sends shivers down my spine, calling to my body in the most indecent way.

Reaching behind me, I unzip the dress and let it drop to the floor. I deliberately step out of the pool of material, the movement bringing us close enough to touch.

Jamie cups my cheeks, his gentle thumbs skating over my heated skin. But I'm not fooled. The dark vow shrouding his face belies his soft caress.

"Do you like fast cars, Princess?" he asks mockingly.

Slowly, I shake my head. I'm transfixed, unable to look away from the challenge in his eyes. "No."

"Hmm, I didn't think so. Then what do you like?"

This! Fucking this! The way you make me feel alive.

"You," I answer honestly.

A satisfied smile spreads across his face.

"On your knees," Jamie commands, nodding to the floor at his feet. "You know what to do."

I sink down without thinking, a puppet with severed strings. Intent on finishing the job I started earlier, I quickly remove Jamie's belt before turning my attention to his jeans. One by one, I pop open his buttons, making sure to run my fingers along his ridged length as I do.

There's already a dark patch of pre-cum staining his black briefs, and I make sure Jamie's eyes are on me as I inch closer, my quickened breath aimed right at the proof of his arousal.

256

His cock twitches the moment my lips brush against the damp material. Holding his gaze, I wrap my mouth around the tip and gently suck his seed through his briefs.

"Pull it out," Jamie hisses.

I don't listen. Instead, I keep suckling soft and slow while skimming my hands over the rough denim on his thighs.

"Princess," Jamie warns, his voice rumbling through my chest.

"Sorry," I repent, pulling back to flutter my eyelashes at him. "I got distracted."

I give his flared head one more kiss before freeing him completely. I wrap my fingers around his thick girth and lean in to tease his sensitive underside. Jamie punches his hips forward, pushing through my fist to seek more than I'm giving.

I giggle quietly, lapping at Jamie's tip until he twists his fingers in my hair and scrapes his nails across my scalp. He's probably suffered enough. Putting him out of his frustrated misery, I finally, finally, take him in my mouth.

I work his length, sucking hard enough for my cheeks to hollow and taking more of him with every pass. Every so often, I pull back and swirl my tongue around the head, teasing him mercilessly before diving back down to his root.

Jamie moans above me, a wanton sound that echoes through my mind until I can think of nothing else. His fingers tighten into a satisfying sting that only makes me want to take him deeper until, with one final flex of his hips, he pulls away, his cock dragged from me with a crude *pop*.

"On the bed," he pants, lifting me off the floor and dropping me onto the pillows stacked across my headboard.

Instead of climbing on top of me like I want, Jamie turns to my dresser and opens the drawer I cleared out for him.

He rummages around, looking for something that seems long forgotten.

When he returns to me, he's holding two ties, one silky black and the other an outrageous shade of blue.

"Want to try something new?"

Yes, yes. Fuck yes! I want to scream. But all I can do is nod my consent, squirming in a desperate bid to relieve the ache pulsing in my clit.

Jamie wastes no time. He eats up the floor between us while pulling out a condom from his back pocket and throwing it onto the bed next to me.

Carefully, he takes my right wrist and wraps it in the length of silky material. He lifts it up and ties it to my bedframe, tight enough that I won't be able to work myself free but not so tight that it'll leave a mark. In other words, *perfect.*

"That okay, Princess?" Jamie asks.

I nod again, eager for him to carry on. He slowly circles to my other side and repeats the intricate process with my left hand.

My chest is heaving, my body trembling with need. I may be tied up and helpless, but I'm the one with the win tonight.

Satisfied, Jamie surveys his work from the end of my bed. "You look unreal," he says, his dark eyes clawing down every line and curve of my body. "I can't wait to be inside you."

You're the one holding things up!

I nearly sob with relief when Jamie finally moves to undress. He flings his clothes behind him, revealing every sculpted inch before climbing onto the bed and prowling towards me.

Grabbing my ankles, he pushes my legs apart so he can fall between my shaking thighs.

"Ungh," I keen as he traces his fingers up my body, over my stomach, my chest, my neck, before landing to tap impatiently at my lips.

"Suck. Get them nice and wet for me, Princess." Jamie pushes his fingers into my mouth, and I do exactly as he asks. Who'd have thought it?

I give Jamie's fingers a few hard sucks before he pulls them free. Then, slowly, oh so slowly, he trails his soaked digits over my nipples, coating the sensitive flesh so that the midnight air can tease them cruelly. I try to arch into him, needing something, anything, as long as it's *more*.

Then, when all I can focus on is this torturous bliss, he pushes his fingers inside of me.

I tug at my restraints, my body lighting up beneath him. I want this. Need him. He fucks me carefully, every thrust skilfully calculated to drive me to the edge, but no further.

The desire builds steadily inside me, simmering at the surface, unable to spill over.

"Please, Jamie. Please. Please!" I chant as he works that beautiful spot inside of me.

"Well, since you asked so nicely," he says with an evil grin.

With his fingers still working me higher, he uses his free hand to pick up the little foil packet and tear it open. After a few more teasing thrusts, he pulls out his fingers to roll on the condom and get himself in position.

I expect him to slam home, which, of course, means he does completely the opposite. Jamie eases in slowly, determined to torment me with the glide of his cock against my tight heat.

"Jamie, I need more," I croak, pulling at the ties pointlessly.

"I know, Princess."

Jamie pulls out of me completely before thrusting so hard that I see stars.

Yes!

He's relentless, pounding into me with such force I cry out with every flex of his hips. It's too much. I can't think. I can't breathe. All I can do is *feel* as I start to pulse around him.

"Shit, you feel so good," Jamie groans.

His pace quickens, the frantic thrusts brushing my sweet spot to send me hurtling over the edge. My orgasm slams into me, my body clenching around him as every part of me explodes.

Jamie follows, his own hard climax shooting into the condom as he buries himself deep inside of me. My tightening body grips him until he's spilt every last drop.

With a final groan, Jamie's shaking arms give out, and he collapses onto my spent body. His weight grounds me, settling me as I gradually come down from my euphoric high.

Jamie takes a few deep breaths against my chest before pushing himself up to release my hands from the bedframe.

Once I'm free, he lifts my wrists into the lamplight and checks the skin where I was bound. I want to tell Jamie how amazing that was. How amazing *he is*. But my mind is still warped from my intense orgasm.

Jamie brings both of my wrists to his lips and gives each a tender kiss.

I melt against him, purring like a kitten when he wraps his arms around me and guides us down to the mattress.

"Princess," he murmurs when I've settled on top of him. "The next time you try and make me jealous, I'll tie you to this bed and won't let you up for a week."

I roll my head back against his chest, staring into his sex-blown eyes. "You think that's a threat?"

Jamie nips at my neck, sending aftershocks dancing through my stomach. "That's a promise. Do with it what you will, as long as you remember you're mine."

"Yours?"

"Mine, Princess. Is that clear?"

"Does this mean I'm your girlfriend?" I ask impishly.

"No," he growls, digging his fingers into my hips and pressing the length of his body into mine. "It means you're my fucking wife."

Chapter Twenty-Five

Jamie

All my life, I've been a man of two halves. I'm a people person. I'm charged just by existing in a bustling space, watching a hundred different lives unfold before me. Given the chance, I'll happily catapult myself into a group of strangers and leave with a bunch of new friends.

But I also need my space. Even when Anthony and I shared a flat, I'd end the night by shutting myself in my room and unplugging for a while. I have never had the urge to share my bed, let alone on an ongoing basis.

In fact, I used to think there was nothing worse than sacrificing my personal space.

Yet here we are.

I barely recognise myself. I'm thriving in domestic bliss. Emma and I have fallen into a little morning routine. We wake up tangled in one another, and then I bring her coffee while she sets the room back to its pristine condition. Over breakfast, we moan about the needless meetings we have that day and then kiss goodbye at the front door.

It's sickening. And I'm not even mad about it.

But it's also a strange feeling to have found my home in

the last place I ever dreamed of stepping foot. I'm loving it, but it still sometimes slips my mind that I *live* with Emma. I've been on my own for so long and worked so hard to get my first place that I keep forgetting I've moved!

Occasionally, I find myself heading for the wrong line on the underground, and this afternoon, I had a text from my cousin to say he'd signed for some parcels at my flat. It's a reflex to send my orders there, especially when I can never remember Emma's postcode. I've been going back and forth on whether to get my post permanently redirected. Which is ironic when I didn't give that much thought to the wedding that got us here in the first place.

I used to feel awkward when I spent time alone in Emma's flat. Like I was invading a space where I didn't belong. Now, my stuff is everywhere. Pictures of Nan decorate the bookcase, and my horde of football mugs is stashed haphazardly beside Emma's more grown-up collection. The bedroom wardrobe is threatening to collapse under the weight of all our clothes, and I even made a special trip back to mine to pick up the ugly shell lamp that my niece decorated for me last year. It now casts a gruesome shadow around our lounge.

I have successfully infiltrated every nanometre of Emma's life. It would take an incredibly skilled surgeon to get rid of me.

Emma should be home from work any minute now. And since *I* shut down my laptop at a reasonable time, I've managed to tidy the flat and make a quick chilli in the slow cooker. When Emma gets home, all she has to do is relax.

I don't mean to brag, but I am really good at husbanding.

There are still days when Emma works too late or can't sleep because she's running through a mental checklist in her head. A few weekends of fun aren't a miracle cure, especially after years of anxiety and pressure. But she's finally drawing a line and deciding for herself when she wants to cross it.

Not so long ago, I was worried that Emma was only using me to balance out her work life. A convenient bit of fun she could turn to whenever she felt stressed. But after the way she preened when I called her my wife, I'm starting to hope she sees us as more.

I want all of her. Every beautiful curve, every whispered moan, every organised list, and smutty romance book. I'll greedily take whatever she'll give me.

I just need to work up the courage to tell her that when neither of us is drunk on orgasms. That stipulation does limit my options somewhat. It's very hard to keep my clothes on when Emma's around.

I hope the gift I picked up this morning will help show Emma I'm all in. I've found a beautiful alternative hardback cover of her favourite questionable book. She's going to love it. I'm not going to lie; I'm feeling pretty proud of myself. Yet more husband points coming my way.

Ping.

Any thoughts of my better half are cut short by a chime from the depths of the lounge sofa. I dig my phone out from between the cushions to find a text from Bridget and an earlier missed call from Anthony.

Bridget: Are you still alive?

A pang of guilt pulses in my chest. My sister and I spoke almost every day when Nan was in the hospice. We used the excuse of coordinating our visits as a pretence to check in on one another.

But our texts have tapered off since the funeral, and I realise I've no idea how she's doing. When did I become such a shitty brother? Feeling terrible, I quickly hit the call button.

Bridget takes a long time to answer, especially when she text me less than a minute ago. A part of me thinks she's making me wait on purpose.

"He lives!" Bridget yells dramatically when she finally picks up the phone.

"Har har, very funny. You could have called me too, you know?"

"I know. But as the oldest, I get to take the moral high ground."

"Surely, as the oldest, you should be taking care of me?" I ask with feigned innocence.

"That sounds awful. No deal."

"Fine," I laugh. "I promise to call you more. Happy?"

"I'm taking that as an admission of guilt. So, yes."

"Great. Now, how are you? What've you been up to?"

"I'm alright," Bridget sighs. "Same old, same old. Work interspersed with increasingly crappy dates. What about you? Are you still walking on eggshells at Emma's place?"

"Not quite," I admit reluctantly. Bridget is going to have a field day with this.

"Go on…" I practically hear her ears prick up.

"We're… sort of together."

Bridget gasps dramatically. "Oh my God. I never saw that coming." Her staccato speech implies exactly the opposite.

"Oh, whatever."

"No, really. Who'd have thought living with the woman

you've been obsessed with for years would be a recipe for fireworks?"

"Urgh, you're annoying," I groan, flopping onto the sofa. "I knew you'd be like this."

"I'm sorry, I'm sorry. I just can't believe you thought you could live together without this happening. Your drunk ass had already decided it was a good idea," she snorts. "So, how serious is this? Have you labelled anything yet?"

"It's pretty serious," I reply. "Emma's my girlfriend." *Wow, how do I say that without sounding like a twelve-year-old?*

"A girlfriend who is also your wife," Bridget adds. "What are you going to do about the whole marriage thing?"

Thankfully, a heavy pounding on the front door saves me from opening *that* can of worms. Emma and I haven't even broached the subject yet.

"Listen, I've got to go. There's someone here."

"Okay, but we'll be coming back to this," she says. "And don't you dare use that as an excuse not to call!"

"I wouldn't dream of it," I lie. "Bye, Bridget."

Another persistent turn of knocking drowns out the muffled sound of Bridget disconnecting.

I glance at the clock. Emma should be home by now. Could it be that Princess Perfect has forgotten her keys? I hope so. If I gloat hard enough, I might be able to annoy her into christening the entryway table. It's the only spot left unsullied in the entire flat, and I'm dying to rectify that oversight.

Just to be extra irritating, I wait for a third set of thumps to sound on the door before I throw it open, a smug grin already plastered on my face.

Except it's not Emma.

"Anthony!" I choke out.

It doesn't bode well for me that he's *not* surprised to find me here. Instead, he radiates anger. His fists are clenched into tight, vibrating balls, and his jaw works from side to side, chewing on his contempt.

There's no doubt in my mind. Anthony knows.

Shit.

"You weren't home." His accusation is strained, his voice shaking over every word.

"Yeah, erm..." I hesitate, struggling to find any words that won't make this worse.

"The wedding breakfast menus were delivered to your flat this afternoon," Anthony explains scornfully. "When you weren't answering your phone, I figured I'd just pop by and pick them up on my way home."

Dammit.

"When a Mini-Payne answered the door, I just assumed one of your cousins was staying with you. Imagine my surprise when he told me he was living there because you'd *shacked up with your wife.*"

Ah. What an unfortunate way for him to find out.

How could I forget that Anthony had asked to use my address for wedding deliveries? It had made so much sense all those months ago, considering I work from home more than he does.

"Did Robby have the menus?" I ask tentatively, bracing myself for the inevitable.

"Yes, he had the menus," Anthony spits. "Did you marry Emma on my stag do?"

I swiftly consider my options. There's no way to damage control this, not when he's found me at Emma's place, my hideous lamp standing proudly in the background. That leaves me with option two. It's time to bite the bullet.

"Technically... yes."

"Technically," he imitates. "What do you mean, technically? You're living in her fucking flat."

"Well, that sort of happened after—"

"Could you not have let me have this one thing?" Anthony interrupts abruptly.

"What?"

"I know you're not used to sharing the limelight, but were you so jealous that you had to beat me to it?"

I can feel his rage crashing over me, cresting waves of anger in a storm. It's pulsing in the air between us, a living, breathing thing just waiting to tear us apart. But it's the pain beneath his harsh words that cuts deep, the profound betrayal in his voice.

"Anthony, it wasn't like that."

"You know how hard we've worked to pull this wedding off. The money, the planning, the sweat and tears. And yet you still went behind my back to make it all about you."

I don't know where this is coming from, but Anthony's really hurt. He's never spoken to me like this before. Whether this is some underlying insecurity at play or he really believes I'd sabotage his wedding, the anguish slipping through his fury is making my heart ache.

Anthony was always shy, but I never realised he felt overshadowed. Have I really been stealing the limelight for all these years? God, why didn't I see this before?

"Why Emma?" Anthony asks, begging me to help him understand. "Was it because you knew it would get the biggest reaction? What were you going to do? Announce it at my reception? Drop the bomb in your best man's speech?"

"No, of course not." I close the gap between us, only for Anthony to retreat further into the communal corridor. I hear a heavy door creak open at the end of the hall.

Wow, the neighbours are really getting a show tonight.

"Then why marry the person you've hated your whole life? Why marry the person that just last week you called *the most insufferable, vile bitch you've ever had the misfortune of meeting?*

"You didn't want me to leave you alone with her because you were scared she'd either bore you to death or skewer you with a cocktail straw. Why did you marry Emma, Jamie? Why?"

Damn Operation-Status-Quo. It has caused us *nothing* but trouble.

"It wasn't real, okay," I snap, tugging at my hair in frustration. "It was just a crappy, drunk decision. The only reason it happened is because Emma got me hammered on tequila. You have to get over yourself, Anthony. This had nothing to do with you."

My words are met by a strangled gasp, a faint sound that echoes thunderously around the corridor. For a single blessed second, I think it's come from Anthony. But one look at his guilty face reveals the truth.

The creaking door. It wasn't a neighbour. It was Emma. And she's home at the worst possible moment.

I turn my head slowly, trying to fortify myself against the sight that awaits me. But all the time in the world couldn't have prepared me for what I find.

Instead of fury, there's defeat. Instead of fire, there's resignation. Emma's stylish bag hangs from her limp hand, the silver clasp accenting the unshed tears glistening in her hollow eyes.

I'm frozen with fear, rooted to the spot as my world falls apart around me.

Emma says nothing. Not one word. She simply spins on her heel and takes off down the stairs.

I did that. I drove her away from her own home. Away from me.

"Emma, stop!" I call after her. My heart tries to tear

269

itself from my body, desperate to pursue the woman it belongs to. And I don't blame it.

I race back into the flat, shoving my feet into my trainers and scrambling through the bowl for my blasted keys. The second I wrap my fingers around the cold, jagged metal, I'm out of the door, slamming it closed behind me.

I make it two steps before a strong hand wraps itself around my wrist. I stumble, barely managing to catch myself before I end up on my ass.

"Let me go," I growl, yanking my arm out of Anthony's grip.

"Did you mean it?" Anthony asks, the fight drained out of him.

"Mean what?"

"That it wasn't real?"

"Clearly not," I huff, my every muscle itching to chase after Emma. But I can't leave Anthony without knowing he'll be okay.

"Why did you lie to me?"

And there it is. The crux of my betrayal. We've never kept secrets from each other before, let alone *lied*. Not once. But this hadn't just been my story to tell. Because admitting my mistake would have meant exposing Emma too, and I couldn't do that to her. Not even when we 'hated' each other.

And yet, by constantly covering my tracks, I've managed to hurt two of the most important people in my life.

This really is a fucking mess.

"I'll explain everything soon," I promise, reaching out to squeeze his shoulder, "but I really need to go."

I wait for Anthony to respond, desperately wanting some kind of sign that we'll get through this. The moment drags on and on until, after what must be a year of my life, he finally gives me a tense nod.

I breathe a sigh of relief and pull him in for a stiff, awkward embrace. I'm sure this is what it would be like to hug a log, but I'll take it right now.

"I'll speak to you later," I say, letting him go.

Without further ado, I race down the corridor to catch the woman who's stolen my heart.

"Call me," Anthony shouts like some lovesick teenager.

I allow myself a small, sad smile.

Anthony and I are going to be okay. Our friendship will survive this.

I only hope the same can be said for my marriage.

Chapter Twenty-Six

Emma

A crappy, drunk decision. I was a crappy, drunk decision. The reason that Jamie married this *insufferable, vile bitch* can be found at the bottom of a tequila shot that *I'm* responsible for.

I wish I could say that I'm angry. That Jamie has lit a furnace of rage inside me, just as he's done so many times before. But he hasn't. Ever since he spat out those vicious words, I've felt nothing. Numb. The burning in my lungs is my only reminder to breathe as my heart sets about rebuilding every wall Jamie tore down.

As Anthony so kindly reminded him, Jamie and I don't fit. I '*bore people to death*', and it's only a matter of time before Jamie finds someone more like him. Someone outgoing, and sociable, and fucking fun.

So, I didn't stick around to confront Jamie. I didn't rant and rave and call him every name under the sun. Instead, I did the only thing I could to protect what was left of my heart.

I ran.

I was down the stairs and out of the building before my first tear could fall. The instant I stepped out onto the street, I hailed a black cab and asked the driver to take me somewhere, anywhere, as long as it was far away from Chelsea.

That must have been hours ago. At least, that's how it feels after walking around and around this small, neglected park in a daze. Pulling out my phone, I find it's actually been less than an hour since I overheard Jamie and Anthony's little *chat*. This park must be smaller than I thought. I've passed the same slime-green pond about six times already.

Unsurprisingly, I have a dozen missed calls from Jamie and the same number of texts.

I don't bother to read them.

What a mess. I can't believe that shit's hit the fan the week before Cindy's wedding. I've said it before, fate's a bitch. Couldn't she have given us a few more days' grace before revealing all to Anthony?

Spotting a tired bench underneath an overgrown silver birch, I plonk myself down and kick out my aching feet.

Usually, I'd cringe at the thought of setting myself and my leather handbag anywhere near something as disgusting as this dilapidated bench, especially with the baked-on layers of pigeon mess cemented to its cracked wood. But tonight, I can't find it in myself to care. A hitched skirt and a dirty bag are the least of my worries.

What the hell am I going to do?

I can't look at Jamie right now, let alone exist in the same space as him. Which is going to be a problem since Anthony finding out about us doesn't mean this entire ruse is over. Jamie's family still thinks our marriage is legitimate.

So did you an hour ago, the snide voice in my head reminds me.

Am I an idiot? Was I building this relationship up to be

something it's not? Jamie seemed so sure of us, so possessive of me. Was I misreading the signs?

God, I need to speak to Cindy. I just hope she still wants to speak to *me* after what I've done.

There's no doubt in my mind that Anthony will have told her what transpired this evening. I have to make Cindy understand that I never wanted to hurt her. I've not worked out exactly why I married Jamie, but I know for sure that it wasn't out of spite.

All I can do is pray Cindy can see past the shock and hear how much my heart is breaking. With trembling hands, I dial her number.

"Emma?" Cindy answers immediately.

"Yeah, hi."

"Oh my God, where are you?"

I glance around the empty park as if the answer will reveal itself. "To be honest, I'm not sure. I asked the taxi driver to take me somewhere outside of Chelsea."

Cindy mutters a curse under her breath. "Find the coordinates on your phone. I'll come and get you."

Sure, because every bride has the time to traipse the length of London during the week of her wedding.

"Don't worry about it, Cindy. I spotted a station not too far from here." *Probably.*

"Seriously, what the hell is going on, Emma? Did you really get married in Vegas?"

"I'm so sorry," I say, my voice wobbling with my admission. I thought I'd feel lighter once Cindy knew the truth, but I don't. Instead, the weight of my deception is ruthless.

"Yeah, I'm going to need you to explain how that happened," Cindy replies, sounding more confused than anything else.

"How long have you got?" I sniff. The dam is cracking,

the first tears spilling down my cheeks in unrelenting rivulets.

"Oh, Emma. What's wrong?"

"I thought we were going to be something," I sob.

"You and Jamie? He *is* the guy you've been seeing, right?"

"Yeah," I say, slumping back against the protesting bench. I take a deep breath and spill the whole unbelievable tale.

I tell her everything. From waking up married to the fallout of Bridget's bombshell. From Maggie's inheritance to Jamie losing his flat. I relive every precious moment that led to me giving my heart to the boy who hated me.

By the time I've finished, my words are shaking, and my face is wet. "I really liked him, Cindy," I hiccup. "Why did I think this could work? Why did I think I'd be enough for him?"

A bewildered old man walks past my bench, his eyebrows raised so high they've disappeared beneath his peaked cap.

"We kept this stupid secret for so long because we didn't want to hurt anyone. And look how it's turned out. God, this is awful. I just want to crawl into a hole and live there forever."

"Are you done yet?" Cindy asks.

Not quite.

"Can you call Jamie and ask him to move his stuff out? I don't think I can see him yet."

"Why would I do that when you're going to find your-self a nice cosy hole to live in?" she asks sarcastically.

"Cindy," I whine.

"No, you've had your pity party, and now it's time to listen. Am I hurt that you lied to me? A little. I've found out

I've missed a whole chapter of your life. A really important one."

"I'm so sorry," I whisper again, trying in vain to speak past the lump in my throat. "I never should have lied to you. Are we going to be okay?"

"Of course we are," she says gently. "And you know Anthony will understand when he calms down. He's just a little high-strung right now."

Well, that's one way to put it.

"I don't really blame Anthony," I admit begrudgingly. "It must have come as a bit of a shock."

"Emma, you're phoning me in tears after running away from my hot-headed fiancé and his idiot best friend. You don't even know where you are. I'm going to blame him a little."

"It's not Anthony's fault," I sulk. "It was all Jamie."

"Hmm..."

"Hmm? What does that mean? Hmm?"

"It means I'm not asking Jamie to move out for you."

"What?" I shriek, bolting upright on my creaking bench. "Why not?"

"I hate to say this, but I think you're self-sabotaging."

"Did you hear the part where Jamie called me vile and insufferable *last week*?"

"Yes," she says patiently. "But I also have eyes. You should have seen the way Jamie was looking at you last Saturday. Hell, I thought he was going to crush a glass with his bare hand when that guy started to hit on you.

"I think you've already decided that Jamie isn't in this for the long haul. You've convinced yourself you're not exciting enough for him, and you're using tonight as proof you're right."

Cindy's trying to put hope in my heart, but the fear that is starting to bubble in my stomach is the perfect antidote.

Because what if Cindy's right? What if Jamie said those hurtful words to spin our web of lies? It's certainly possible. Which means I've just walked away from the best thing that's ever happened to me.

He called you a crappy, drunk decision less than an hour ago.

"I don't know, Cindy," I sigh tiredly. "He was hardly going out of his way to defend my honour."

"You heard a snapshot of a very heated conversation. Clearly, Jamie didn't handle this well, but you should at least hear him out. You owe it to yourself, Emma. And if he really is just a jackass, I'll come over there and kick his ass myself."

I want more than anything to believe Cindy's right. I really do. I want *my* Jamie back. My fiercely loyal protector who'll do anything to make me smile. But I can't let Cindy's hope take root. Because *that* Jamie wasn't standing on my doorstep tonight. *That* Jamie didn't trample all over my heart.

"Promise you'll come and kick his ass if he's a dick?" I finally relent.

"You can count on it. He might be a hundred foot tall, but I can take him."

I manage a dull smile. Setting Cindy on Jamie would be as effective as sending a bunny rabbit into battle.

"So, here's what you're going to do," Cindy continues. "You're going to march your perky ass back home and tell Jamie just how much of a twat he is. You're going to make him grovel, and then you're going to put this whole thing behind you.

"And try to find a bathroom en route. If you look anything like you sound, you're probably a snotty, blotchy mess by now."

"I'm not that bad," I lie, rummaging in my bag for a

packet of tissues. Thank God I have some spare make-up with me. My angry soliloquy won't be as effective with mascara smeared halfway down my face.

"Oh my God," Cindy suddenly screeches, halting my search. "I've seen Jamie's dick!"

I can't help but laugh at the strange mix of horror and awe infused in her realisation. "Maybe that'll teach you to stop being so nosey."

"Wow. No wonder Anthony was so pissed with Jamie," she muses to herself.

A sombre bleep in my ear alerts me to my phone's dying battery. I need to look at a map and work out where I am before it conks out completely.

"Thanks for everything, Cindy, but I have to go. I'll call you later, okay?"

Cindy doesn't let me hang up until I've promised to text her the second I find a station and the moment I get home. We disconnect after saying goodbye a few more times, my battery protesting all the while, and I feel a thousand times brighter.

So much so that I finally have the presence of mind to recoil from the pigeon toilet I've been sitting on for the past half hour.

I brush myself off as best I can and use my phone as a mirror to fix my blotchy face. It's a bodge job, but hopefully it will spare me the concern of any passing Londoners. Not that this seems a particularly busy part of the city. Wherever *this* is.

Needing to find my route home as quickly as possible, I open a map and search for the nearest underground. Even though I might still decide to avoid the crowds and hail a cab, it'll be easier to catch a driver near the station. Taxi or train, my first step home is the same regardless.

Ah, bingo. There's a line about fifteen minutes away from this overgrown jungle.

The roads are surprisingly quiet tonight, the lingering smoke from a seldom-used barbeque the only sign of life. It's not a bad area; it's just that there's not much here to draw a crowd. No cafes, no shops, only narrow streets of terraced houses and one park that you probably shouldn't walk through after dark.

I weave through the streets, my nose in my phone so I don't miss a turn on my ever-winding route. The robotic voice directs me to *take the next right* down a long lane that will quite literally save me from walking around the houses.

My cautious steps on the uneven slabs echo off the shadowed walls, the cool shade a welcome relief from the hot summer night sun.

I take a deep breath of thick, smoggy air, and, at that moment, I'm knocked completely off balance.

I don't have time to think, let alone brace myself, as I'm pushed face-first into the rough wall beside me.

The wind is punched from my lungs, and my forehead ricochets off the cold, coarse brickwork. Pain lances through my skull, a sharp bite that makes me wince.

Acting on instinct alone, I try to push myself away from the wall. But a heavy arm lands across my back, immobilising me while my phone is torn from my hand.

My mind glitches into a panic of white noise, my mouth open in a silent cry and my crushed body struggling for air. For one sickening moment, I'm back in that hotel corridor, vulnerable and helpless at the hands of those vile men.

Except this is worse. Much, much worse. Because now there's not a hope in hell that a knight in shining armour will swoop in to save me.

I squeeze my eyes tight and plead for the fight to spark inside me. Struggling against the wall, I suck in as much air as possible while trying to escape the impossibly powerful weight of my attacker.

"Help," I croak in vain. "Help!"

I almost feel relieved when my bag is yanked from my shoulder, my back unpinned the instant the straps untangle from my shaking arm.

It's over in a second.

The solid footfall of my assailant disappears down the lane before I can even think of peeling myself away from the wall. I stumble backwards, the toe of my shoe catching on a loose slab to send me crashing back to where I started.

I turn to rest against the brick, my heart pounding as my mind tries to process what's just happened to me. What the hell do I do now? I can't think straight, let alone remember the convoluted route to the station. Not that I can pay for any transport once I'm there.

A warm bead of sweat cools on my brow, and I swipe at the annoying trickle before it can drip into my eyes.

"Ah," I gasp, flinching away from my own fingers.

Not sweat. Blood.

Great.

Can this day get any worse?

Chapter Twenty-Seven

Jamie

I t turns out I was wrong. It didn't take the services of an incredibly skilled surgeon for Emma to be rid of me. Oh no. All it took was for Anthony and me to open our big mouths.

I've been running around the streets of Chelsea like a headless chicken for over an hour. I've trodden in more patches of gum than I can count, been terrorised by a pack of savage sausage dogs, and given directions to clueless tourists who couldn't give a crap about my life crisis.

What I said to Anthony was stupid. More than stupid, it was downright wrong. But I couldn't think straight with my best friend yelling at me. All I wanted was for him to calm down and see that this wasn't some ploy to ruin his wedding day.

Emma has to know I didn't mean what I said. She *has to* because the thought of spending a single day without her by my side is torturous. I finally have Emma, and I'm not letting my moronic words and an absurd situation get in the way of that.

I won't give her up without a fight. I *will* fix this.

My frustration is rising with every passing minute. It

comes as no surprise that wandering aimlessly around London isn't helping me find Emma. For all I know, she's jumped on a train and is halfway to Scotland by now.

The fourth time I pass her building empty-handed, I give up. No, that's not right. I don't give up. I restrategise.

I decide to wait for Emma at her flat. No matter where she's gone, she *has* to come home at some point. And when she does, I'll make her understand. I'll beg, and grovel, and do whatever it takes for her to see she's the most important person in my life.

Then, I'll yell at her for running away and tie her to our bloody bed until she's learnt her lesson.

When I burst into our lounge, my heart sinks. Everything is exactly as I left it.

Pristine and perfect.

Cold and empty.

Even the rich aroma of slow-cooked beef doesn't welcome me home. Instead, it teases me with what could have been if I'd kept my cool with my best friend.

Knowing I'll go mad if I have to sit around and wait for Emma to come back to me, I send a text to Anthony.

> Me: I couldn't find Emma so I'm waiting for her at the flat. Has Cindy heard anything?

> Anthony: Sorry, mate. Cindy says she spoke to her but has no idea where she is. If I hear something, I'll let you know.

A dull ache spreads through my chest. The girl I love will speak to Cindy but won't even take my calls. That hurts.

Wait... The girl I love?

The girl I fucking love?

Huh. Shouldn't this be a monumental moment? Shouldn't the first time those words enter my psyche steal my breath or send my heart soaring out of my chest? Instead, I feel nothing but contentedly calm, at peace with the revelation of what I've probably known for a very long time.

I love her.

I love Emma.

Unfortunately, I'm snapped out of my beautiful realisation when my phone vibrates in my hand. I'm so desperate to hear Emma's voice that I rush to answer without even checking the caller ID.

"Emma?" I hope.

"Hello. Is this Jamie Payne?" I instantly deflate at the very official, decidedly *not female* voice.

"Yes. Who's this?"

"I'm Officer Jones with the Chelsea Police."

My ears prick up. Officer Jones certainly has my full attention now. I quickly wrack my brain, trying to think of any reason the police might want to contact me. I borrowed Anthony's car a while back. Did I miss an emissions charge? Was I caught speeding?

"I'm here with your wife," the efficient voice clarifies.

"Emma?!" I blurt into the phone for the second time. "Is she okay? Is she hurt? What's going on?"

"Your wife's absolutely fine, Mr Payne. Just a few bumps and scrapes."

"Bumps and scrapes?" I ask in disbelief. She was flawless the last time I saw her. Bumps and scrapes do not constitute *absolutely fine.* "What the hell happened?"

"I'm afraid your wife was the victim of a mugging earlier this evening. She got away with minor injuries, but her phone and her bag were stolen."

Mugged? Emma was mugged? I don't know whether to scream or burn down the entire city until I find the person responsible.

Someone touched Emma. *My Emma.* Someone hurt her, and robbed her, and if I don't see her with my own fucking eyes right now, I'm going to lose it.

"She's at the station?" I confirm through gritted teeth.

"Yes. She asked us to call so you could be here when she's finished giving her statement. Do you know where to find us?"

Once I check I have the correct address, I hang up and hastily order a taxi.

In a cruel case of déjà vu, I'm yet again shoving my feet into the first pair of shoes I find and scrambling from the flat in search of Emma. At least this time, I know where to find her.

My curb-side wait for the taxi is the longest three minutes of my life.

I must resemble an unhinged lunatic because when the car pulls up, I hear the wary driver engage his locks. The way I sprint for the passenger side door probably doesn't help his first impression, especially when I gesticulate wildly for him to wind down the window.

"For Jamie?" I ask frantically, trying to sound as sane and nonthreatening as possible.

"To the police station, yes?"

I nod, diving into the back seat as soon as I hear the doors unlock.

My mind is reeling, fluctuating between sheer terror over what could have happened and a guilty burst of hope that Emma wanted to call *me.*

That has to mean something, right?

I stamp down the selfish thought as best I can and try instead to think of ways to be there for Emma tonight.

My nerves are shot by the time we pull up to the shabby grey station. I've bitten my nails to the quick, and there's a flurry of nerves in my stomach that makes me want to yell into the darkening sky.

I barely remember to pay the driver before I launch myself out of the taxi and straight into the depressing building.

"I'm here for Emma," I pant, clinging onto the reception desk.

"Mr Payne? I'm Officer Jones. We spoke on the phone."

"Okay. Where is she?" I ask impatiently.

"They should be out any minute now."

Sure enough, an irritating buzz interrupts Officer Jones, reverberating around the small lobby to signal the arrival of Emma and a paunchy, older officer.

My heart drops the second I lay eyes on her. She looks small, defeated. Her shoulders are rounded, and her head is bowed as she steps through the heavy door from the station beyond.

"Emma," I breathe, racing towards her.

There's dried blood smeared across her forehead. It's matted into the front of her hair and even dotted down the front of her pastel green blouse.

Before I can utter a word, Emma closes the distance between us, throwing her arms around my neck and clutching onto me for dear life. A wave of relief flows through me. It's more powerful than anything I've felt before.

I hold her close and bury my nose in her hair, vowing to never let her go again. Not ever.

"I'm so glad you're here," she whispers.

"So am I, Princess. I'm here, and we're going home."

Emma nods into my shoulder, silent tears soaking through the material of my T-shirt.

"Mr Payne, I'm Officer Harper." The gruff older man holds out his hand, and I reluctantly peel myself away from Emma to offer my own.

"Jamie," I answer. Because if one more person calls me *Mr Payne*, I'm phoning my dad to ask him to come and deal with this.

"You'll be glad to know we have a lead on the man who attacked your wife. We believe the mugging is linked to a wider spate of thefts in the area."

Feeling Emma tense beside me, I wrap my arm around her waist and pull her close. *Glad* isn't a word I'd use to describe anything about this situation.

"Do you think you'll catch him?" I ask, running my hand up and down her arm, not really sure if I'm trying to comfort Emma or myself.

"I'm confident we'll have him in custody by the end of the week."

"Will Emma get her things back?"

"Anything we recover will be needed as evidence. I'd look into making an insurance claim if I were you."

"My Kindle was in my bag," Emma mumbles, breaking my heart that little bit more.

"I'll order you a new one as soon as we're home." The best one, with all the covers, stickers, and books she wants. I'll have it plated in gold if it makes her feel better.

"Thank you for your statement, Emma. If you remember anything else, please do let me know. We'll keep you updated with any developments."

Without fuss, Officer Harper excuses himself to return to whatever mountain of paperwork awaits him. I'm sure he'll have forgotten us by the time he makes his next cup of coffee. This might be traumatic for us, but this is a reality he faces every day.

Though, that still doesn't excuse the state in which he's left my wife.

"Excuse me," I call to Officer Jones. "Do you have a first aid kit I could borrow?"

"Yeah, of course." He reaches under the desk to retrieve an old green container embossed with a big white cross. "Do you want me to call the first aider?"

Bit late for that now.

"All I need is a plaster," Emma interjects, clearly wanting to get out of here as quickly as possible.

Officer Jones nods sympathetically, passing me the plastic box. "You'll find the bathroom through there on the right."

I lead Emma down the dingy corridor and steer her into the small disabled toilet. The moment the door closes behind us, I pull Emma into my arms and hold her against my chest.

"Oh my God, are you okay?"

"Not really," she admits shakily. "Thank you for coming for me."

"I'll always be here for you, Emma," I say, pulling back so she can see the truth in my eyes. "No matter what."

"I'm sorry I ran away. If I hadn't, then maybe…" I feel the break in her voice like a stab to my chest.

"No, don't say that," I beg, cupping her cheeks. "This wasn't your fault."

I itch to kiss away her pain. But that's not what Emma needs from me right now. What Emma needs is to get out of here. "Come on," I say softly. "Let's get you cleaned up so we can go home."

A cursory glance around the small bathroom tells me that while it's not the most modern facility in the world, it's at least clean. Still, it feels weird to administer first aid while she's sat on a toilet or leaning against a public sink. So, I gently guide her to stand under the bare lightbulb hanging from the spongy ceiling.

Carefully, I flick the clips on the first aid kit and open the lid, half expecting moths to fly out of the old box. Instead, I find a well-stocked inventory of everything I need to get Emma home without raising too many eyebrows. I grab a large plaster and a handful of antibacterial wipes before closing the box and placing it on the floor.

Tentatively, I wipe around the graze on Emma's forehead. At first glance, it looks a lot worse than it is. Most of the blood has come from one long but shallow scrape along her hairline. Still, I don't want anything to get infected on our way home. So, I unwrap the plaster and carefully press it over Emma's cuts.

"You've had a hell of a few months," I say, brushing as much of her hair away from the dressing as possible. "Have you always attracted so much trouble?"

The tiniest, most reluctant smile pulls at her lips. "Considering I've not been able to get rid of you after all these years, I'm going to say yes."

I raise my brows disbelievingly. "Me? I'm the poster boy for good behaviour."

Emma scoffs, music to my ears. Then, just when I think she's about to say something snarky in return, the fight leaches out of her.

It kills me.

"How about I run you a bubble bath when we get home?" I suggest, jumping on the first thing I can think of that might help. "I'll even read you one of your smutty books while you're in there."

The way Emma's eyes glisten at my offer makes me want to do anything—anything in the world—as long as she keeps looking at me like that.

Like I'm everything.

"You'd do that?" she asks quietly. "You'd stay with me, even after..."

Even after all the shit I said this evening? After my massive cock up?

I really do have a lot of making up to do.

"Of course, Emma. I'd do anything for you."

Emma's watery eyes search mine, but still, she stays quiet. And that's okay. I know it'll be hard for her to believe me, but I'll spend as long as it takes proving to her that she's my world.

"Let's get out of here," I say, unlocking the door and leading her into the dank corridor. "I'll ask Officer Jones to call us a cab."

"Will they do that? This isn't exactly a hotel," she says behind me.

"They let you give a statement without cleaning you up first. The least they can do is order us a taxi."

Sure enough, in under ten minutes, I'm bundling Emma into a black cab and buckling myself into the middle seat to be as close to her as possible.

This is where Emma belongs. Right beside me.

And I'll never be stupid enough to risk that again.

Emma

I'm exhausted. I can't think, let alone try to string a sentence together.

All I want to do is shower. Jamie's hunting around my bathroom in a panic, trying to find the right combination of bubbles and bath salts to ease the pain of my night. But I just can't face it. Now I'm home, all I want to do is go to bed.

I think I tell Jamie not to bother, but I can't be sure.

Either way, I turn on the shower and wait for steam to fill the room before stepping under the scorching spray.

Even though Jamie cleaned me up pretty well at the station, I still feel filthy. I sigh as the hot water sluices over my skin, washing layers and layers of blood, and grime, and dirt into the drain. I scrub myself until my skin is pink and then scrub again for good measure.

I don't know when Jamie left the bathroom. I don't even know how long I've been standing here. Everything is happening in my periphery, completely out of focus. The only thing that's real is the throb in my head and the relentless jet of water pounding down my spine.

When my legs start to tremble beneath me, sick of holding up my weight, I stop the shower and towel off before slipping into the cosy flannel pyjamas that Jamie set out for me.

I can hear him clattering around in the kitchen, probably salvaging whatever smelt so good when we walked in. I bet he's trying to make me a plate, but I can't eat anything right now.

All I want to do is sleep.

I crawl into bed and nestle into my overstuffed pillows, wrapping up in my heavy duvet and shielding myself from the world. It's far too hot to be so well covered, but I need the familiar weight to settle me tonight.

I lie in bed, staring at my blank walls until Jamie's steadfast footsteps sound in the hallway. Quickly, I shut my eyes, trying my best to look like I'm asleep.

I can't handle Jamie's concern right now. I'm too fragile. All it will take is one kind word or tender look, and I'll crack. I'll start to sob and won't be able to stop until tomorrow comes and draws a line under this hideous day. I can't do that tonight. I've not got the strength.

Whether Jamie is fooled by my amateur acting or not, I

don't know. If he does see through my scrunched-up eyes and exaggerated breaths, he doesn't let on. He just leans down and kisses my cheek before placing something heavy on my bedside table.

I wait until Jamie's safely out of earshot to end my charade. My room might be dark, but I can still make out the familiar outline of what Jamie's left for me.

It's a book.

A beautiful, smutty, thoughtful book. A couple of weeks ago, Jamie asked me about my favourite author, and I showed him the first romance novel I ever bought. It's well-loved and well... wrecked. But books are like boyfriends. Your first will always have a special place in your heart.

And now, there's a brand-new copy in all its hardback glory sitting proudly on my bedside table, ready to be loved. I can't believe he remembered.

Great. Now I'm going to have to pretend to be sleep-crying.

Damn you, Jamie. Why did you have to go and be so fucking perfect?

Chapter Twenty-Eight

Emma

Over a decade in London, and last night is when fate decided to turn me into a city statistic. I got my heart broken, and my bag snatched, all within the space of an hour.

Just peachy.

It was sheer luck that a gentleman found me in my sorry state. A very kind old man called Bill Jenson saw a hooded figure run past his house while he was watering his patio plants.

Being eighty-seven years old and with nothing else to do, dear Bill decided to investigate. Lo and behold, he found me down that damned lane, propped against a wall with more blood running down my face than an extra in an apocalyptic thriller.

Immediately, Bill called the police on a phone that still had actual buttons and stayed with me until the patrol car arrived.

The world needs more Bill Jensons.

And more Jamie Paynes.

I'd never felt more precious than I did last night. More protected. The moment Jamie rushed to my side, everything felt better. His light banished the darkness hanging over me and breathed life back into my chest.

Wrapped in his arms, I knew the nightmare was over. That everything was going to be okay.

Of course, the independent woman inside me baulks at the idea. But, hey! Even the biggest, burliest strongman would need a hug after being stranded in the middle of London with literally nothing but the clothes on their back and a cut on their forehead.

I'm just glad I didn't need stitches. That would have been just my luck. Cindy choosing the greatest bridesmaid dress known to man, only for me to show up having gone ten rounds with a heavyweight champion.

I woke up feeling better this morning. Less jumpy and defeated, more angry than anything else. Last night, I would wake at the smallest of sounds. I had this awful feeling someone was watching me, lurking just out of sight and waiting to pounce.

Today, I'm not feeling so exposed, especially after Officer Harper called to say they'd arrested the culprit. Hopefully, my dickhead mugger is cursed with perma-garlic breath and incurable sniffles for the rest of his life.

Still, I want to stamp my feet and throw a temper tantrum whenever I think about my cancelled credit cards, complicated insurance claims, and having to tell my boss I need a new work laptop.

It doesn't help that Jamie found the most ridiculous plaster under my sink, so I'm walking around with what is essentially a sanitary towel stuck to my forehead. Let's just say this isn't the sexiest I've ever felt.

Though, Jamie did find himself back in my good books when he phoned his office to take the day off. He explained to his boss that I was mugged, and whilst surprised to hear about our marriage, Julie was very sympathetic. She even had some beautiful sunflowers sent to my flat. They arrived at nine o'clock, just before the shiny new Kindle that Jamie ordered for me last night. Talk about efficient.

Optimistic after Julie's kind delivery, I've finally worked up the courage to call my own boss. I've timed it perfectly so that Howard's desk phone will ring the second his late ass hits his chair.

Unfortunately, he's not being quite as understanding about my situation...

"What do you mean you need the day off?" he sneers. "You're down to the wire as it is, Emma. You can't afford to lose time because you're a bit upset."

I take a deep breath, swallowing the urge to scream down the phone. I hold back for Jamie's sake because he looks about one bad word away from storming out of here to deal with Howard himself.

"I know it's not ideal," I say through gritted teeth, "but I won't be able to work today. I can send a doctor's note and crime number to HR if you need that information."

I know HR does *not* need that information, especially if I'm back in a couple of days. And Howard knows that, too.

"How long will you be gone? Clough wants a report from me by the end of the week!"

An ache starts to pulse behind my eyes. It reminds me that whatever I don't do today will make tomorrow hell.

I nearly cave. I mean, I could take a few calls. It's not as if I'm *badly* injured or anything.

Jamie coughs loudly, training his eyes on me as if he knows exactly what I'm thinking. *Don't you dare,* he mouths.

It's enough to snap me out of my old habits.

This will be my first sick day in years, and taking twenty-four hours to process the shock of what's happened is not too much to ask.

"I'm hoping to work from home tomorrow," I compromise, and Jamie groans. He'd keep me at home for a month if he could. "I'll need a new computer sent to me as soon as possible. My work laptop and phone were stolen in the mugging."

A tense silence swells on the line. I can just imagine the prominent vein pulsing on Howard's forehead. Perhaps it's exploded. One can only hope.

"Be ready for a delivery later today," Howard finally grunts. And that's all the sympathy I'm afforded.

I can't hear what my boss mutters when he slams down the phone, but I'm sure it relies heavily on the words *snowflake, sensitive*, and *back in my day*.

The fucking hypocritical fossil doesn't have a leg to stand on. Last winter, he took four weeks off to personally supervise the team of decorators renovating his house. Apparently, they looked untrustworthy. Meaning they didn't speak with a plummy accent or attend boarding school.

I don't need to be a mind reader to know Jamie's furious. He's leaning stiffly against my kitchen doorframe, his eyes brimming with animosity. The set of his jaw tells me *exactly* where he wants Howard to stick his job.

"He's a nasty piece of work," Jamie says, just in case I hadn't noticed.

"I know," I sigh, flopping back onto the sofa. "I suppose you don't claw your way to the top by being nice."

Jamie looks pointedly at the gorgeous sunflowers brightening our coffee table. "Human decency costs nothing, Emma."

I'm sure the florist would disagree...

"If Howard can't see how much you do for him, he doesn't deserve you."

My knee-jerk reaction is to spill the tired narrative I've

relied on for years. Howard gave me a chance straight out of university. There were hundreds of other applicants he could have chosen, and he'd wanted me. I was determined to do anything to earn my place and make myself indispensable.

And I did. My life, my relationships, my sanity, I served them all on a platter so I could feel justified in calling myself a success.

The thing is, I'm not so sure this success is worth it. There's an itchy feeling in my chest, a ball of energy throbbing inside me and vying for my attention. Is this really the life I want? A never-ending stream of projects I have no hand in selecting? Working my ass off for someone who couldn't care less about me?

I think I want more. I want to work with clients who share my vision. I want the freedom to create messages I'm passionate about. And I want to be happy at work, something I haven't been for a long time.

"Cindy's been bugging me about going out on my own for a while now," I admit self-consciously.

Jamie pushes off the doorframe and joins me on the sofa, sinking down as close as humanly possible without landing on my lap.

"Is that something you'd want to do?"

"I think so," I nod. "It's just finding the right moment to take that chance. My contract has a competition clause, meaning I'll have to build up a whole new client base as soon as I leave."

"Emma, I don't think there's ever a *right moment* to take a risk that big," Jamie says gently. "Perhaps now is as good a time as any?"

"Maybe," I agree half-heartedly.

"No, I'm serious. I'm already paying you whatever Robby can spare in rent. I know it's not much, but if you're sure about this, I can work something out with Aunt Brenda. She'd understand, given what's at stake. It's not as if Robby was meant to live at my place forever.

"If I could find a tenant at the proper rate, I could cover the bills here. It would give you some breathing room to build up your client base. We even have my share of Nan's inheritance to fall back on if things get tight."

I can only stare dumbfoundedly at Jamie as he lays out his plan for our future. I'm speechless. Just yesterday, I thought I'd lost Jamie forever. I watched as he denied me to his best friend and cracked my heart in the process. But now he seems so sure about this.

So sure about us.

That is until his eyes fly wide open, struck by the realisation that he's just invited himself to be my permanent houseguest.

"Unless you don't want that," Jamie's quick to add. "I'd understand if you didn't. I mean, after what happened with Anthony last night, I'm surprised you can even look at me."

Before my run-in with The Artful Dodger, I was fully prepared for how this conversation would go. Under Cindy's instruction, I was going to let Jamie say his stupid piece, watch as he talked himself into a hole, and then make him grovel his way out of it. Preferably in the bedroom.

But now? That all sounds exhausting.

Jamie was there when it mattered. He came through when it mattered. Really, there's only one thing that's important to me.

"Did you mean it? Am I really just a bad decision?"

Pain cuts across Jamie's face, a shadow of hurt slicing over his rugged features.

"Not for a single second," he says, his fingers softly brushing my cheek. His voice is low, intense, and laced with remorse. "I'm so sorry, Emma. I panicked and made the biggest mistake of my life. What I said to Anthony is the only thing I'll ever regret. Not you. Never you. That night in Vegas was the best thing that ever happened to me. *You* are the best thing that ever happened to me.

"Haven't you worked it out yet, Princess? I'm in love with you. And I think I have been for a very long time."

Time screeches to a halt.

No, wait. Time is moving fine. It's me who's frozen. There's a gasped breath caught in my chest, and my heart has stopped its incessant beat.

I watch as entire chunks of the universe right themselves around us, the truth of Jamie's proclamation guiding them into their proper place. All of a sudden, we make sense. Jamie and I are two halves of a beautiful whole. We don't work apart. We're too volatile, unstable. But fit us together, and we're perfectly balanced. I harness his crazy, and he pushes me past my carefully constructed boundaries.

I've never been more sure of anything in my life. Here with Jamie is where I'm meant to be. And a few careless words won't change that.

Putting my husband out of his misery, I throw myself at him, wrapping my arms around his neck the second I land on his solid thighs.

"I love you too," I whisper against his lips.

Jamie's answering groan washes over me, rolling over my body and drowning me in its euphoric depths. "Say it again," he begs.

"I love you," I sigh, worshipping every inch of skin I can reach with frantic, open-mouthed kisses. "Jamie, make me yours."

My demand spurs my husband into action, and he slams his lips to mine. The kiss is all-consuming. I feel its blissful tremor from the top of my head to the tips of my curling toes.

And later, once the force of our new love has thoroughly defiled our sofa, Jamie turns to me with a wicked grin on his face. "We should really send Anthony a gift basket."

My mind is still floating, so I'm slow to ask, "What for?"

"For choosing Vegas," he says as if it's obvious. "Imagine if he'd wanted his stag do in Newquay."

Chapter Twenty-Nine

Emma

"Mmm," I moan, taking another big bite of my pastry, the smoothest chocolate I've ever tasted oozing into my mouth.

"Oh my God," Cindy mumbles, spraying crumbs over the crisp, white bedding beneath us. "What the hell did they put in these?"

I gaze down at my pain au chocolat. This has surely been bestowed upon me by the angels of heaven themselves. "Can I change my order for your reception? I want one of these for my starter, main, and dessert."

"Don't forget the fish course," Cindy reminds me, wiping her chocolatey fingers on her silk pyjamas.

"Whatever. Just ask the waiter to make sure I always have one of these in front of me."

Cindy makes a noise of agreement, and we return to demolishing our pastries. I tear off a strip of flaky perfection, and Cindy does the same. I'm sure our manicurist would be having kittens if she could see the state of our previously immaculate nails.

Then, just as we're about to dive in for an inadvisable second helping, the door to the honeymoon suite flies open.

Cindy and I freeze, guilty as charged when her mother finds us with our hands suspended over the basket of buttery goodness.

"Cindy," Janette gasps in dismay. "There are crumbs in your hair!"

One glance at my best friend confirms there are indeed flakes of pastry hanging in her styled curls. I reach over to brush away the evidence while Cindy hurriedly wipes at my chin.

"We couldn't help it," Cindy implores, pointing to the basket by way of an explanation. "You have to try one of these."

"I've only just had my make-up done."

"Pleeease," Cindy pouts. "For me?"

"Oh, good grief. You really are ridiculous," Janette tuts, snatching up a pastry to appease her daughter. The escaping chocolate looks incredibly dangerous against her stunning cream and champagne mother-of-the-bride ensemble.

Of course, it only takes one bite to recruit Janette to our side.

"Oh my God! What the hell did they put in these?" she groans, mirroring her daughter's exact thoughts. Janette devours her pastry in four exaggerated bites, eating over the basket to minimise the threat to the various wedding garments hung all over the room.

White really is an impractical colour.

Once we've had our fill, I pop the cork on another bottle of prosecco to toast Cindy's last hour as a single woman. The three of us settle on the bed, Cindy and I cross-legged against the headboard, and Janette perched stiffly on the edge of the mattress.

"Stupid skirt," she curses, nearly toppling over while attempting to hook one ankle behind the other.

"You should have got ready with us," Cindy boasts smugly. "We're waiting until the last minute to get dressed."

"We are *not* waiting until the last minute," I correct her. We may be relaxing now, but make no mistake—this is a scheduled intermission. Our exact timings for this morning can be found on my phone, Cindy's phone, and a secret sticky note inside my handbag.

What can I say? Old habits die hard.

Talk soon turns to the wedding and, more specifically, to the various people from Cindy's home village who'll be attending. I get a very quick run-down of who's dating who, which neighbours are at war, and how to spot Old Farmer Joe. It's his first time in London, and he's worried his suit isn't 'city' enough. Apparently, his partner had to talk him out of ordering a sequined bowtie.

"Oh, and I saw Jamie on my way up here," Janette says sneakily, her eyes twinkling in my direction. "I have to say he's looking incredibly handsome in that tux. And he's positively glowing."

Recognising a trap when I see it, I quickly jump off the bed. "Well, look at the time. We'd better start getting ready."

"Oh nonsense, there's plenty of time," Janette laughs, pulling me back down to the mattress. "I want to hear all the juicy details. Cindy told me how close you two got in Vegas."

The way she winks when using the word 'close' makes me shudder. But at least she doesn't know about our surprise wedding. As far as anyone but Anthony and Cindy are concerned, Jamie and I have just started to date.

And even that half-truth has raised a few eyebrows...

Janette prods and pokes until I finally relent and give her the gossip she's after. It's a tale as old as time. Man hates woman. Woman hates man. Man saves woman from a group of drunken louts then falls madly in love with her over a bottle of tequila. Once I've told my censored version of events, Janette's practically melted into the sheets, her prosecco gone and her smile loopy.

"I have a very good feeling about this, Emma," she says, patting my thigh knowingly. "Your aura is blossoming. I think fate knew it had to keep the two of you apart until you were ready to make this work. And now, your stars have finally aligned."

Huh. Is it me, or does that actually make sense?

Or maybe I just need to cut back on the prosecco.

Gingerly, I place my empty glass on the bedside table and make a mental note to ask housekeeping to clear the room.

Before long, my phone alarm heralds the final stage of our morning. I shimmy into my spectacular gown and quickly slip on my slinky heels. Then, all attention is on Cindy and completing her transformation from pastry disaster to the most beautiful, blushing bride I've ever seen.

The moment I fasten her last fiddly button, Cindy turns to face her mum. All it takes is one wobble of Janette's lip, and we're all done for. The three of us burst into an embarrassing onslaught of tears, laughing and sobbing in equal measure as we rush to whatever mirrored surface we can find to save our mascara.

When the event planner knocks to announce the arrival of the registrar, we're as composed as we're going to get.

It's time to celebrate the new Mr and Mrs Carter-Reed. And if I have tissues stashed in every conceivable hiding place, well, that's no one else's concern.

Jamie

All morning, my head has been repeating the same crucial list over and over again.

Rings? Check.

Speech? Check.

Emergency condoms in case of Emma looking like fire? Check, check, check.

A little thrill has shot through me every time I've reached into my tux to pull out whatever the situation has called for. I'm feeling incredibly smug. Maybe Emma has a point. Organisation *is* fun.

The whole wedding has gone off without a hitch. The ceremony was short and sweet, the weather was perfect for photos, and my best man's speech went down a storm. I have entitled the masterpiece '*Anthony Reed: Excellent Husband, Terrible Groom*', and I expect recognition from the comedic council any day now.

Of course, another way of saying the exact same thing is that this wedding has been pure torture. All day, I've had to contend with that fucking bridesmaid dress. It looks even more tempting in person. Every time Emma moves, her tanned thigh peeks out from the golden skirt and renders me useless. There's only so much longer I can resist such a seduction. I'm at my breaking point.

When a booming voice announces the bar is open, I'm done holding back. I march over to my wife and latch onto her wrist, much to the amusement of Cindy's parents.

"Wedding emergency," I shout over the thumping music. At least a few eyes are on us when I drag Emma from the room, but I can't muster up the inclination to care.

They've seen Emma. They understand.

Emma says nothing as I lead her along the corridor, the celebratory sounds growing fainter as we veer away from the party. We both know there's no wedding emergency. Not unless you count the one straining against the zipper of my tuxedo trousers.

Finally, in a quiet corner of the enormous building, I find exactly what I'm looking for. Without warning, I yank Emma into an empty room and quickly lock the door behind us.

A quick glance suggests we're in an unused conference room. Bland tables are pushed against dull walls, presided over by those hazardously stacked cushioned chairs you only find in hotels. We must be near the spa because the smell of chlorine hangs heavy in the air, the atmosphere almost damp with it.

"Jamie," Emma chastises. "What are we doing in here?"

As if she doesn't know...

In one seamless motion, I press Emma against the wall, her ethereal dress seeming ever more resplendent against the dreary background. I grab onto her thigh and wrap her leg around my hip, my fingers flexing against her warm, supple flesh. It takes everything in me not to drop to my knees and take a bite out of what's mine.

"Do you have any idea how hard today has been, Mrs Drayton-Payne?" My steely length throbs against her stomach, proving just how *hard* my predicament has become.

A desperate yearning flares in Emma's eyes, and she rolls her hips forward, sating her carnal need with her own mindless grind.

Well, that won't do at all. Not after I've spent the whole day in turmoil over the mere sight of her.

Now, it's her turn.

I grab her chin and lift her gaze to mine. "Eyes on me, Princess," I demand.

Once I'm satisfied her hunger is locked on me, I slowly skim my hand down the front of my shirt, flicking open the

305

top three buttons to reveal the gold chain resting on my sternum. There, against my chest, sit our wedding rings.

"It didn't feel right to go through today without them."

Emma reaches out, reverently stroking her fingers across the embodiment of our vows. We've forged an unbreakable bond. An eternal promise I don't remember making but will never forget. She looks drugged, her cheeks flushed, and her pupils blown from heady lust.

And I'm not fairing much better. Unable to wait another second, I capture her lips and demand she surrender as soon as my desperate mouth meets hers.

"Fuck, Jamie," she moans, her fingers twisting in the delicate chain around my neck.

"Do you need me, Princess?" I purr into her ear.

"Yes," she pants. "Need you."

I'd give anything to indulge in that sweet submission. I want Emma to fall to pieces beneath my hands. I want to bring her to the edge over and over until her screams echo through this entire building.

Alas, the sporadic footfalls in the corridor have me shelving that idea for later. Instead, I bunch up her silky skirt and hoist it around her waist, running my hands up her thighs so I can pull down whatever scrap of material stands in my way. Except, it never comes. My fingers glide uninterrupted until I feel the soft dip of her waist.

Emma looks at me expectantly, waiting for my sex-addled brain to catch up.

"Princess, have you been naked under here all day?"

"Of course," she says innocently. "I didn't want my underwear to show through my dress."

A triumphant smirk graces Emma's sinful lips, and the last remaining thread of my sanity snaps. The fucking temptress has been planning this all along.

A low, threatening growl rumbles in my throat. Gripping her waist, I spin her around and pull her flush against my chest. One well-placed push, and Emma is exactly where I want her, braced against the wall with her ass nestled against my pulsing cock.

All it takes is one flip of her skirt, and she's completely exposed, at my mercy to do with as I see fit. But we're on borrowed time. We've already been gone long enough for people to notice. So, I quickly free my aching length and fumble with one of the emergency condoms stashed in my jacket.

"Hold on, Princess. This is going to be fast." And that's all the warning she gets before I slide home.

"Jamie," she gasps, her back arching to welcome me deep inside her body.

There's no slow burn, no tender build. My every brutal thrust is met by a desperate mewl as the teasing tension erupts between us.

"So good. You feel so good," I moan as Emma chases her release, using the wall to push herself back on my hard cock.

Control freak.

"I'm gonna come," she breathes, gripping me so tightly I see the gates of heaven.

I thrust harder, her impending orgasm driving me closer to my own.

With a final punishing punch of my hips, I unload into the condom, burying my face in Emma's neck to muffle my thundering climax.

One day soon, I'll fuck her bare, fill her up with so much cum I'll be able to sit back and watch as the evidence of my love drips out of her.

"Oh God, I needed that," Emma groans, collapsing against the wall in front of her. "Do you know how hot you look in that tux?"

"Thanks, Princess," I say, quickly kissing her temple.

I step back to deal with the clean-up, thankful I'd had the foresight to pack tissues *as well* as condoms. Though there's nothing to be done about the telltale creases that we've fucked into our clothing.

"Do you think people will notice?" Emma asks.

"I hope so."

Emma hums contentedly. "So possessive." She wraps her arms around my neck and gifts me one last filthy kiss.

But our time has run out. Just as her tongue tangles with mine, we're interrupted by a heavy knocking on the conference room door.

"I know you're in there, Jamie. Open up!"

Ah, Anthony. I wonder how he knew we were here. Did he hear us? Or has he been trying the same line on every closed door in the hotel?

I'm hoping for the latter because the image of Anthony shouting at inanimate objects is just too funny.

"Do you seriously want to come in here right now?" I ask tauntingly. The door handle jiggles in answer to my question.

"Come on," Anthony laughs. He's not nearly as annoyed as he's pretending to be. "Put it away, man. It's almost time for the first dance, and Cindy will be upset if you guys miss it."

I huff, still not making a move to actually leave. "I guess we'd better get going."

Emma pushes onto her tiptoes and brushes a soft kiss across my cheek. "I love you," she whispers. No matter how many times I hear it, my heart still somersaults in my chest.

"I love you too, Emma," I reply. *With all my heart.*

I'm still smiling like an idiot when we meet a frazzled Anthony in the hall.

"You two are gross now that you're all in love," he says, speedwalking us back to the reception.

I slap him on the back. Hard. "Let's go and watch you trip over your feet in front of hundreds of people."

Anthony mutters something that sounds remarkably like *dickhead*, making Emma snort out loud behind me.

In a plot twist I didn't see coming, it turns out that Anthony's been *practising*. Gone is the lanky, uncoordinated man who once accidentally hit a bouncer in the face when dancing in the student union. He spins and twirls Cindy around the room, leading her elegantly and even dipping her low—to the delight of the charmed crowd.

Maybe I should take dance lessons? Would Emma want that? When the slow ballad fades into an upbeat pop song, I gingerly extend my hand to my wife. I'll showcase my non-existent moves if there's any chance it'll make her happy.

"My feet are killing me," she says apologetically, taking my hand anyway. "Want to hit the bar while it's quiet?"

"God, yes," I sigh with relief, steering her away from the dancefloor before she changes her mind. "I'll even buy you a drink."

"At the open bar? How generous of you."

A couple of songs later, and everyone is danced out. There are a few diehard aunties strutting their stuff on the floor, but our Vegas companions soon join us at the bar.

"Shots!" Patrick announces, clumsily carrying an overloaded tray towards us.

"Urgh, nothing good happens after tequila," Marta says, sloshing her shot back at Patrick.

He downs it in one heroic gulp.

"Pfft, tell that to these two," Anthony hiccups, wincing at the afterburn.

I pass a shot to Emma and raise my own in a toast. "To bad decisions," I murmur just loud enough for her to hear.

"To bad decisions," Emma echoes, tapping her glass against mine and knocking back the vile drink.

"Right, that's enough for you two," Anthony slurs, pointing at Emma and me accusingly. "We don't want you waking up accidentally married again."

"WHAT?!" Every head spins in our direction, eyes wide and mouths open.

"Oh, shit. Forget I said that," Anthony chokes, quickly turning tail. He disappears into the crowd to spread his chaos elsewhere, dragging his giggling bride behind him.

"Fuuuck," I groan, stealing the last shot from Patrick's tray. I turn to check how Emma is taking the big reveal, only to find her leaning over the countertop.

"Hi, hello?" she says, waving frantically at the barkeeper. "Hi, yes. I'm going to need another round of these."

Hoots and hollers surround us, and my back smarts from the number of people offering their boisterous congratulations.

Well, I guess our secret is blown. Time to claim my wife.

I wrap my arms around her waist and kiss her for everyone to see. Emma Drayton-Payne is mine.

God bless tequila.

One Year Later

Emma

I couldn't do it. I absolutely could not do it.

Jamie looked so happy when he saw the rickety aircraft that was meant to fly us to our doom, bouncing on his heels and just raring to go.

Me? Not so much. The second the instructor clipped me into the harness, I noped right out of there.

Skydiving is NOT for me.

Jamie didn't look the slightest bit surprised that I was leaving him to jump to his death with Anthony and Bridget without me. Instead, he kissed me on the lips and told me to keep a very pregnant Cindy company.

Why the hell did I think I'd be able to go through with it?

Oh yeah, because Jamie asked me after doing that swirly thing with his tongue... the manipulative bastard.

I suppose it was better to back out now rather than thousands of feet in the air. But that doesn't mean I'm not frustrated with myself.

Jamie's been planning this dive for months, jumping in memory of his nan and raising money for the hospice that took such good care of her. I hope Maggie's looking down on the spectacle today and is proud of the man she helped raise.

At least keeping my feet firmly on the ground means I get to spend time with my best friend. Cindy's almost eight months pregnant, and I'm convinced the shock of seeing her husband piss about with the laws of physics will set off premature labour.

Although to be honest, Cindy's taking this all much better than I am.

"So, how's your first month been as Ms Independent Consultant?" she asks when we're settled in the spectator zone. It's a field in the middle of a bunch of other fields where we can watch the skydive from a safe distance.

"It's been amazing and terrifying at the same time," I laugh. "Luckily, my old boss offered me some freelance work, which is tying me over while I build up my client base."

It took me many sleepless nights and endless pep talks to work up the courage to hand in my resignation. Not a day went by during my three-month notice period when I didn't question whether I was doing the right thing.

But when Robby moved in with his girlfriend, and Jamie found a new tenant for his flat, it felt like now or never.

And, wow, am I glad I took the leap. Sure, it's hard. But the reputation I've built over the past few years has given me more traction than I thought possible. I've already got a few projects underway, and Jamie's even helping me with my social media presence.

I've never been more excited about the future. My busy work life is no longer a draining burden. It's a welcome challenge I can face in whatever way I want.

"Jamie says you're smashing it." Cindy smiles, rubbing

her swollen stomach absentmindedly. "I knew you could do it."

"What? Going it alone, or house training Jamie?"

"Both." The pair of us laugh, our flimsy chairs creaking ominously beneath us. I don't know what I expected from a spectator zone, but some plastic garden chairs in an enormous field weren't it.

Wherever I rest my gaze, all I can see is grass. It's a bit daunting for someone who's lived in the heart of London for over a decade. I forgot there was so much sky!

"Where do you think they'll land?" I ask, scanning the endless green for any sort of distinguishing landmark. I find none.

"The instructor said north, I think."

"Oh... Which way's that?"

"Not a clue," Cindy shrugs. "I thought we'd figure it out when people start to fall from the sky."

Who knows if it's north, south, or somewhere in between, but half an hour later, my husband throws himself out of a minuscule plane, strapped to the chest of what I hope is a very competent skydiver.

It's hard to tell with literal vertical miles between us, but I think Jamie jumps first, followed by Anthony, and finally Bridget. The closer they float to the ground, the louder their cries of celebration become. Whoops and cheers fill the empty space that separates us, carried on the gentle breeze to where Cindy and I now stand transfixed.

My heart is in my throat, unable to settle until its missing piece touches down in an inelegant heap a few fields over.

"I can't believe they did it!" Cindy claps excitedly, jumping up and down as well as her bump allows. "I'm so jealous. Next year, I'm going too."

I'd love to return the sentiment, but I know myself

better. Thrill-seeking is *not* something Jamie and I share, and I've made my peace with that. Luckily, I have plenty of other ways to keep him on his toes.

"I'll wait here and cheer you on with my new little godson."

Once the three jumpers detangle themselves from parachutes and instructors, they hop in a readied golf cart. Cindy opens a little cool bag she's brought with her, producing a bottle of champagne and even some sparkling apple juice for herself.

What a good idea! I just thought Cindy was keeping a stash of pregnancy snacks to hand.

Jamie is glowing when the little golf cart pulls up and drops off its hyped-up passengers. His smile is so bright the pilot can probably see it from the sky. The moment his shining eyes land on mine, his happiness grows impossibly, and I barely register my feet moving until I land in his outstretched arms.

"I'm so proud of you," I say, my voice shaking against his neck. "Nan would have loved it. I'm so sorry I couldn't be up there with you."

"Don't worry, Princess. What happens next will be more than enough excitement for you today."

"What?" I ask. My confusion lasts until Jamie drops onto one knee, reaching into his trouser pocket to pull out a small leather jewellery case.

Oh my God, is this happening?

"What are you doing?" I whisper.

"Setting things right," he whispers back, winking at me roguishly. He opens the box to reveal a gold engagement ring, three breathtaking diamonds adorning the delicate band.

"Emma, I know we didn't have the smoothest start," he admits to a round of quiet laughter. "But Nan was never wrong. When she said you were the one, I knew it had to be true.

"If she's looking down on us today, she'll be proud. Not because I kicked ass jumping out of a plane, but because of you. You're kind, beautiful, and so fucking fierce. I can't believe I get to call you mine.

"You've made me the happiest man in the world, and I promise I'll spend the rest of my life making you feel the same."

I can't speak. Jamie has stolen all the words.

"Princess, will you marry me... Again?"

The world stands still around us, blades of grass frozen mid-breeze and bubbles of champagne caught where they fizz. It's an infinite moment that's completely unnecessary because this is the easiest decision of my life.

"Yes!" I burst out, throwing myself at Jamie with enough force to send us falling onto the dried grass.

Cheers and applause fill the air, but I only have eyes for my husband.

"I love you so much, Emma," he says adoringly, gently sliding the stunning diamonds to rest atop my wedding band. "Want to start doing things in the right order?"

"I don't know," I laugh. "The wrong order has worked out pretty well for us so far."

Maybe we'll head back to Vegas. Make our vows in the city that stole our memories but gave us our hearts. Or maybe we'll have a small ceremony here with everyone we love. Either way, it doesn't matter as long as Jamie's the person at the end of the aisle.

When I look to the future, all I feel is hope.

My life is full, and my soul is light.

And all because I fell desperately in love with the man I accidentally married.

Coming Soon...

What happens when your older brother's best friend can't hold down a PA?

You step up, of course! If anyone can tame the grumpy millionaire, it's the girl who's always had him wrapped around her little finger.

And if you can outrun your girlhood crush in the process, then all the better.

Except, what if he realises his best friend's little sister isn't so little any longer?

Join Amory and Lennon in a brand-new office scandal.

I promise love, spice, and all things nice.

Coming Autumn 2024

Be the first to know!

You can follow me on TikTok and Instagram at the handle @emmilysorelle

You can also join my mailing list at www.emmilysorelle.com to hear more about upcoming releases!

Acknowledgments

To Mum and Dad,

Thank you for being the most supportive and encouraging parents a girl could ask for.

Without you, this couldn't have happened.

To my amazing partner,

Thank you for believing in me and this bonkers dream... And for putting up with the late nights and lonely evenings on the sofa.

I love you!

And lastly, to my BookTok friends and wonderful ARC readers,

A year ago, I joined the bookish community, and never in my wildest dreams did I expect it to be the beginning of such a wild journey that would ultimately lead to Emma and Jamie's story being born. But here we are, many friends and one book later. Here's to the next one!

About the Author

I'll keep this short and sweet because I'm British, and talking about myself makes me feel me feel uncomfortable.

I'm Emmily, and I live by the sea with my fiancé, three adorable children, a cat who thinks he's Houdini, and a chihuahua who shakes. A lot.

It goes without saying I don't get out much. But when I do, you'll either find me in a bookshop or hiding from my responsibilities at a drive-thru.

I'd love to be bookish friends with you! You can follow me on TikTok and Instagram.

You can also join my mailing list at www.emmilysorelle.com to hear about upcoming releases!

Thank you for reading Do You Need Me? I can't wait to hear what you think.

Love,

Emmily

tiktok.com/@emmilysorelle
instagram.com/emmilysorelle

Printed in Great Britain
by Amazon